# KNIGHT SCHOOL

## THE ATLANTIS WARS
## BOOK ONE

# RICHARD M. LOHREY

Black Rose Writing | Texas

ISBN: 978-1-68433-373-8
PUBLISHED BY BLACK ROSE WRITING
www.blackrosewriting.com

Printed in the United States of America
Suggested Retail Price (SRP) $18.95

*Knight School* is printed in Chaparral Pro

*The final word count for this book may not match your standard expectation versus
the final page count. In an effort to reduce paper usage and energy costs, Black Rose
Writing, as a planet-friendly publisher, does its best to eliminate unnecessary waste
without lessening your reading experience.

*To my wife.*

# KNIGHT SCHOOL

# Contents

# Prologue

Plato was lowered down the thousand-foot cliff by rope and harness to the dock below where a crewman waited in a skiff. From there, the renowned Greek philosopher and scholar was rowed out to the *Delphinus* anchored a quarter-mile offshore. It was the same ship that clandestinely delivered him to Atlantis several weeks earlier. Once on board, Captain Strongthorne ordered the anchor pulled and a course set for Greece.

Plato looked up at the late afternoon sky, faintly dotted with the brightest stars in the galaxy. He scrutinized one particular object for a moment but was distracted by the screech of a seagull overhead.

An hour or so passed and Plato remained on deck contemplating his trip to Atlantis as they traveled away from the mysterious island continent still in view. The crystal-clear twilight sky harmonized with gentle seas and a light breeze caressed by a warm undertone. The ship effortlessly glided across the surface of the ocean as a marble rolling across a glass table.

Captain Strongthorne approached Plato holding a strange object in his hands. Plato estimated the captain to be half his age. Standing over six feet tall and muscular, he had a full mane of sandy-blond hair tied back in a ponytail. His arms bore scars, either from sailing or battle or both. He was a man of formidable presence and stature. The captain handed him a tapered brass cylinder about three feet in length capped by a sphere of glass on each end.

"What is this?" asked Plato.

"It's called a telescope," said the captain.

"What does it do?"

Captain Strongthorne laughed. "Hold it up to your eye and you'll see."

Plato was shocked at how the device magnified distant objects. "Incredible!" he exclaimed. Nothing like it existed in his country.

He reflexively jerked his head up at the sound of an explosive BANG followed by a low rumble. He fixed the telescope on an object perforating the Earth's atmosphere. Friction set it ablaze leaving a long trail of molten flames and smoke in its wake.

The meteor was huge. The concussion of the impact alone would surly kill all on the ship, let alone destroy Atlantis and maybe even other parts of the world. There was no time to panic. Plato felt death was imminent and there was nothing he could do to stop it.

He closed his eyes and waited. For a brief moment, there was no movement of any kind. Time itself stood still. Plato opened his eyes again. The meteor had disappeared—and Atlantis with it.

The crew went on manning the ship as if the whole incident had been a figment of Plato's imagination. He stared at the sea where Atlantis stood moments earlier. He could not comprehend what happened. Was he still alive? Was this all a dream?

Plato remained cemented to the deck as if any movement would spontaneously eject him overboard. Another hour passed and the evening air cooled enough to make him shiver. Captain Strongthorne ordered a crewman to bring Plato a blanket.

He finally snapped out of his stupor and approached the captain. "What happened to the meteor? What has become of Atlantis?"

Strongthorne answered, "Master Lumens says, 'Information is not always useful. Knowledge often blinds us to the essence of truth. Destiny is found in the heart, not the mind.'"

The journey back to Greece took ten days. No crewman nor the captain spoke of the incident during the remainder of the trip. Master Lumens' definitive words prevented Plato from making further inquiries and in fact directed his attention to fulfilling the purpose of his visit—chronicling Atlantis. No one would ever believe him though, especially without empirical evidence. How would he explain an entire land mass just disappearing? They would say he had gone mad and Atlantis would become nothing more than the ranting of a lunatic.

He then thought of something Master Lumens said to him directly during his visit which at the time seemed more of a philosophical aside than pragmatic guidance: *We believe in myths, not because fantasy is preferable to our past, but rather, fantasy is the mortar that keeps us connected to it.* Plato knew how to preserve the mysterious island continent's existence. Perhaps no one would believe in Atlantis itself—but they would believe in the *idea* of it.

# ADRIFT AT SEA

Cameron Costello took out a compass from his pea-coat pocket, placed it on top of the nautical chart, made a quick calculation and adjusted his course five degrees west. Born and raised in Chadbourne, Maine, he was the son of a shipbuilder and took to all things maritime. Growing up, he worked with his father at the shipyard after school and over summer vacations.

When it came time for college, Cam was accepted at the U.S. Naval Academy in Annapolis, Maryland. He graduated top ten in his class and was commissioned as an ensign. Over the course of his military career, he was promoted to the rank of captain and given command of a heavy cruiser during World War II.

Cam saw a lot of action during the war. He served bravely and was awarded several accommodations. In 1943, he decided to retire from the Navy once the war was over. Of course, the nurse he met while docked in Pearl Harbor that same year may have had something to do with his decision. The war ended in 1945. They married the following year. That was over a decade ago.

"Ahright, ye scalawags, hoist the jib before I beat ya with me peg leg," shouted Cam.

Janice Costello was having none of it. "Cam, I swear to God, one more pirate reference and you'll be shark chum before you can say 'Walk the plank.'"

Cam frowned. "You really know how to ruin a pirate's fun, don't you?"

"If you're a pirate, then show me the buried treasure," quipped Jan.

"Ye drained me dry of me treasure when ye remodeled the shanty!" Cam shot back. "Arrrrrr!"

Jan rolled her eyes. Her husband did a terrible pirate impression but she couldn't help but love him. He was an honest man with a good heart and most important, he could make her laugh, even after convincing her to sail round trip across the Atlantic from Maine to the UK on a restored fifty-five-foot John Alden Yawl. Cam named the vessel *Atlantis Pearl*, an amalgam of the mythical island continent supposedly inhabited by a seafaring people and the pet name he gave Jan on their first date while sipping pineapple juice at a tiki bar in downtown Honolulu.

They were on the return leg of their trip but still over two thousand miles from home. The temperature was brisk with clear and sunny skies. Jan looked toward the horizon and spotted something floating on the water. "What's that up ahead?"

"It's your mother," joked Cam. "She's desperate to come live with us."

"Stop it." Jan rolled her eyes yet again. "Seriously, what is that?"

"Let's find out." Cam adjusted course for the floating object and pulled the *Atlantis Pearl* right up alongside what appeared to be a raft.

Cam noted the logs making up the ten-foot by ten-foot structure had a green hue but weren't stained or painted. The pigment penetrated the full depth of the grain. From working in the shipyard, Cam assumed he had been exposed to every kind of lumber there was but he had never seen wood like that before.

On top of the raft was a blanket concealing a mass of something underneath. Cam used a gaff to hold the raft steady while Jan stepped onto it to pull back the covering. "Oh my God!" she gasped.

"What is it?" asked Cam.

"It's—it's a girl." As a trained nurse, she checked the girl for a pulse, broken bones and other injuries, then immediately swooped her up into her arms and held her with care.

The girl seemed to come out of a deep sleep. "It's okay, sweetheart, we've got you! You're going to be all right," Jan assured her. Dressed in a tattered tunic, the girl was badly sunburned and weatherworn but mustered up a brief smile before passing out.

"Here, give her to me!" Cam gently took her from his wife. "Is she okay?"

"I don't know yet," Jan said with concern. "She's got all the symptoms of severe dehydration and exposure. It's a miracle she's even alive out here in the middle of nowhere."

Next to the blanket was a small burlap sack. Jan grabbed it and got back on the boat. She laid the sack on the deck and took the girl from her husband.

"What's that?" asked Cam.

"There's something in it, some kind of box or something," said Jan.

"I'll take a look. Maybe it will help us identify who she is or where she's from." Cam opened the sack and as his wife suspected, there was a wooden box in it about ten inches cubed. "Would you look at that?" Cam said. "It's made out of the same green wood as the raft!" There was a latch on the front of the box. Cam tried to open it.

The box almost slipped from his hands. In a lightening second, the girl lurched forward and grabbed the box. Jan was caught off guard by the sudden movement and almost dropped the girl. "It's okay, honey, I've got you! Don't worry, we won't let anything happen to your box. Right, butterfingers?" Jan directed at Cam.

"Hey, I was an All-American shortstop at the academy!" Cam saw that Jan was in no mood to reminisce about his college baseball accolades. "Yes, of course. Don't worry," Cam told the girl. "I promise I'll be more careful with it." The girl handed it to him and looked into his eyes. Without her having to say one word, Cam knew that whatever was in the box was extremely important to the girl, as if it was a matter of life and death. She passed out again.

"I'm going to take her below and get her some fresh water," said Jan.

Cam took off his pea-coat and wrapped it around the child. "We'll head home but we're still a few weeks out. I'm sure someone is desperately worried about her."

"Before Jan went below with the girl, she turned back to her husband. "I don't think anyone will be looking for her. I don't why. I just know."

A million questions ran through Cam's head. How did this girl end up in the middle of the Atlantic Ocean? Where were her parents? Where did that strange green wood come from? When they got back to Maine, of course, they would contact the authorities and try to find her family but Cam had a gut feeling as well the girl was all alone in this world.

He sat on the deck and carefully examined the box before opening the latch and lifting the lid. Inside was soft velvety cloth providing cushion for what lay in the middle—a pristine nautilus shell.

# J ᴀ C K

Jack Pepper lived in the Northern Californian suburb of Sunvale and attended eponymous Sunvale Jr. High School. Once a thriving agricultural community, fruit orchards had long been replaced with microchip manufacturers, strip malls and tract homes. Still, not a bad place to grow up, if he had been allowed to grow up like most kids.

Jack had a photographic memory and an IQ sixty points higher than the majority of his teachers. He could have taken college courses—probably could have taught college courses, but the school system was gravely underfunded and programs for gifted students were cut years earlier. It was just as well for Jack who didn't really like to draw attention to himself for any reason, but he had a hard time fitting in with his peers just the same. He was treated as an intellectual pariah, an outcast even among the nerdy kids.

He tried to play it cool at the start of $8^{th}$ grade but his plan quickly fell apart when Ms. Ackley's social studies class watched *The Time Machine*, based on the H.G. Wells novel. After the movie was over, the students got into an animated discussion about time travel. What would they do if they could travel to the future? How far back in the past would they like to go? What major event would they try to change? Jack usually stayed out of these group discussions but having read the latest paper from the theoretical physicist Dr. Michio Kaku on the multiverse theory, he couldn't contain himself and jumped right in.

He questioned whether the time machine in the movie had actually traveled in time, but rather, may have traversed an alternate universe existing in a different frequency. He had some other theories, of course, but that one seemed the most plausible. About twenty seconds into his dissertation, he realized two things: 1) everyone was staring at him, including his teacher; 2) there was a small handful of people in the world (think Steven Hawking) who could actually understand what he was talking about—and none of them were in the classroom.

Jack never knew his father and his mother, Emily, never spoke of him. From what he could piece together, his father was an officer in the military. He once found a picture of a man who shared similar physical attributes, wearing an army uniform with the Green Beret insignia. When asked about it, his mother snatched the picture from his hand and refused to discuss it further. Before Jack was even born, his father left them. His mother never gave him the full story but it had something to do with Emily's mother. Jack never met his grandmother nor did his mother ever discuss her either.

Whatever happened left Emily severely depressed. When Jack was a young child, she was a loving and devoted parent but she became more sullen and withdrawn over time. She was also extremely controlling when it came to her son and she projected her own fears onto Jack which left him with several phobias. Among other issues, he had a horrific fear of heights and was a staunch germaphobe. He carried hand-sanitizer at all times.

Though Jack was small and wiry for his age, he had good hand-eye coordination and probably would have been adept at sports—had Emily allowed his participation. She was terrified he'd get hurt so she restricted him from playing kick ball, soccer, football … any sport with a ball … basically any sport.

By the time Jack entered elementary school, his mother had taken to drinking a glass or two of wine after work and on weekends to "relax." By his first year in junior high, she drank half a bottle of vodka a day. When he awoke in the morning, he often found her passed out on the living room couch. Jack wanted desperately for her to get help but she refused it. With no one to turn to, he endured the situation as best he could.

He instead lost himself in movies, especially adventure films. He lived vicariously through the main characters, traveling to strange lands and surviving near-death experiences despite the crippling odds against him.

Jack was also a voracious reader. Of all he read and studied, one subject stood out as his favorite—Atlantis, the ancient island continent that allegedly sunk into the ocean in a single day due to a natural catastrophe.

As far back as 360 B.C., learned men like Plato had written about Atlantis, but with no real evidence of its existence, scholars throughout the ages concurred that Atlantis was a made-up place, perhaps a metaphor for something the Greeks had aspired to become, an enlightened society. Real or not and much to his mother's chagrin, Jack was inexplicably obsessed with it.

Jack looked over his notes one last time before presenting in front of Ms. Ackley and the class. Each student was required to give a five- to ten-minute presentation on something related to Ancient Greece. A week earlier when assigned the project, Jack convinced Ms. Ackley to let him do it on Atlantis. She preferred students stick to Greece itself, but after Jack explained how he would "establish an allegorical context from which then to draw factual initiatives based on ..." Ms. Ackley stopped Jack mid-plea. She saw how much it meant to him and she really couldn't understand what he was saying anyway so she capitulated.

Jack's PowerPoint presentation covered Plato's description of Atlantis in his two dialogs *Timeaus* and *Critias*, how Plato's work regarding Atlantis guided Ancient Greece in its socio-political evolution, scientific and speculative theories about its disappearance and the significance of Atlantis to our modern age. Jack considered that he risked further ostracism by presenting something so detailed. Most of the other students were doing their presentations on subjects like Greek yogurt and toga parties. Already alienated with no real friends, Jack figured he'd have nothing to lose so why not enjoy it.

As Jack suspected, his presentation went over like a lead balloon. Some of his classmates fell asleep, others battered him with spit balls and the rest looked at him as though worms were crawling out of his ears. Yawning uncontrollably, Ms. Ackley stopped his presentation midway making the excuse they were running short on time. "Well, Jack, you certainly did your research!" she said sweetly, attempting to assuage his disappointment for cutting his presentation short.

"I could finish it later," offered Jack.

Ms. Ackley waved off his plea. "And the idea Atlantis existed is quite romantic."

"Romantic?" Jack was confused. "I don't understand."

Ms. Ackley completely redirected Jack's presentation. "Well, yes, romantic! Imagine if you were a Greek princess back then!"

"They didn't really call them 'princesses,'" asserted Jack. Ms. Ackley ignored him. He had seen that glazed look in her eyes before. Ms. Ackley was an incurable romantic, notorious for straying from any topic into a discussion about love—unrequited love, lost love, enduring love, ever-lasting love ...

Even though Ms. Ackley was a reasonably attractive woman in her early thirties, she was chronically single. She lived in a one-bedroom apartment with her tabby cat Mr. Whiskers. He had his own stroller and she regularly walked him around the park and talked to him like he was her child. This scared men. Her last boyfriend tolerated her eccentric behavior for a while but liked dogs better and left her a week before their one-year anniversary for a woman who bred Dalmatians.

"And what if you met a handsome, charming prince from Atlantis?" soliloquied Ms. Ackley. The girls in the class were glued to every word. The boys were clueless.

"There's really no reference to any princes in Atlantis," said Jack to no avail.

Ms. Ackley continued, "But your father, the king, didn't like this Atlantis prince and started a war."

Jack conceded a little, "Plato did refer to a war between Atlantis and Athens—"

Ms. Ackley cut him off. "Your prince is forced to choose between you, the woman he loves, and his homeland." The girls sighed.

"Did you say how they met?" asked Jack trying his best to get involved in the story.

Ms. Ackley headed for the finish line. "He chooses you!" The girls sighed again. "He heads back to tell his father but is ambushed by the enemy and killed." The girls in the class went wide-eyed. One shrieked, startling the boys.

Ms. Ackley's eyes welled up. "The love of your life is dead. He died for you! And now you can never be together." Some of the girls started crying. The boys just sat there petrified, stupefied, and had they been covered in batter, deep fried.

Ms. Ackley turned to Jack, tears streaming down her face, looking for a word of comfort, some indication this tragedy had redemption. Jack had nothing. He grabbed the box of tissues on the edge of the desk and handed it to her. "I'll go back to my desk now."

# BOWIE

Jack walked with an umbrella that was useless. The rain pelted him sideways thanks to unrelenting wind from the storm of the decade. He was soaked from head to foot, but didn't really mind. Or more appropriately, his mind was on something else—the threat earlier in the day from the school bully, Eric Header.

Because of the wet weather, Ms. Ackley kept her students indoors for recess. Jack was pretty good about staying out of Eric's way on the playground, but in close quarters, it was like being trapped in a sardine can and trying to avoid the smell of fish. Eric took it upon himself to pick on Lucy Davis, a very shy and timid girl. Eric called her "Juicy Lucy" and poked her to make juice come out. It was too much for Jack. He tried being diplomatic at first, "Come on, Eric, you can do better than that!"

"What do you mean?" asked Eric.

"She's an easy target," replied Jack.

"So?" Eric was an equal-opportunity bully. He picked on the tall, the short, the fat, the fit, girls, boys ... if you were breathing, you were a candidate for "Header and the Henchmen" as the victims called Eric and his gang of thugs.

Jack got frustrated. "How do you argue with an idiot?" he said to himself, though unfortunately, he said it out loud to himself—and everyone within a twenty-foot radius.

Since Jack referred to him in the second person, Eric didn't catch on at first because his shoe size was larger than his IQ, and he didn't have big feet to begin with. "What idiot?" asked Eric.

Jack may have been able to talk himself out of it with Eric but one of the Henchmen, Artie Buckman, overheard the insult and came right over. "Eric, I think our boy here needs to be taught a lesson!" Eric finally caught on and snarled. A few of the other Henchmen gathered around Jack just as the bell rang. Ms. Ackley ushered everyone back to their desks.

"We'll see you after school, Jackie Boy!" Eric cackled that ubiquitous bully cackle as he and his gang dispersed.

Jack had never been in a fight before and didn't feel like breaking new ground just yet, but he knew avoiding the conflict would only make it worse. He'd have to watch his back constantly and at some point, he'd still have to face the music. While Jack walked home, he thought about how much he missed having a father at times like these.

Jack knew Eric and his crew were going to give him a beating. When and where were the questions. He certainly didn't look forward to it, but strangely enough, he wasn't afraid of it either. He also considered his opinion might change after the beating.

"Well, who do we have here?" Eric stood at the corner under the awning of a storefront with four of the Henchmen in tow, Artie being one of them.

"I'm Jack, and you are?"

Eric was dumbfounded. "You don't remember my name?"

Artie nudged Eric. "He was screwing with you."

Eric shook it off a half-second too late. "I knew that!"

The Henchmen encircled their victim. Artie snatched the umbrella from Jack's hand and threw it on the sidewalk. The wind picked it up and carried it down the street. It was strangely mesmerizing to watch the umbrella dance along the asphalt. For a brief moment, there were no friends or enemies, only the random interplay of man and his environment. But such philosophical ponderings don't last long in the minds of miscreants and they quickly refocused their attention on the task at hand, beating up Jack.

The umbrella tumbled past the last building on the block, catching the attention of a hooded figure crouched down in the alleyway. The stranger watched the umbrella pass by, then turned his attention toward Jack and the group of boys surrounding him. He emerged from the shadows and approached the group.

Three of the Henchmen grabbed Jack as Eric closed in. Jack instinctively scanned for his assailants' potential weak points. The one holding his left arm had a foot within stomping distance. The one holding his right arm had his you-know-whats vulnerable to a quick downward strike. Even if he got knocked to the ground, Jack thought he could get in a good kick or two. In the end though, he would get pulverized. There were just too many of them.

"What's going on here?" a voice asked with a rather thick Scottish brogue. The stranger walked through the circle of boys and stood between Eric and Jack. He pulled back his hood and looked Eric in the eye. The stranger was a head taller than Jack and half a head shorter than Eric. His clothes were drenched from the rain and sagged on his body, which was rather brawny for a teenage boy. His weathered sandy-blond hair was pulled back in a ponytail with a rubber band.

"Who are you?" asked Eric.

The stranger just stared back at him.

Eric was slightly intimidated by this act of defiance but garnered strength from the sheer number of his friends. "This doesn't concern you!" he asserted.

The stranger didn't flinch one bit. "Didn't you just ask 'Who I am?'"

Eric looked to his gang. They were perplexed. He grew more uncomfortable and desperately clung to the notion of saving face. "Okay, who are you?"

"Your biggest problem if you don't let him go," said the stranger.

Eric turned to Jack. "He a friend of yours?"

"He is now," responded Jack.

Eric didn't know what to do. Being the predator he was, he wasn't used to anyone turning the tables, getting in his mug and challenging him. He didn't like it one bit. He pointed his finger at the stranger in warning. "If you know what's good for you—" Eric's finger touched the stranger's chest and before he could finish his sentence, a lightning-fast right hook laid him out cold.

The Henchmen were paralyzed in disbelief. Jack was paralyzed in disbelief. The stranger looked down at Eric splayed on the sidewalk. "You'd better get him to a hospital. I'm pretty sure he's got a concussion. Maybe a broken jaw as well."

Artie spoke up, "What did you do that for?"

The stranger walked up to Artie. "Five of you and one of him?" he looked over at Jack. "I wanted to even things up. Maybe you'd like to have a go?"

Artie backed off and the other boys let go of Jack. They picked up Eric who was still out cold and dragged him to the urgent care center a few blocks away.

"I really appreciate what you did," said Jack to the stranger.

"He had it coming and I was glad to give it to him."

"Can I get you something to eat as a thank you? That's the least I can do. By the way, I'm Jack, Jack Pepper." Jack extended his hand.

"Bowie Blackwood." He was no longer a stranger and shook hands with Jack.

"Would I be correct in saying you're from Scotland?" asked Jack.

"Aye, lad, you'd be farnin' the square cot." Or at least that's what it sounded like to Jack.

"I'll take that as a 'yes.' The cafe down the block has the best burgers in town," said Jack.

"Excellent!" said Bowie. "Lead the way!"

# Scotland to Sunvale

Jack and Bowie ordered burgers and spent time getting to know each other. As Jack had guessed, Bowie was from Scotland, a small town called Dunnach on the eastern seaboard. He was just a few months older than Jack.

Bowie was the only child of Fraser and Alana Blackwood. Fraser was a world-class boxer at one time. He was a mountain of a man, loyal to family and friends, boisterous and arrogant but always coming to the defense of the underdog. From an early age, his size and athletic ability segued his entry into Highlands games competitions. He also never lost a schoolyard fight, which led to detention on more than one occasion. As chance would have it, his secondary-school principal had boxed while serving in the Royal Air Force and recognized pugilistic talent when he saw it. He introduced Fraser to a family friend who was a boxing coach and trainer.

In the boxing ring, Fraser was a brute. His devastating right hook earned him the moniker "Fraser the Fist." In the heavyweight division, he quickly rose up through the ranks winning all fifteen of his professional fights via knockout and becoming a surefire contender for the title belt. Some of Bowie's earliest memories were of his father teaching him to box. By the age of four, Bowie had a devastating right hook of his own!

In contrast, Alana was petite in stature and soft-spoken, but had a huge heart and unlimited capacity for kindness and compassion. She was also a gifted musician and singer. Music was a big part of Bowie's upbringing and his mother taught him to play the guitar.

The Blackwood family life was seemingly perfect—but all that changed one night. Fraser was out with friends and had one too many McEwan's ales. He and his posse stumbled out of the pub and decided to go for a swim in the frigid waters of the North Sea. Water temperatures were cold enough to kill a man through hypothermia but Fraser never made it to open water. He tripped down an embankment and fractured his leg. The injury summarily ended his boxing career.

At first, Fraser took it in stride and accepted his own stupidity. When his leg healed well enough for him to walk again, he looked for regular work, but none was available to him. Because of boxing, he had dropped out of school and didn't have an education or trade to fall back on. He was strong as an ox but his leg never healed entirely and he walked with a pronounced limp so manual labor was out of the question. When he couldn't find work, he turned to the bottle for relief.

It quickly got to the point where he drank all day and any little thing would set off his temper. He readily broke into violent outbursts, yelling, throwing dishes and punching holes in the walls. Alana was able to comfort him initially, but over time he became more bitter and despondent. This went on for years.

Bowie came home from school one afternoon and as soon he walked through the front door, he sensed something was wrong. His father stood at the top of the staircase holding a three-quarters empty bottle of scotch in one hand while gripping the banister knob with the other to steady himself.

"Hey, Da," said Bowie.

"Son," responded his dad.

"Where's mum?" he asked.

Bowie paused the story. His eyes welled up.

"You don't have to tell me any more if you don't want to," said Jack.

Bowie regained his composure. "Long story short, I crammed a bunch of stuff into a backpack along with my life savings of forty-three euros and left. I walked to the terminal and took the ferry to Gourock. From there, I hitchhiked to Port Glasgow."

It was early evening and quite chilly when Bowie arrived at the port city. He wandered around for a while thinking about his next move. Along the boardwalk, a cartography shop caught his attention and he decided to go inside to warm up.

The shopkeeper sitting behind the counter greeted him cordially. He was an elderly gentleman and wore standard-issue Scotsman attire—forest-green wool walking sweater with suede patches on the shoulders and elbows, and tweed trousers.

Bowie strolled over to a section of the shop displaying U.S. maps and picked up the one for California. He had always wanted to go there to check out the music scene, girls in bikinis—basically all the stuff teenage-boy dreams are made of. On the wall above the display were framed black-and-white photographs taken locally—cargo ships, a couple on a sail boat, sailors on shore leave and other visitors to the port.

"Can I help you find something?" The shopkeeper materialized right next to Bowie which startled him. Despite the man's age, he was quite spry.

"Bowie showed him the map of California. "I was thinking about—I mean my family and I were thinking about going there." Bowie felt awkward lying to this man.

"Never been there myself but always wanted to go." The shopkeeper took the map from Bowie, opened it up and pursued it. "Ah!"

"What is it?" asked Bowie.

The shopkeeper pointed to a city in Northern California. "Right here, Sunvale, just populated enough to appear on the map. I know someone who lives there. Don't know if it's much of a vacation spot, but seems like a nice place to visit nonetheless." He handed the map back to Bowie and pointed to a docked cruise ship through the window. "That vessel there is headed back to New York tonight. It's scheduled to leave port at 8pm."

Bowie thought the non sequitur curious. "How much for the map?" he asked.

"It's yours," said the shopkeeper.

"I can't accept a gift—"

The shopkeeper cut him off. "I insist."

Bowie thanked the man and tucked the map away in his backpack. He left the shop and started plotting ways to get on board the cruise ship to New York. He wanted to get out of Scotland as soon as possible and Sunvale was his ultimate destination. It was as good a place as any at that point. He didn't know what he'd do once he got there but having a specific place to go gave him a goal and purpose for the time being.

There were two gangways leading up to the ship but well-guarded by security personnel checking IDs. Even if he could sneak on board somehow, where would he sleep? He didn't think he could avoid detection the entire trip. While sitting on a bench mulling over different scenarios, a cab pulled up and four young men in their mid-twenties got out. Bowie determined from eavesdropping they were musicians and by the look of them, probably a rock band. Two of the members were in a heated argument with each other.

"I'm telling you for the last time, we're playing cover songs for the entire cruise!" said the band's leader. "That's what they're paying us for! You want to play your own stuff, find a coffee shop and have at it!"

"I'm bloody sick of this, mate. In fact, I'm bloody sick of the lot of you! I quit!" said the other band member. When he turned to storm off, he bumped into Bowie. "Watch where you're going, ya twit!"

"That's just great. What are we going to do without a lead guitarist?" asked the band's drummer.

"It's your lucky day," said Bowie. "I play guitar and I'm between gigs right now."

"Shouldn't you be in school? How old are you?" asked the band's leader.

"Old enough to play with you lot," answered Bowie.

"We play mostly 70s and 80s rock—AC/DC, Arrow Smith, Zeppelin. We call ourselves Pitchfork, you know, like a devil's pitchfork. We thought the demonic undertone sounded more rock n' roll," said the bass player.

"Truth is we're all Presbyterians," confessed the drummer.

"Not a problem," said Bowie. "I can play the old stuff."

"What is a problem is getting you on board," said the band's leader. "You'll need a ticket and we can't afford to spring for one. We don't get paid until we hit the States and our pre-paid tickets are in our individual names."

Bowie revealed the wallet he lifted off the lead guitarist. He opened it up and pulled out the ID. "Will this work?" Pickpocketing was a skill he learned from his dad's brother, Uncle Fergus, a seven to ten-year *guest* of Her Majesty's Soughton Prison.

The band leader's snigger turned into a guffaw. He pulled out a pair of sunglasses and gave them to Bowie. "Here, put these on—they'll make you look older. Welcome to Pitchfork, mate!"

# DEVOVA

Jack lived a sheltered life with no adventure. Bowie lived a free-spirited life with too much adventure. Yet, here they were together. They spoke to each other with total honestly and without judgment. Despite Bowie's hardships, he was optimistic and fearless. On the opposite side of the coin, Jack was more cynical and timid. They were such polar opposites in appearance, temperament and personality, naturally they hit it off.

Though Bowie had survived quite well on his own, Jack felt compelled to help his new friend in any way he could. If the authorities found out about Bowie, they would surely ship him back to Scotland. Jack didn't know the whole story behind his leaving, but running away like he did implied Bowie had nowhere to go. At best, he'd end up living with some distant relative or in a foster home. Bowie was too independent for that to work. Jack saw their friendship as a fresh start for both of them.

Bowie wasn't used to accepting help from anyone but he liked and trusted Jack and was moved by his sincerity. He had achieved his goal of reaching Sunvale. Frankly, he didn't know what else to do.

Jack didn't really know what to do himself once they got home. He should probably call his mom to see— Call? "Oh, shoot!" It wasn't like Jack to forget checking in. His mom would be freaking out!

"What's wrong?" asked Bowie.

Jack riffled through his backpack and found his cell phone. His mom had left three messages and as many texts. He called her right away. "Hi Mom, I just got your messages."

Bowie couldn't hear what Jack's mom was saying but he could tell she was giving him the third degree.

"Mom, hold on, don't get upset, There was a bad connection because of the storm. I stayed at the school library to finish up my homework."

Bowie was impressed how Jack fabricated such a convincing impromptu lie. "Not bad," said Bowie.

Jack shushed him and returned his attention to his mother. "Are you leaving for work soon? In a little while? Okay, I'll be home in about thirty minutes. Oh, I have a friend with me, bye." He disconnected the call before his mother could protest.

Jack was nervous as he approached the front door of his home with Bowie beside him. He noticed Bowie's backpack, which looked like it belonged to a homeless person—which it basically did. "We'd better hide that outside," Jack pointed to the well-worn pack. "It looks suspicious."

"Right," said Bowie and placed it under a shrub by the walkway.

The front door was partially open. Jack heard his mother yelling at someone.

"You have no business being here! I don't want you within a mile of my son!" said Emily. Jack walked in with Bowie in tow.

His mother and an elderly woman whom Jack had never met turned to face the two boys. Emily sat on the couch holding a glass of vodka. The other woman sat in a chair opposite her. When the elderly woman saw Jack, her expression shifted from angst to soft joy. She was elegant in appearance though her tanned face and penetrating brown eyes conveyed a rugged gravitas.

There was an awkward moment of silence which Bowie shattered. "Hello! I'm Bowie," he said to Emily assuming she was Jack's mom. "I'm a friend of Jack's from school." Emily shook his extended hand, albeit curtly. Bowie looked at the drink in her other hand and grimaced. It brought back bad memories of his father.

"Jack's never mentioned you before," said Emily.

Jack chimed in, "He's new to the school, an exchange student from Scotland. His host family lives just a few blocks away."

Bowie extended his hand to the other woman. "And you are?"

"I'm Devova, Jack's grandmother." Jack's jaw dropped. Bowie and Devova shook hands. She couldn't place it but Bowie reminded her of someone.

"It's a pleasure to meet you," he said. "Can I call you 'Gram Devova?' You're Jack's grandmother after all. It feels less formal." Bowie was brazen in his request. Jack was awed by it. Gram Devova delighted in it. Emily hated it.

"'Gram Devova' it is," she said. She turned to Jack and opened her arms to hug him. 'It's so good to finally—"

"I said stay away from him!" asserted Emily. Devova reluctantly honored her daughter's wishes. "You'll ruin his life just like you did mine and I won't have that!" She took a gulp of her vodka.

Watching Emily drink pushed an old button in Bowie. "It's a little early for that, don't you think?" he said.

Emily's shock turned to anger. "Who the hell do you think you are telling me what to do in my house!"

Bowie didn't apologize but swallowed his harsher sentiments. "I meant no offense."

Devova addressed Emily. "I know you hate me for what I believe in and—"

"What you believe in is nonsense! What's worse is you had me believing it for so many years!" Emily teared up. "It's why Dad left us and it's also why Robert walked out on me the week before I found out I was pregnant!"

"Honey, what I told you was all true! In a month, the truth will come to light, I promise you!"

Bowie couldn't help but get involved in the conversation even though he had no clue what they were talking about. "What happens in a month?" he asked anyone who would answer.

"My birthday, for one thing," said Jack as if prompted by an invisible force.

"That's right!" Devova went to pick something out of a large canvas bag she had lying next to the chair. "I need to give you—"

Emily stood up and got between Devova and Jack. "You are not going to give him anything! Get out now or I'll call the police!" Devova peered into her daughter's calloused eyes, trying to find a glimpse of the love Emily once had for her. There was none to be seen. Taking the bag with her, she exited the house without saying another word.

Emily reached for her drink but saw Bowie eyeballing her and changed her mind. She rubbed her head as if trying to ward off a migraine then noticed the time. "Damn it, I'm going to be late. I have to go."

She grabbed her purse and coat. "I need to speak to my son alone for a moment," she directed at Bowie.

"I'll wait outside." Bowie exited the house.

Emily waited until Bowie was out of earshot. "I don't trust that boy and he is not to set foot in this house again!"

"But Mom, he's my friend! You can trust him!" pleaded Jack.

"Don't backtalk me, young man! He's no good. I can tell," said Emily.

"You don't know him!" Jack held his ground. "He's staying if I say he's staying!" Emily slapped her son hard across the face. She had never struck him until that moment and they were both stunned by it. Jack's eyes filled with tears.

"We'll talk about this later," remarked Emily. She turned away from her son, wiped a tear away from the corner of her eye and left the house. Jack followed her to the door and watched her drive off.

He stepped outside to look for Bowie but didn't see him. Maybe he had taken off. Who could blame him? Then he remembered the backpack. He went to the shrub where it was hidden. He pulled it out just as Bowie came around the corner.

"Are you going to do my laundry for me?" asked Bowie.

"I was actually going to burn the whole backpack." Jack took a whiff of it. "It smells like spoiled cheese!"

"I like spoiled cheese!" retorted Bowie. "I guess your mom and I really hit it off, eh? What did she say to you when I left?"

Jack winced a bit. "Something to the effect of *you're not welcome in our house.*"

"I see," said Bowie. He noticed the red welt on Jack's face. "Did she hit you?"

"It's nothing." Jack was embarrassed.

"I don't want to cause any trouble——"

"You're not and don't worry about it. Her shift goes to 1 am. My home is your home and I won't hear anything different. At night, you can sleep in the attic. She never goes up there and there's an entrance from my closet. She's usually passed out in the mornings so it shouldn't be too hard to sneak you out. She's off on Sundays and Mondays. We'll figure out something for then."

Bowie was immensely appreciative. "I owe you big time."

"You don't owe me anything. And I'll help you do your laundry but I'm not touching your underwear!" emphasized Jack.

"I don't blame you! I swear, one pair almost got up last week and walked away on its own!" said Bowie half seriously.

The two boys had already been through a lot together in just a short period of time. Their bond was solid and everything to follow would only serve to make it stronger.

# hIDING OUT

Over the next month, the plan worked flawlessly. In the mornings, Jack snuck Bowie out the back door. Jack went to school during the day while Bowie hung out at a local park, the mall or around town. When an adult questioned why he wasn't in school, he said he was visiting from Scotland and his relatives were at work. His accent sold them on the story.

Jack came home from school and waited for his mom to leave. After she left, he met Bowie in the backyard, which faced an open field so it never aroused suspicion from the neighbors. Together, they fixed up a make-shift bedroom in the attic, complete with an air mattress, sheets, comforter and lamp.

Jack had quite the collection of DVDs. He first played his favorite movie *Raiders of the Lost Ark*. Bowie had never seen the film before but it became his instant favorite as well. There was one scene in particular they replayed at least a dozen times: the hero Indiana Jones frantically searches for his love interest Marion who was kidnapped by hired thugs via the Nazis in Cairo, circa 1936. Cairo was a frenetic city with many of the inhabitants dressed in turbans and kaftans so it was hard to distinguish the actual kidnappers who also wore turbans and caftans. And the basket in which they were holding Marion looked like every other basket holding goods and supplies.

In the famous scene, Indiana Jones turns a corner looking for her. The crowd clears and there standing in his path is a fierce and foreboding swordsman-assassin dressed in black waiting to dispose of him. As the assassin stares down Indiana Jones, he tries to intimidate him with fancy swordplay, shifting his oversized scimitar from hand to hand and swinging it with martial precision. Indiana Jones is fatigued and annoyed. He needs to find Marion but this brute stands in his path. He's no match for the swordsman. But his revolver is. He pulls out his gun and shoots the swordsman dead. Done deal. Obstacle gone.

The first time Bowie watched that scene, he laughed out loud for a full minute. "Freakin' brilliant!"

"I know, right?" said Jack.

"Hey, I want to show you something!" Bowie went into the attic, rummaged through his backpack and returned with something wrapped in an old t-shirt and stuffed in a Ziploc bag. He opened it up and inside was a Smith & Wesson .357 Magnum along with one bullet.

"Whoa! Where did you get it?" asked Jack.

"It belonged to my Dad. I think he won it in a poker game. He used to keep it in his nightstand. When his drinking got really bad, I hid it in the garage, just in case. I took it with me when I ran away," said Bowie.

Jack was both enthralled and fearful of the weapon. He had never seen a gun up close. "Did you ever fire it?"

Bowie picked it up and aimed it at an invisible villain. "One time, I was sitting under a freeway overpass in Iowa and these four guys started yelling at me and threatened to beat me up if I didn't turn over the can of tuna fish I was eating. I pulled it out and shot it in their general direction a few times. They took off."

"That must have been scary!" projected Jack.

"Sure it was," confirmed Bowie. "And then when I was going through Utah, I got so hungry, I tried to shoot a squirrel."

"Tried?" questioned Jack.

"I wasn't that good a shot," admitted Bowie. " Even if I had shot it, I wouldn't have known what to do with it." Bowie held up the solitary bullet. "I have one left." He looked at it pensively. At one point, Bowie had thought about using the bullet on himself. He had experienced deep despair after running away. He figured what would be the difference if one less person was on this planet? But Bowie was a fighter with an indelible spirit. In his heart, he believed he was put on this earth for a purpose and he was going to find out what it was. A few months ago, he had nothing. Now, he had a friend, a best friend. Jack made sure he had food, clean clothes, and more than any material thing, Jack helped him realize he had worth and value, else why would someone go to so much effort on his behalf?

Jack picked up on the vibe and tried lightening the mood. "Save that one for an evil swordsman!"

"Sounds like a good idea." Bowie smirked. "Have you seen any lately?"

Jack played along. "There was one at the Starbucks this afternoon, but he's probably gone by now."

At first, Jack didn't know what to do about Bowie when his mom had time off from work. She usually hung out around the house, drank and would occasionally run errands, but nothing with any consistency. It was too risky for Bowie to stay in the attic when she was home for the day. Then Jack remembered in the open field behind their house stood an old oak tree and among its branches was an abandoned tree house built by some neighborhood kids over a decade earlier. Jack had never been in it because of his fear of heights so Bowie climbed up to inspect it. The structure was open on one side but enclosed on the other three sides. Save for one loose floor board, which Bowie nearly fell through, the tree house was in pretty good shape.

It took Bowie a few hours to kill off the spiders and clean out the inside to make it generally livable. The sleeping bag, tarp, flashlight and bucket Jack found in the garage went a long way to making it downright homey.

The tree's canopy was very dense so Bowie was well concealed. The boys developed a rope-and-pulley system for supplies and refuge, though Jack refused to handle Bowie's "personal hygiene" bucket, which both of them were fine with to keep their friendship on speaking terms.

On Cinco De Mayo, Jack and Bowie celebrated by making Bowie's new favorite dish, nachos. There was a knock on the front door and both boys froze for a moment. "It's not my mom," surmised Jack. "She wouldn't need to knock. Probably someone selling something."

"You want me to get the gun?" asked Bowie.

"That's okay, but if the person has a scimitar, I'll yell for you." Jack went to the door and opened it. There stood his grandmother holding a green-hued wooden box. They stared at each other without speaking. Bowie came up behind Jack. "Well, if it isn't Gram Devova! Don't be rude, Jack. Invite her in!"

Jack hesitated for a moment remembering his mom didn't want her in the house. But it was his grandmother after all and he was a bit curious. "Yes, please come in." Devova walked in and sat in the living room holding the box.

"Do you want some nachos?" offered Bowie.

"No, thank you," she said.

"Something to drink then?' persisted Bowie. "I can get you a glass of water and I think we have a Fresca left, which I have to say tastes horrible, but well, maybe you Americans like it."

She smiled faintly. "Just some water, thanks."

"Coming right up!" Bowie went to get her the water. Jack took a seat opposite his grandmother.

"Why are you here?" asked Jack directly.

"It's your birthday in two days," she said.

"You showed up after all this time to celebrate my birthday?" Jack didn't know where this was going but he thought the unusual box she was holding had something to do with it. "Why now? Why are you here now?" asked Jack with some edge. He was angry she never visited him earlier in his life. Since his mother had fallen into deep depression and alcoholism, no one had ever tried to ease his burden, until Bowie came along.

Devova looked hurt but maintained her composure. "There's too much to explain right now."

Bowie came in with the water for Devova and a plate of nachos. "Last chance on the nachos," he said and extended them to her. She gently waved her hand in refusal. "Jack, how about you?"

"Not right now," said Jack, keeping his eyes on his grandmother.

"I'll leave you two alone for a while." Bowie went into the kitchen to give them space.

Devova handed the box to Jack. "This is for you."

The wood was dense and the box had some weight to it. "What is it?" he asked.

"What's inside is extremely important," answered Devova somberly.

Jack opened the box. Inside laid a pristine nautilus shell. He picked it up gently and looked at it from all angles. He was confused. "A nautilus shell? What's so important about this shell?"

"Maybe it's a metaphor!" an eavesdropping Bowie yelled from the kitchen.

"I got this one, Bowie, thank you," answered Jack. He turned back toward his grandmother. "What am I supposed to do with it?"

She let out a sigh and closed her eyes to collect herself for a moment before speaking. "On your birthday, at the exact moment you were born, 12:03 A.M., you need to hold the shell up to your ear." Jack waited for the punchline but none came.

A skeptical look swept across Jack's face. "What's going to happen?"

"In truth, I don't know," answered Devova. She changed the subject. "Has your mother told you anything about me, how close we once were or why we don't talk anymore?"

Jack thought for a moment. "No, not really. She only said you were crazy." He could tell his words cut Devova deeply but he thought better to answer truthfully.

"'Certified whack job' were the exact words you said she used!" yelled Bowie from the kitchen.

"Thanks for the clarification!" Jack yelled back.

"I'm afraid if I told you everything, you would think I was crazy, too," admitted Devova.

"Well, you show up for the first time in my life just as I'm turning fourteen years-old and give me a shell so on my exact birthday I can hold it up to my ear and then you don't know what will happen but it's very important," he summed up concisely.

"He's got a point!" yelled Bowie from the kitchen.

"Thanks for the assist, but I'm doing fine by myself!" replied Jack.

"No worries!" answered Bowie.

Devova couldn't contest the facts. "I realize it's a lot to ask, Jack, but I'm asking you to trust me. Will you do it?"

Jack held the shell up to his ear. "I don't hear anything special now, just the sound of the ocean, which is really not the case." Jack entered professor mode. "Scientists used to believe it was the echo of our blood pumping but was later discovered to be the echo of the air around us, also known as ambient noise."

"Just say you'll do it!" yelled Bowie.

Jack didn't answer him this time. Why should he listen to a mad woman, even if it was his grandmother? She came out of nowhere and asked him to do something that if anyone found out, he'd be the laughing stock of Sunvale.

"I guess it won't hurt to do it," conceded Jack.

"Oh, thank you, Jack!" She jumped out of her seat and hugged him, but was careful not to crush the shell. Devova's embrace was warm and loving. He hadn't felt anything like that in years.

She pulled away from him and held his gaze. "Remember, it has to be exactly at 12:03 A.M. or else!"

"Or else whatever is supposed to happen won't happen," iterated Jack.

"I'll go now. We'll talk soon." Devova cupped his cheek in her hand then turned toward the door and left.

Bowie came out from the kitchen and looked at the shell. "That's cool! Hey, what do you think will happen?"

"I don't think anything will happen. You really think something is going to happen?" asked Jack.

"Heck no, but as we say in Scotland, "Whit's fur ye'll no go by ye!"

"Say what?"

Bowie translated, "It means what's meant to happen will happen."

Jack didn't want to think about it any further for the time being. "Where are those nachos?"

"I've got another round in the oven as we speak," said Bowie.

Jack mustered up his best Scottish accent, "That's freakin' greeeat!"

"Were you imitating me?" asked Bowie.

Jack smiled. "No, William Wallace."

"If that's what he sounded like, I understand why he was drawn and quartered!" Bowie walked back into the kitchen.

Jack laughed until he realized Bowie just insulted him. "Hey!"

That night, Jack dreamt he held the nautilus shell up to his ear and was suddenly sucked into darkness. He woke up with a start and turned on his nightstand light. He checked under his bed and pulled out the wooden box. He opened it up and there sat the nautilus shell. He thought his grandmother may truly be insane. But he told her he'd hold it up to his ear at exactly 12:03 A.M. on his birthday and he would be true to his word. If his mother found out about the shell, she would smash it to bits, which wouldn't be a big deal considering *probably* nothing was going to happen anyway. Jack put the shell back in the box and placed it under his bed. "Probably?" he thought to himself. "Of course nothing will happen!" He shrugged it off and went back to sleep.

Five miles away in a hotel room, Devova sat by the window looking up at the starry sky. As she took in the beauty of the universe, she softly chimed the same verses over and over:

*Ging-de-lot-dot-de-dig*
*Fung-hey-dey-lot-de-dot-dora*
*Shung-gonna-fot-te-zing*
*Fong-bay-te-le-dot-de-vova*

*Grare-te-lot-don-fu-te*
*Ang-wan-bay-la-taun-vay-fuega*
*Lom-gonna-zot-she-tang*
*Gome-ply-werti-som-sot-sora*

# JACK'S BIRTHDAY

"So, tonight's the big night!" said Bowie while he and Jack played a video game in the living room.

"What do you mean?" asked Jack, though he knew exactly what Bowie was talking about.

"The shell!" said Bowie.

"What shell?" answered Jack sarcastically. "Oh come on! You really don't expect anything to happen, do you?"

"Maybe the shell will give us the winning lottery numbers!" said Bowie. "You have to admit, a wee part of you thinks just maybe something will happen." Bowie searched for confirmation in his friend's eyes.

Jack turned away. "I don't have to admit anything." They heard someone at the front door. "It's Mom!"

"Why is she home so early?" asked Bowie.

"No idea. Better get into the attic!" said Jack. Bowie practically sprinted into Jack's bedroom closet and up the attic stairs, pulling the collapsible steps behind him.

Jack turned off the video game and hid one of controllers under the couch. Mom, is that you?" he called out.

"Come help me, Jack!" she said through the front door.

Jack opened the door. His mother was on crutches with her ankle wrapped up in an ACE bandage. "What happened?"

"Grab my stuff," she replied. Jack took her purse and car keys and helped her onto the couch.

"The idiot janitor was mopping the floor and forgot to put down the caution sign. I turned the corner and my foot slipped right out from under me, sprained my ankle. It was so embarrassing. They forced me to get an x-ray then sent me home with crutches."

"Can I get you anything?" asked Jack.

"I'm thirsty," she replied.

"Do you want some water?"

"You know what I want," she said. Jack knew. She wanted a glass with ice. While he went into the kitchen to get it, she pulled out a half-full bottle of vodka from the coffee-table drawer. She also pulled out a bottle of pills from her purse.

Jack came back and set down the glass with ice on the coffee table. He noticed the pills. "What are those for?"

"They're pain pills, silly! Your mother isn't a spring chicken anymore. Sprain ankles hurt!" She filled the glass.

"Just be careful, okay? You know, mixing—"

She cut him off. "I'm a nurse for God's sake. I think I know my way around pills!"

Jack changed the subject. "How long will you be out of work?"

"They told me at least a week, maybe longer," she said.

"A week?" said Jack distressed. Bowie would have to hide out in the tree house the whole time his mom was laid up and Jack would be nothing short of a man-servant, waiting on her hand and foot. He'd have a hard time sneaking away.

Emily could tell Jack wasn't happy about the prospect of her being home for an extended period. It hurt her feelings though deep down, she knew she was the cause of it. "Do me a favor, Jack. Go into my bedroom and on the dresser is a small box. You can't miss it. Bring it here, please."

Jack complied. On the dresser was a small box tied up with ribbon. He brought it back into the living room as his mom was taking a slug of her drink to wash down four pain pills. "What is it?" asked Jack holding up the box.

"Your destiny," she said severely.

Jack was shocked. "My destiny?" Maybe she was in collusion with Devova and the whole estranged relationship situation was completely staged to test his character. He had a vivid imagination.

Emily held out a few seconds longer before laughing. "I'm just kidding, Jack. The expression on your face ... you look so serious! It's your birthday present. Open it." His mom smiled sweetly and ran her fingers through his hair. Jack was taken back. He couldn't remember the last time she had been affectionate with him.

"Well, aren't you going to open it?" she asked.

"But it's not my birthday yet," said Jack.

"A technicality. Your birthday is three minutes after midnight. We'll probably both be asleep by then. Just open it," she insisted.

Jack opened the gift. Inside was an antique, albeit functional, compass attached to a sterling-silver chain.

"It belonged to your great grandfather," she said. "When I was a little girl, he often took me sailing. He was very funny and very smart. He even taught me how to read nautical charts and navigate using this compass."

"That's so cool!" Jack rarely heard his mother speak about her childhood.

"I was actually pretty good at it, but I've forgotten. That was a long time ago. Anyway, I'm sure he would have wanted you to have it," she said and placed the chain around Jack's neck. "He was a good man, just like you." She gently kissed him on the cheek.

Jack hugged her. "Thank you, Mom." She hugged him back and held him tight. There were many things they both wanted to express to each other but words failed them in the moment. A hug would have to do. Emily let go of Jack and wiped the tears from her eyes. "It's getting late. You should probably go to bed."

Jack got up to leave but a thought made him pause. "Maybe we could go sailing sometime." As soon as he said it, he felt stupid. "Or we could do something else together—it doesn't have to be sailing."

Emily looked at her son with soft eyes. "I'd like that, Jack."

He knew they would never go sailing together but for a brief moment, he allowed himself to hope. "I love you, Mom."

"I love you, too, Jack." Her eyes teared up again and she waved him away.

Jack went into his bedroom closet and pulled down the attic stairs. He looked in on Bowie who was crashed out on the air mattress and decided not to wake him.

He set the alarm for midnight, figuring he'd need a few minutes to fully wake up before holding the nautilus shell to his ear. "This is nuts!" he said to himself out loud. His grandmother was probably crazy just like his mom said, but why would she show up after all these years? If she really was crazy, wouldn't she have been institutionalized by now? Had she really waited decades just to give him a shell? Without knowing much about their falling out, he couldn't draw any concrete conclusions. Jack laid his head down on his pillow and drifted off to sleep.

The alarm went off at midnight waking Jack with a start. "Whoa!" He was so disoriented at first, he didn't know where he was. After a few breaths, he got his bearings and looked at the clock—12:01 A.M., two more minutes until his birthday. Jack reached under his bed and recovered the wooden box. He pulled out the shell and gave it the once over. The clock read 12:02 A.M. "I still think this is crazy," he said to the shell. "Oh, great, now I'm talking to shells." Jack held the shell up to his ear and heard the familiar echoing sound of ambient noise. He waited for twenty seconds and nothing. Then it happened.

The echoing turned into a static-like vibration, then words were spoken, though Jack couldn't tell if he was actually hearing words or thinking the words: "31 degrees, 24 minutes, 25.58 seconds north, 24 degrees, 32 minutes, 9.08 seconds west, *lunius* 21, 2:13 post meridian."

Jack grabbed a pen and paper. The phrase repeated and he wrote it down verbatim. The static-like vibration returned, transitioned back to the echo of ambient noise and that was it. The message had been delivered.

He was pretty sure the first part was nautical coordinates. He would have to check Google maps. The second part was "lunius 21." Jack had heard "lunius" before. He'd have to look that up as well. The third part, 2:13 post meridian, was the time of day, 2:13pm. So, maybe the middle part was the date. Jack got up and went to his laptop. Just as he suspected, *lunius* was Latin for "June." June 21st then, the summer solstice. He typed in the coordinates. The map took him to the middle of the Atlantic Ocean. Nothing there, not so much as a tiny atoll when he zoomed in. "Middle of the Atlantic Ocean, June 21st, 2:13 P.M. It's official, I'm crazy." He closed his laptop and returned to bed.

Jack took off the compass which was still hanging around his neck and laid it on top of his nightstand. He quickly fell into a deep, dreamless sleep.

\*\*\*

The alarm went off at 6:30 A.M. Jack woke up hard. Bowie came down from the attic rubbing sleep from his eyes. He had a small present wrapped in crate paper and twine in his hand and gave it to Jack. "Here you go then."

Jack took the gift. "What's this for?"

"Your wedding, genius, what do you think?" said Bowie.

Jack laughed. "You didn't need to do anything for my birthday."

"I wanted to. That's why they call it a gift and not a chore," responded Bowie.

Jack opened up the present. It was a Ghostrike Fixed Blade Deluxe tactical knife with ankle holster. "This is awesome! Thank you!"

"I figured you wouldn't get a lot of weapons for your birthday this year, so I thought a knife was a safe bet," reasoned Bowie.

"Can't argue with you there," said Jack. "Hey, how were you able to afford this?" Jack knew better than to accuse his friend of stealing it. Yes, Bowie had pickpocketed a wallet to get on the cruise ship and shoplifted some food when he was crossing the country—but only when he was absolutely starving and couldn't find food anywhere else. Still, he was curious as to how Bowie acquired the funds.

Bowie sensed Jack's suspicion. "There was a bloke in town who was cleaning out his shop last week and paid me to help him. Made a few bucks."

Jack held his finger to his lips for Bowie to be quiet. They were talking louder than usual and he didn't want to wake up his mom. A moment later though, he sensed something was wrong. "Wait here, I'm going to check on her." He went into the hallway and listened for any noise. It was quiet. Too quiet. He continued walking into the living room where his mom was passed out on the couch. The empty vodka bottle sat on the coffee table along with the opened pill container. Only a few pills remained. His mom looked pale as a ghost. Jack gently touched her cheek. She was cold to the touch. "Mom?" He pulled his fingers away. He put his ear by her mouth. She wasn't breathing. "Mom!" he shouted.

Jack grabbed her cell phone lying on the coffee table. His hands were shaking but he managed to dial 911. Bowie ran into the room when he heard Jack yell. "What's wrong?" he asked. He looked over at Emily and knew it wasn't good.

Jack didn't answer him. He waited for the emergency operator to pick up. After what felt like an eternity, a woman's voice came on the line. "911, what's your emergency?"

"My mom isn't breathing!"

Bowie pushed back the coffee table and gently lowered Emily to the floor.

"What are you doing?" Jack yelled at Bowie.

"I'm going to try CPR," replied Bowie. He was a Scout at one time and had earned his first-aid merit badge.

"Does she have a pulse?" asked the emergency operator.

"Check for a pulse!" said Jack. Bowie checked for a pulse at her carotid artery. He shook his head. There was no pulse.

"She doesn't have a pulse. My friend is performing CPR. Send someone quick. Please!" Jack gave her the address.

"We have paramedics in route," said the operator.

Bowie kept up CPR until the paramedics arrived ten minutes later. Jack held the front door open for them as they rushed in. Trailing them in the driveway was Jack's grandmother. "Emily?" asked Devova.

Jack was speechless. He returned to the living room but left the front door open.

He watched as the paramedics injected her with adrenaline. Nothing. They tried the defibrillator several times but couldn't get a sinus rhythm. The paramedics looked at each other grimly. They quickly loaded her onto a gurney though her body was limp and lifeless. The junior paramedic put an ambu bag over Emily's mouth and squeezed it regularly to force air into her lungs.

The senior paramedic addressed Devova. "Are you relations?"

"I'm her mother," she confirmed.

"We're taking her to General."

"Is she alive?" asked Devova in a quivering voice.

"We're not getting any vital signs," said the senior paramedic.

The paramedics loaded Emily into the ambulance. Jack was overwhelmed with feelings. Devova stood quietly, tears in her eyes, looking at Jack.

Bowie was exhausted after administering CPR. "I tried to save her, Jack. I really tried."

Jack smiled at his friend. "I know you did. Thank you for that."

Devova drove them all to the hospital where they waited in the emergency room. After forty-five minutes without a word spoken, Devova broke the silence. "Did the shell give you a message?"

Jack shot her a contemptuous look. With everything going on, he had completely forgotten about the shell. "I don't want to talk about it right now!" he said curtly.

Devova pressed on despite Jack's mood. "It spoke to you, didn't it?"

"I said I don't want to talk about it," repeated Jack. She looked at him and waited. "All right, yes," said Jack disdainfully. "It spoke to me."

Bowie looked surprised. "Well, I'll be a rusty nail!"

"What was the message?" asked Devova.

Jack's eyes filled with anger. "I don't want to talk about it right now!"

"It's important!" insisted Devova.

"More important than your daughter?" countered Jack.

Devova didn't have a response. Whatever message Jack received from the shell was more significant than he could possibly imagine. If she pushed him though, he may resist doing what needed to be done. She was also sure Jack distrusted whatever the message was. It was one thing to receive a message from a shell. It was an entirely other matter to follow it.

After several minutes of deafening silence, Jack finally gave in and told her the message in its entirety.

Devova's eyes lit up. Bowie saw her reaction and said, "You know what the message means, don't you?"

Devova was just about to answer him when the doctor walked in.

"Are you Emily's family?" asked the doctor.

"I'm her mother," said Devova. "And this is her son, Jack. And a close family friend, Bowie."

"I'm sorry to tell you this, but Emily is gone," said the doctor. "She had probably been deceased for several hours before she arrived here."

Even though they had suspected as much, it was still shocking to hear it confirmed. The doctor continued, "She likely had a bad reaction to the combination of Oxycodone and alcohol in her system." He paused to let them assimilate the news. "Take whatever time you need. When you're ready, Valerie at the nurse's station can help you make arrangements. I'm very sorry for your loss." The doctor left them.

Devova legs collapsed underneath her but Bowie caught her before she hit the ground. Her only child was dead. She felt responsible and sobbed uncontrollably. Bowie helped her to a chair. Jack still didn't trust his grandmother but he shared her pain. He walked over and hugged her hard. She hugged him back and together they cried. Bowie put his arms around both of them.

Jack had never been through the death of anyone close to him before. Everything happened so fast, he initially felt numb to it. He was preoccupied with a million thoughts running around in his head on the way home from the hospital. What was he going to do? What would happen to him? Should he look for his father? Was his father even alive? Was his grandmother going to ask him to live with her? Where did she even live? What would happen to Bowie?

They arrived back at the house and went into the living room but no one sat on the couch were Emily had been found. "I need to talk to both of you," said Devova. She sat on one of the chairs. Jack took the other and Bowie grabbed a chair from the kitchen.

"We'll listen," Jack said warily.

Devova looked relieved. "That's all I can ask."

"Does anyone want some nachos before we get started?" asked Bowie.

Jack rolled his eyes. "Really, Bowie? Nachos?"

"I have a feeling we have a lot to talk about, is all." said Bowie unapologetically.

Devova capitulated. "We haven't eaten all day. It may be easier to hear what I have to say after a little nourishment."

"One plate of nachos, coming right up!" said Bowie.

The nachos were very comforting after the day they had been through. After a few bites, Devova bluntly said, "We have to leave as soon as possible."

"The school year isn't over yet," said Jack. "And what about the funeral—"

Devova cut him off, "There's no time for any of it! In a few weeks, none of it will matter anyway."

Jack was furious. "Mom's death won't matter?"

"That's not what I meant!" she said exacerbated. "I can't explain it all!"

"Where do you want to go then?" asked Jack.

"To our family house in Maine," she answered.

"You just want to leave Mom's body here?" Jack put his foot down. "I'm not doing that!"

"We can't afford to waste any time, Jack. I'm going to call the airlines and get us on the next flight out of town," she said.

"One slight problem," chimed in Bowie. "I can't fly."

"Why not?" asked Devova.

Bowie thought about a polite way to say it. "I may be sort of wanted."

Devova was taken aback. "Sort of? Wanted for what?"

Before Bowie could respond, Jack interjected, "Never mind that! You drove here, didn't you?"

"Yes," she confirmed.

"So, we'll drive back in a few days," concluded Jack.

Time is crucial!" insisted Devova.

Bowie had an idea. "You both could go now and I could catch up with you in a few weeks."

"That might be best," said Devova.

Jack closed his eyes for a few moments to focus. When he opened them, he looked directly at his grandmother. "We'll make arrangements to have Mom cremated. If it takes a few days, so be it. Just last night, she spoke fondly of sailing with her grandfather. We'll spread her ashes at sea. I think she'd like that. Also, I'm not coming with you unless Bowie comes, too. So we're driving."

This is not what Devova wanted. If Jack knew what was at stake, he wouldn't require such concessions, but to burden him with any more at this point might have broken him. And Bowie was critical to this whole thing. Devova didn't know how or why, but she felt it intuitively.

"Very well," answered Devova.

It took four days to get Emily's ashes. During the wait, Jack tried as best he could to clean up the house and garage. It wouldn't make much difference if he was just going to abandon everything but the process provided him with some sense of closure.

It was a strange feeling for Jack to up and leave the only home he had ever known to go with his grandmother, whom he barely knew, across the country. *Thank God for Bowie* he thought to himself. Bowie made him feel like everything was going to be okay. At the same time, he was concerned for his friend. Even though Bowie seemed up for the adventure, Jack didn't want to put him in a dangerous situation. For all he knew, his grandmother was some kind of psycho and she'd drive them all off a cliff on the way to Maine!

Jack set down a box of old photos in the garage and turned to his friend. "Are you sure you want to do this? You're taking an even bigger leap of faith than me. The shell didn't speak to you. I may be going crazy but I don't expect you to follow along."

"Didn't you know?" asked Bowie.

"Know what?" wondered Jack.

"I was *born* crazy," remarked Bowie.

Jack shook his head. "That much I know."

# Maine

The drive to Maine was a bear. The trio spent eighteen hours a day on the road, barely stopping for food or to answer the call of nature before checking into a motor lodge for a few hours of sleep before hitting the highway again.

Despite Bowie's plea to "learn as I go," Devova insisted on doing all the driving since she was the only licensed driver. Because of the urgency, there were no side trips to take in America's natural wonders or even novelties like the biggest ball of twine.

Instead, they played all kinds of car games to pass the time like twenty questions and Jack's favorite, biography. The latter is played when one drives by a vehicle and then in one or two sentences, makes up the biography of the person or people in that car. After everyone's turn, the other participants vote on whose biography they liked best. They drove by a middle-aged man wearing a bright orange baseball cap. Jack gave his bio—"After failing his audition as a pylon for an upcoming TV miniseries, Mr. Brightly took a full time job at the airport to help planes land in the fog."

Jack usually won but Bowie got pretty creative as the trip went on, like the time they drove by a rather corpulent woman in a convertible, blasting the radio and singing along out loud. Bowie gave her bio—"She used to be an opera singer but got hit in the head by a strobe light on opening night of Don Giovanni, causing partial amnesia. When she awoke, she could only remember songs she'd heard on the radio."

"Hit in the head with a strobe light?" questioned Jack.

"Oh sure, strobe lights kill more people than coconuts each year!" said Bowie matter-of-factly.

Devova and Jack both lost it. Devova was laughing so hard she almost ran their vehicle off the side of the road.

"How do you know about Don Giovanni?" asked Devova.

"My mom wrote a folk version of one of the songs in the opera," explained Bowie. "She used to sing it to me when I was a bairn."

"Sing it to us!" suggested Jack.

"Ach! No! I wouldn't do it justice!" insisted Bowie.

"Please, Bowie," said Devova. "We could use a song."

"It's kind of a 'chick' song," emphasized Bowie.

"And what am I?" asked Devova with a derisive undertone.

Bowie couldn't refute that. "Fair enough, but if the windows start to crack, don't blame me."

"I'll get the duct tape ready just in case," offered Jack.

Bowie took a swig of bottled water and cleared his throat:

*Hush now, sad heart, from grievin'*
*The days of joy are through*
*The traitor with wiles deceivin'*
*Hath broke mine heart in two*
*His words strangely affect me*
*Sweet love, thou do direct me!*
*But never can I believe again*
*Believe in thou again*
*For this my heart has panted,*
*Shall I refuse or give it gain?*
*By some enchantment spell-bound,*
*Quite fled is my disdain*

The song brought tears to Devova's eyes. "That was beautiful, Bowie. Sad and beautiful."

Close to midnight on the fourth day of marathon driving, Devova pulled into the driveway of a two-story Cape Code waterfront cottage. Bowie was sound asleep in the back seat. Jack got out and closed the door gently so as not to wake him. He deeply inhaled the salt air and was mesmerized by the moonlight shimmering across the surface of the canal. The cool breeze gave him a slight chill.

Devova got out on the other side. "This is it. Why don't you and Bowie bring in the luggage? I'll go in and get the heater going."

Jack opened the car door. "Bowie, wake up, we're here!"

With his eyes still closed, Bowie grumbled, "I was dreaming I was the judge in a beauty contest."

"Who were you going to pick?" asked Jack.

Bowie opened his eyes. "Miss Scotland, of course!"

"Ach!" mocked Jack.

Bowie helped Jack unload the luggage and bring it into the house.

"Reminds me of home a bit," remarked Bowie. "We lived close to the water as well."

The home was decorated with a heavy nautical theme comprised of authentic maritime objects—a brass deep diver's helmet, fishing net on one wall, signal lanterns, buoys and various nautical regalia.

An antiquated map hanging on the wall caught Jack's eye. Devova walked up behind him. Jack felt her presence but remained transfixed on the map. "This is Athanasius Kircher's map of Atlantis."

"That's correct," confirmed Devova.

The map was oriented upside down. Part of the map showed the eastern portion of the North American continent and the western portions of Africa and Hypania respectively, separated by the Atlantic Ocean. In the middle was Atlantis, depicted as an island roughly the size of Spain.

"You'd better get some sleep," suggested Devova. "We have a big day tomorrow."

After four days of marathon driving, Jack was in full agreement though something gnawed at his subconscious. He decided to postpone his normal neurosing for the time being and figured he'd have plenty of time to really worry about everything in the morning.

*\*\*\**

The boys slept in the guest bedroom which had two twin beds. Jack woke to the smell of breakfast steaks cooking on the stove and Devova singing. It was actually more of a chant than a song.

*Ging-de-lot-dot-de-dig*
*Fung-hey-dey-lot-de-dot-dora*
*Shung-gonna-fot-te-zing*
*Fong-bay-te-le-dot-de-vova*

*Grare-te-lot-don-fu-te*
*Ang-wan-bay-la-taun-vay-fuega*
*Lom-gonna-zot-she-tang*
*Gome-ply-werti-som-sot-sora*

Jack gently shook Bowie awake. They shuffled out to the kitchen where Devova was making breakfast. "Good morning, you two," she said energetically. She couldn't haven't slept more than a few hours herself but showed no outward signs of exhaustion.

They nodded good morning, still not coherent enough to actually speak. She served them each a breakfast steak cooked in olive oil with onions. It smelled pretty darn good and after four days of fast food, it was absolute heaven. They both dug in. "Thank you, this is great!" said Bowie as an onion tried to escape his mouth down his chin.

"Yes, thank you," said Jack more reserved.

"You're both very welcome. It's nice cooking for more than one for a change," she said nostalgically.

They gorged themselves on the steak and onions, toast, fresh butter and blueberries. After they finished, they took their plates to the sink. "We'll clean up," offered Jack.

"I'll take care of it," insisted Devova. "You and Bowie get dressed. I went out earlier and got you some clothes."

"But we have clothes," said Bowie.

"Not for what we're doing," said Devova resolutely. "You'll see the bags in the hallway. Go get dressed while I finish up here."

Curiosity propelled the boys into the hallway to check out their new wardrobe. There were three bags resembling oversized beanbag chairs. Bowie opened the first bag and pulled out a pair of bright red Gortex overalls. Jack opened the second bag and pulled out bright yellow overalls, also made of Gortex. The last bag contained two pairs of Henri Lloyd waterproof boots. "Are we hiking to the North Pole?" asked Bowie.

"These are for sailing," said Jack. That's when panic set in. "Wait a minute, you don't think ... Devova intends ... sailing to those coordinates ... no way!"

Devova finished cleaning up the kitchen then donned her own sailing gear, which included her adopted father's pea-coat. She had a box of provisions with her and led the boys out to the dock behind the house. Tied up was a well-maintained fifty-five-foot John Alden Yawl. Jack walked around to view the transom which bore the vessel's name: *Atlantis Pearl*. "She's beautiful!" said Jack.

"This boat looks familiar," said Bowie. "Must have seen one like it back home."

Prior to releasing the bow and stern lines securing the boat to the dock, Devova sat the two boys down for a little talk. "There are two things I need to say before you embark on this next phase of your journey: the first is the ocean is unpredictable. It can be calm as glass one minute and the next you could literally be fighting to stay alive amidst a storm generating waves twice as tall as this boat is long.

"There's a second thing after that?" asked Bowie.

"More than you know depends on this," expressed Devova with utmost seriousness. "Learn everything you can and there's a chance—" she cut herself off.

Jack looked concerned. "You sound as if you're not coming with us."

There was a long pause before she answered. "I can't," said Devova.

"What?" Jack was shocked.

"Believe me, I would if I could."

Even Bowie looked concerned. "Look, Gram, you've figured out by now I'm a risk taker, but I have to say in all honestly, yer aff yer heid!" Without knowing the translation, it was safe to assume Bowie just said she was out of her mind. "Sorry, just had to get that off my chest," he added. "Please, go on."

"Before we set sail today, I'll go over the vessel itself, safety protocols and teach you some of the basics. The rest you'll have to learn as we go. It took me years to become a competent sailor. You'll only have a few weeks," she said.

For twelve to fourteen hours per day, Devova taught Jack and Bowie how to sail as well as navigate. Maine provided an excellent training ground with its rough winds, cross currents and choppy seas. Whether it would be enough for what lied ahead remained to be seen.

# THE LIGHT

The intensive sailing was exhausting but invigorating as well. Jack and Bowie became quite adept at handling the vessel and were on the fast track to becoming old salts. But despite their sailing abilities, two weeks was nowhere near enough time to adequately train novice sailors to travel across open ocean. That fact alone should have been enough to keep Jack in a perpetual state of anxiety. Yet, to his own disbelief and credit, he also felt more comfortable in his own skin than he had ever felt before.

On the morning marking the end of their second week in Maine, Jack awoke later than usual and went out to the kitchen where Bowie was cooking up steak and eggs.

"Good mornin', sleepy head," said Bowie.

"Mornin'. Hey, is Gram up yet?" asked Jack.

"Haven't seen her yet this morning."

"Hmmm, that's odd. She's always up before we are. I'm going to check on her." Jack headed upstairs to her room.

He knocked on her bedroom door. No response. "Gram?" he called out, then knocked again. After what happened to his mother, he feared the worse. Jack mustered up the nerve to open the door. What he saw was even more shocking. "Bowie, get up here!"

Hearing the distress is Jack's voice, Bowie turned off the stove and ran upstairs to Devova's room. "What is it?" Jack opened the door wider so Bowie could see.

Devova was lying on her double bed, surrounded by a chrysalis of gently pulsing white light. Jack and Bowie approached the bed cautiously. She was breathing shallowly and appeared to be sleeping. As if sensing their presence, she opened her eyes.

"Gram, are you okay? What's happening?" asked Jack. "Should we pull you out?"

"No!" said Gram forcefully which immediately weakened her. "The transmutation has begun. It will take much longer though without the *auroris* to channel the energy."

Jack was confused. "Auroris? What are you taking about?"

"Never mind," she dismissed. "Are you both ready?"

"We're as ready as we'll ever be but we're not leaving you like this!" asserted Jack.

"You have to!" she retorted.

"Gram, we need to get you to a hospital," said Bowie. "Though I don't think they'll have a lot of experience with, um, whatever this is."

"Boys, this is not something that needs to be cured. It has to be this way and it's why I can't go with you. You both have to get on the *Atlantis Pearl* and set sail for those coordinates. Time is of the essence and if you waste any more of it, all this will be for naught."

"I'm not leaving you like this!" insisted Jack.

Gram softened her tone. "Jack, listen to me, what's happening is necessary for what you and Bowie have to do. Please trust me."

Jack cringed at the word "trust." Trust had lead him to abandoning his home, traveling across the country and training to sail across the ocean to a destination given to him by a shell! But while he had some serious doubts about everything, instinct told him he was doing the right thing.

"Can we do anything for you before we leave?" asked Jack.

Gram smiled, "You've already done it."

Bowie was deeply saddened by leaving her. He had grown quite fond of Gram Devova in the short time they had spent together. "Are you in any pain?" he asked.

Gram Devova smiled. "Not at all."

Jack's mind turned to the journey ahead. If they survived the trip, and the odds were highly against that happening, he had no idea what they would find once they arrived at the coordinates or what would happen next, if anything.

The only consolation was that he was doing it with Bowie. Fate had brought them together for better or worse. Whatever other thoughts or concerns he had, he'd have to bracket them off for a while because there was a task in front of him that required his total focus.

"We'll go now," said Jack. A look of great relief came over Gram's face. "Good-bye, Gram."

"Good-bye, Jack," she said. She closed her eyes but opened them quickly remembering something. Take it," she motioned toward the pea-coat draped over a rocking chair. Jack pulled the coat off the back of the chair and put it on. It was made from heavy wool and hung awkwardly on his small frame.

"Don't worry," she said. "You'll quickly grow into it."

"She turned to Bowie and spoke to him for the last time, "Cha d'dhùin doras nach d'fhosgail doras."

"Aye!" replied Bowie. He bowed slightly then waited outside in the hallway for Jack.

Jack looked at Gram Devova with conflicted feelings. He still didn't know what to make of her or of everything that had happened since she appeared in his life. "Gram, I just want you to know that I don't blame you for what happened to Mom. She lost faith in you and what you believed and she had every reason to be skeptical. But she didn't have to take the path she did. It was her choice."

Gram's eyes teared up. "Thank you, Jack. I appreciate that more than you know."

"It's the truth," said Jack. "But I still miss her."

"I do, too," said Gram. "Jack, be true to yourself. It seems obvious, but it is no small thing. To be yourself takes great courage. It's in you."

There were a million more things to say but no words left to say them. Gram Devova closed her eyes and gently chanted:

*Ging-de-lot-dot-de-dig*
*Fung-hey-dey-lot-de-dot-dora*
*Shung-gonna-fot-te-zing*
*Fong-bay-te-le-dot-de-vova*

*Grare-te-lot-don-fu-te*
*Ang-wan-bay-la-taun-vay-fuega*
*Lom-gonna-zot-she-tang*
*Gome-ply-werti-som-sot-sora*

Jack never got around to asking her the significance of the chant, but it stuck in his head like a dream. He closed the door behind himself as he exited the room, never to see Gram Devova again.

"I'll start loading the supplies while you double-check the navigation charts," said Bowie.

"Good idea," said Jack as they headed down the stairs. "Hey Bowie, what did she say to you up there?"

"'Cha d'dhùin doras nach d'fhosgail doras.' It's Gaelic for 'No door ever closed, but another opened.'"

\*\*\*

Mild seas and light winds graced the initial leg of their maritime journey. They each took four-hour shifts at the helm while the other performed routine maintenance, prepared food or slept. They saw incredible things at sea, a rich and diverse abundance of birds, turtles, whales, dolphins, sharks and other fish. It was an awesome experience being out in the middle of the ocean under the power of the wind on a relatively small boat. To entertain themselves, they sang songs, staged pirate battles and even made music videos with Jack's iPad.

Using his great grandfather's compass, Jack became an expert navigator, skillfully plotting their course and tracking their position. A week into their journey, he realized they'd be cutting it close per the time and date given by the shell. They had no Plan B, so Plan A had to work!

The seas were relatively calm at daybreak of June 21$^{st}$ but a light drizzle began to fall, hinting of tumultuous weather ahead. Within an hour, the wind picked up considerably. Jack had an uneasy feeling gnawing away at the pit of his stomach. "I don't like the look of that sky." He pointed to a vast expanse of billowing black clouds closing in at a brisk pace.

"How much further to our destination?" asked Bowie.

"At our current rate of speed, we have about three and a half hours to go. That only gives us a twenty-minute window to find whatever we're supposed to find at the coordinates from the shell. The heading though is taking us right into the middle of that mess coming our way." Jack looked very concerned. "If we hit strong headwinds, we may fall behind."

"What if we arrive late?" asked Bowie.

"The shell didn't go into details," said Jack. Doubt began to set in for him. Being stuck in the middle of the Atlantic Ocean with few provisions left, an ominous storm quickly approaching, the only directions coming from a shell and the only guidance coming from his estranged grandmother were starting to chip away at his beliefs. Even more burdensome was the fact that he was putting his best friend's life in jeopardy. Yes, it was Bowie's choice to come but it was still Jack's responsibility. Jack could accept whatever his fate was but to drag Bowie into this? He couldn't forgive himself if something tragic happened. Of course, he probably wouldn't be around himself to lament it.

The impending doom looming didn't appear to phase Bowie in the slightest. "Well, at least we haven't been attacked by a giant squid yet."

"It's still early," quipped Jack. "I suppose there's no turning back now, giant squid or not."

"That's the spirit! Stuck in the middle of the ocean headin' into who-knows-what, a huge storm ahead, little hope of being rescued and the likelihood of survival slim, there's only one thing left to do."

"What's that?" asked Jack.

"Make nachos."

Jack straightened up like a soldier. "Commence making of nachos."

"Aye, Captain!" Bowie about-faced to go below deck and make nachos.

"Bowie?" Jack called out. Bowie turned to face his friend. Jack's eyes were serious and filled with fear, but mixed in was a steely determination and courage. "Better grab the wet-weather gear while you're down there." Bowie knew from Jack's expression they were in serious trouble, but he also believed if anyone could get them through this, it was his best friend. He trusted Jack as much as he trusted himself, maybe more. He believed in Jack and sometimes that belief in someone can move mountains. Whether it could navigate treacherous seas was another matter.

Two hours passed and the light drizzle graduated into a veritable downpour. The wind picked up significantly and the swells with it, but nothing they hadn't been through before sailing with Gram Devova off the coast of Maine. Into the third hour, things got ugly.

The fifty-five-foot vessel suddenly felt minuscule to the junior seamen. Being tossed up and down twenty-foot sea-sick-inducing swells, the nachos didn't seem like such a good idea in retrospect but the impending threat of the storm took their minds off the potential threat of making chum for the fish. Wearing his grandfather's pea-coat with the cuffs rolled up, Jack held the wheel steady while Bowie battened down the hatches and adjusted the sails. They did their best but there was no substitute for experience—experience neither of them had.

A thirty-foot wave nearly crashed full-force onto the starboard bow of the *Atlantis Pearl*. Jack's quick-thinking of turning straight into the wave saved the vessel from getting capsized, though the force of the impact broke the front mass clean off the bow and into the water.

Bowie yelled over the deafening wind, "Easy, cowboy! We've only got one sail left!"

"You think?" Jack shot back.

Another wave broke quicker than Jack anticipated, pounding him and Bowie hard into the deck. The chart table was swept overboard, along with the charts which bore their course.

"GPS is offline and those charts were our only other means of pinpointing our destination!" exclaimed Jack.

"You took a heading five minutes ago," said Bowie. "Just head into the wind a bit. Eyeball it. We can't be that far from the destination and we've only got fifteen minutes to go."

"That's actually a good idea," said Jack.

"I've been known to have those from time to time," retorted Bowie.

"And your timing couldn't be better." Jack smiled as a blast of salty wash filled his mouth.

"Hey, no water breaks until we're out of this," jested Bowie. Jack spit out the salt water and adjusted their course three degrees northeast.

The *Atlantis Pearl* took pounding after pounding. Jack held the course as steady as possible, timing the waves as best he could to minimize the impact. With a little over ten minutes to go, Bowie caught a flash of something in the distance. Was it another ship or a ray of sunlight that found its way through a pinpoint opening in the clouds? He couldn't be sure. "Jack! Look over there! I see something!" Bowie pointed toward the source.

Jack momentarily took his hands of the wheel to foil his eyes from the piercing ocean spray. It was no illusion. There was something there, a light or beacon of some sort gently pulsating amidst the storm. Without the charts, Jack couldn't tell if the light was emanating from their destination but intuition told him it was. "We're heading to it. If that's what we're supposed to find, then we have seven minutes to get there. We should be good. Just a few—" before Jack could finish his thought, the wind shifted abruptly pushing the vessel sideways. The wheel spun out of control. Jack couldn't figure out how to stop it without ripping his arms off.

Bowie grabbed the gaff hook and rammed it between the spokes. The pole handle bent hard but stopped the wheel, toppling Bowie over in a summersault. "Are you alright?" yelled Jack.

"Never better!" replied Bowie.

Jack struggled to remove the bent pole from the wheel. It was jammed solid. A large wave hovered ominously. Their starboard flank was totally exposed. If they couldn't turn into the wave, they were finished.

Bowie jumped up, stumbled a bit and then worked with Jack to remove the pole handle. They yanked it out of the wheel but it was too late. The thirty-five-foot wave pummeled the *Atlantis Pearl* hurling Jack and Bowie overboard and capsizing the vessel. They plunged into the frigid ocean but the buoyancy of their life jackets propelled them to the surface. The yacht was about ten feet away and sinking fast. Exhausted beyond belief and coughing up sea water, the boys were at their ropes' end. "Rope!" Jack suddenly remembered. "We're tied to the yacht!"

"What do you mean?" Bowie could barely focus.

"We're tethered to the boat! The safety line!" Jack's fingers were numb from the bitterly cold water but he went to work on Bowie's line first. He felt the carabiner connector but couldn't close his fingers around it to release the clasp.

"Get yours off first!" insisted Bowie, but Jack ignored him. The boat started to go under and dragged the two boys down with it. Three feet, five feet, his ears were screaming from the pressure but Jack wouldn't give up. He mustered all of his strength and whatever remaining heat he could find in his body and mentally channeled it to his hands. He pulled on the clasp and released Bowie from the watery grave. Jack looked up at his friend rose toward the surface. He suddenly felt warm inside as if every worry had suddenly dissolved. Bowie would survive, he just knew it. And he could die knowing that he hadn't let his friend down. Jack closed his eyes and waited for the abyss to consume him.

A strong grip caught hold of Jack's wrist. It was Bowie, sans life jacket, holding Jack with one hand and reaching for Jack's ankle with the other to grab the knife he had given him for his birthday. He unsheathed the blade and sliced at the rope cinched around Jack's waist. On the first swipe, he cut a few threads—the second swipe, a few more. On the third swipe, he caught the rope just right and severed the line completely. Jack was out of air but kicked as hard as he could for the surface. Bowie followed. Jack blacked out for a moment then broke the surface and started coughing up sea water. Bowie broke the surface a few seconds later but was having a hard time staying afloat.

"Put your arm around me," insisted Jack.

It gave Bowie the much-needed buoyancy he needed without compromising Jack. They both took in some deep breaths to replenish their muscles with oxygen. In spite of everything, Bowie was smiling. "I forgot all about your knife when we started going down! As soon as you released me, I remembered you had it!"

"Like I said before, you have great timing." Jack smiled as much as his frozen face would allow. He looked down at his watch. "Bowie, we've got three minutes left and the light looks like it's fading. We've got to swim for it."

"Seeing as how we don't have a lot of options, let's do it!" Bowie kept one arm around Jack and they literally swam for their lives. They expended what little energy—what little life they had left. Slowly, they made headway. The light was another chrysalis about ten feet across, domed over the surface of the water. Jack and Bowie swam into the middle of it. It felt warm but nothing else happened.

"Now what?" questioned Bowie.

"Beats me!" Jack looked down at his watch. Twenty seconds left.

A large wave rolled toward them. Jack noticed it first. "Bowie, I don't like the look of that one."

Bowie's eyes widened. "Holly Mother!"

The wave reached a height of fifty feet and hovered a moment before crashing thousands of pounds of ocean water down on them. They closed their eyes, anticipating the full force of the impact. The sound was deafening and they could feel the initial weight of the water press down on them. The rumble reached a crescendo but before being knocked into oblivion, they found themselves pressed against a hard, rocky surface, some residual of the wave splaying them flat.

Jack opened his eyes slowly and peered up at a clean, blue sky, not a trace of rain or storm clouds to be seen. They were in a mountainous area of some sort. He looked over at Bowie who was lying on his back smiling.

"It got a little dodgy at the end there," said Bowie, "but you have to admit, we're the luckiest people in the world right now!"

Two long spears appeared an inch from each of their chests. They looked up at a pair of mounted soldiers holding the weapons. "Get on your knees and put your hands behind your back!" said one of the horseman.

Bowie turned to Jack. "I guess I spoke too soon."

# FRONISI

The soldiers, Terrim and Scalt, shackled Jack and Bowie's hands behind their backs and escorted them at spear point. Part of their journey led them through a patch of dense forest filled with soaring green-hued trees. The boys were soaking wet, banged up and generally miserable. On the bright side, they were also hungry and thirsty.

As they entered the clearing, they saw a compound surrounded by a wall comprised of thick gray cubes of granite. Towering above the wall was the top of a structure glistening in iridescent splendor. Jack ventured to ask, "Sir, what is this place?"

Terrim laughed. "Fronisi, lad! Come now, the spy doesn't know the name of the place he's spying on? Perhaps you'd like me to believe you just dropped out of the sky."

"If the shoes fits," Bowie said under his breath.

"I'm not a spy! We're not spies!" pleaded Jack.

"Granted, spies don't usually like to stand out and those garments you're wearing are rather conspicuous!" conceded Scalt

"We're not spies!" protested Jack.

"Where did you come from then?" asked Scalt.

Jack thought for a moment. "It's a long story."

"I'm sure it is," replied Scalt amusedly. "He pointed his spear at Bowie and remarked to Terrim, "He's from Laidir for sure."

"Where's Laidir?" Bowie asked sincerely.

The soldiers looked at each other and shared a laugh as if Bowie was trying to pull a fast one on them.

"You're both very amusing. It's a shame you'll be executed," commented Scalt.

"Executed? For what?" asked Bowie.

"For spying! Haven't you been following the conversation?" said Jack annoyed.

"But we're not spies!" replied Bowie.

The soldiers laughed to the point of crying. After a minute or two of comic relief, Terrim chuckled out, "I must thank you both. I haven't laughed like that in quite a while."

Scalt wiped a tear from his eye. "Very true. They deserve a quick death as a reward."

"Very kind of you," said Bowie, "but what about the possibility of not executing us?"

The soldiers laughed again. Scalt almost fell off his horse. "Stop, I can't take it anymore! My armor's starting to rust!"

Jack whispered to Bowie, "You're a real comedian."

"Hey, if you're going to die, leave 'em laughing, I've always said!"

"Oh, you've always said that?" questioned Jack.

"I've always said that!" said Bowie. "This just may be the last time is all."

Despite how dire their situation was, Jack couldn't help but admire Bowie's humor under fire.

The boys were escorted to the front gate of the compound. The gate was quite impressive, crafted from thick, carved slats of the green-hued wood. Archers and other soldiers stood at the ready as the escort entered the courtyard. On the opposite side of the courtyard was another gate equally impenetrable. The courtyard was designed to create a bottleneck and confine an attack should assailants ever manage to get through the first gate. With no cover, they would face a barrage of arrows and other projectiles from above.

Once the first gate was secured, the second gate was raised, opening to the compound proper. In the middle stood a shrine built from opalescent rock called *auroris*. More soldiers on horseback joined the escort. Jack felt like they were America's most wanted, or most wanted wherever they were. "Who are they and where did they get those funny clothes?" one of the guards asked Terrim.

"We don't know yet," answered Terrim, "but the cocky one there sounds Laidirian."

"Take off these cuffs and I'll show you cocky," responded Bowie.

"He's definitely got the accent and the temperament!" said the guard.

Jack's mind was racing as to what to say to these people. He had no idea who they were or whether they were friends or foes. If he made up a story and they suspected as much, he and Bowie could be put to death right away. Even if their captors believed a concocted story, Jack wasn't sure what story he should tell. Also, he didn't know what Bowie would say if they were questioned separately. They hadn't really rehearsed any of it—being held at spear point from the moment they arrived didn't allow much of an opportunity to make a plan.

Guards stood apart every twenty feet or so along the wall, many with bows and nocked arrows aimed at the two boys. The entire garrison was on high alert for the arrival of the *spies*.

Walking through the courtyard, the boys observed many other buildings, shops and living quarters to support the community but none compared to the beauty of the shrine with its articulated architectural elements and intricately carved surfaces. Both Jack and Bowie were mesmerized by the shrine's large jade doors encrusted with emeralds.

"Are we going in there?" asked Bowie.

"Yes," replied Scalt. "The shrine is a place of sacredness. Master Lumens insists all trials be conducted where the energies of truth are cultivated."

"Tried?" questioned Jack. "May we speak to Master Lumens?"

"You may not," said Scalt curtly but then softened. "Which is unfortunate because he has a way of getting to the truth without the 'usual' methods." Jack didn't like the euphemistic application of the word "usual."

"Will we be imprisoned until our trial?" asked Jack.

Terrim chimed in, "Sorry, but no. If it was an ordinary crime, you would be confined until speaking with Master Lumens. But with espionage, we are a bit more strict—we conduct the trial as soon as possible then proceed with torture and execution."

"That is a bit strict," affirmed Bowie.

"Rest assured, you will receive justice first," said Terrim. "Magistrate Morsus is sitting court today."

Bowie turned to Scalt and asked, "Nice guy, this Morsus?"

Scalt vigorously shook his head in the negative. "His wife was killed by a spy."

Bowie had an inspired thought, "Let me guess, a Laidirian spy?"

"I'm afraid so," answered Scalt.

Jack glared at Terrim. "So when you said we'd have justice first, what exactly did you mean?"

Terrim looked remorseful. "I was just being polite."

Inside the shrine stood a dozen guards but many more people who were engaged in various types of mediation. A group of nine men wearing tall golden conical *sikke* hats and *tennure* skirts were *whirling*, a type of meditation in which one "whirls" in a counter-clockwise direction to center the self and experience new levels of consciousness. In one corner, a woman chanted a gibberish song, very similar to the chant his grandmother sang in Maine. The words had a chime-like quality:

*Chu-gonna-got-ta-ting*
*Fing-fa-dela-dod-de-neara*
*Shing-tada-tong-det-ting*
*Bey-fa-de-la-det-de-dora*

Next to her sat a man with an *ucchai*, a type of instrument resembling a silver pen. It had an emerald-colored tip and narrow cylindrical base with a fluted opening at the other end. The man stuck the tip of the ucchai into a nautilus shell and told the woman to repeat the chant. He then took a *ravna*, an instrument identical to the ucchai but with a ruby red tip and placed it into the shell, then put his ear to the fluted end and listened for several seconds. "Good," he said. Jack surmised that must have been the way his message was embedded in the shell.

The hall featured many statues and other great works of art. One statue carved from marble stood out. It was a depiction of a Centaur, the mythical half man/half horse creature driving its spear into the flank of a chimera, another mythical creature purported to have the head of a lion, the body of a goat and the tail of a serpent.

Toward the back of the hall stood a curved table with a dour man sitting smack dab in the middle, Magistrate Morsus. He wore dark gray robes and a hat that looked like a cross between a turnip and smashed pumpkin. Morsus was middle-aged with a muscular build and short-cropped auburn hair. His fierce brown eyes and scarred complexion suggested he was no stranger to combat. He was flanked by two men at the table. The man on his right was a scribe. The man of his left served solely as a figurehead of menace.

Terrim and Scalt presented the boys, then pushed them to their knees in submission. Magistrate Morsus slowly approached them. "So, it appears we have some visitors among us today," he said.

"Yes, sir," they said in unison.

"Yes, sir? So polite," the magistrate said condescendingly.

"Magistrate, we found them on the southern slope," offered Scalt. "We were patrolling the area for most of the morning. For spies to penetrate that far without being detected took some skill. They were soaking wet when we found them. They may have used one of the tributaries for cover."

Magistrate Morsus raised an eyebrow. "Are you spies?"

The boys shook their heads no.

"Of course not," said the magistrate. "You're traveling minstrels from Fens looking for the next show. Or maybe you're chimera hunters from Kentauros who got lost. Or perhaps you're emissaries from Andaar!"

Bowie couldn't take it anymore. "I don't know what you're talking about but we're not spies!"

Scalt raised his arm to backhand Bowie in the face but Morsus motioned him to stand down.

"You sound like a Laidirian," remarked the magistrate.

"I get a lot of that," said Bowie.

Morsus yelled explosively, silencing the hall. "My wife was killed by a Laidirian spy!"

Jack shook his head in resignation. "We know."

"Yeah, sorry about that," Bowie threw in unconvincingly.

Morsus regained his composure, then paced back and forth at a controlled cadence. "What are your names?"

"I'm Jack and he's Bowie."

"Where did they get names like that?" asked the scribe.

"Probably from the same place they got those clothes!" said the figurehead of menace. His comment set off a round of laughter in the chamber.

Magistrate Morsus allowed it for a bit before motioning everyone to cease and desist with the slightest lift of his index finger. "Jack. Bowie. Is there anything you'd like to say before I have you tortured and put to death? Mind you, the quicker you talk, the less painful your life, and death, will be."

"That's very kind of you," said Jack desperately hoping they would be spared. No such luck.

"It's my generous nature," answered Morsus.

"What about a trial?" asked Bowie.

Morsus smiled playfully. "Oh, well, that was it! Fast, isn't it?" Morsus motioned the guards to escort the spies to the torture chamber.

Jack was paralyzed with fear. After all he and Bowie had been through, he couldn't believe this was their fate. Jack wished he had smashed the nautilus shell the second his grandmother had given it to him. Nautilus shell ... Jack looked over at the man with the nautilus shell holding a pen-like instrument gently inserted into the opening as the lady next to him began chanting.

"Magistrate," Jack motioned to the man and woman. "I was given a shell like that one from my grandmother and it delivered a message to me. It's the reason we're here," he said as a last-ditch effort to preserve their lives. He had nothing to lose at that point.

"And who pray tell is your grandmother?" asked Morsus.

"Her name was Devova," responded Jack.

A few of the guards looked at each other and for a split-second the magistrate's poker face leaked a hint of surprise. "Do you have the shell with you?"

Jack remembered he had secured the nautilus shell in the cabin of the *Atlantis Pearl.* "No, Sir."

"That's a pity," said Morsus. He turned to Scalt. "I don't know where they got such detailed information, but make sure you find out!"

"Yes, Magistrate!" confirmed Scalt. The guards grabbed the boys to remove them from the shrine.

Goaded by Gram Devova's memory, Jack recited her chant, though he had no idea what the sounds or words meant.

*Ging-de-lot-dot-de-dig*
*Fung-hey-dey-lot-de-dot-dora*
*Shung-gonna-fot-te-zing*
*Fong-bay-te-le-dot-de-vova*

*Grare-te-lot-don-fu-te*
*Ang-wan-bay-la-taun-vay-fuega*
*Lom-gonna-zot-she-tang*
*Gome-ply-werti-som-sot-sora*

The chant echoed throughout the entirety of the shrine. The whirlers stopped whirling and the room fell silent once again as Jack continued the chant. Morsus looked like he had seen a ghost. When Jack finished, Morsus addressed the man holding the shell with the ucchai inserted into it. "Azru, did you record that?"

Azru was confused for a moment and then realized he was holding the ucchai in position. "Let me check, Magistrate." He set the ucchai down and pulled out the ravna, inserted it into the shell, put his ear by the fluted end and listened intently.

"Maybe we can get you on *Fronisi's Got Talent,*" Bowie said to Jack sotto voce.

Azru looked up at Morsus with tears in his eyes, "By the Beyond, he is Devova's grandson."

"Everyone out, now!" commanded Morsus as he grabbed Scalt's arm. "Summon Master Lumens at once!"

***

Master Lumens arrived about an hour later, clad in a purple robe embroidered with gold scrolling. Appearing to be in his seventies, he was tall of stature and lean. He face was gaunt with a well-manicured white goatee and intense green eyes possessing an amalgam of warmth and sadness. He studied the two boys for a moment before saying, "Magistrate Morsus, please remove their bonds. They're our guests and most welcomed here." Morsus hurriedly took out a key and remove their shackles.

"Thank you, sir," said Bowie and instinctively bowed to Master Lumens.

"You are quite welcome, Bowie," he said as he returned the bow.

Master Lumens stood before Jack, taking him in. Jack couldn't read his expression until Lumens revealed the slightest smile. "Jack," was all he said. Lumens addressed both boys. "Please accept my apologies. I hope you weren't mistreated in any way."

"Well, it wasn't exactly a picnic, but they didn't smack us around too much!" said Bowie.

"They were going to torture us and have us executed!" Jack reminded him.

"Oh, yeah. I forgot about that part!" said Bowie.

Master Lumens raised an eyebrow at Morsus who lowered his head in shame. Lumens continued, "We weren't quite sure how you would arrive."

"You were expecting us?" wondered Jack.

"In a manner of speaking," said Lumens. "It's rather complicated."

"Maybe we could talk about it over dinner? You do have dinner here, don't you?" said Bowie, not-so-subtly conveying the notion that a good meal would be welcomed after being shipwrecked, shackled and almost tortured and executed.

Master Lumens nodded. "Yes, we have dinner here. And I think that's an excellent idea." He turned to Morsus. "Would you show our guests to their lodging?"

"Of course, Master Lumens," answered Morsus.

Master Lumens turned to the boys. "I'll give you some time to get settled in and then we'll reconvene over the evening meal." They thanked him. Master Lumens turned to exit, then paused and faced the boys. "I am most pleased to have you both here. Most pleased."

Morsus led the boys to a room within the shrine itself. Inside the room were two beds on either side and a large open window looking out into a tranquil garden illuminated by the sun shining through the open roof. The walls of the room were also carved from auroris which gave the dwelling an iridescent glimmer.

The room was furnished modestly but the bedding was quite plush. A small doorway opened to the adjoining bathroom. The bathroom *sink* was actually a sea-shell encrusted trough with a constant stream of water running into it on one end and draining from the other. There was also a toilet with the same fill-and-drain design, nothing to flush. There was no shower but rather a tub as large as a Jacuzzi, also with the same fill-and-drain design.

Morsus explained that a natural hot spring ran underground and they utilized the "plumbing" accordingly. He uncomfortably pointed to the commode with a stack of furry-looking leaves next to it. "I trust you know what that whole set-up is for?"

Jack rightfully assumed it was a Fronisi toilet and bathroom tissue. "We do," he assured him.

Morsus looked relieved. "Thank the Beyond." He bid them ado and left them to bathe and rest.

The warm natural spring water soothed their aches and pains. After a good soak, they dried off and came back out to their beds where folded clothes and boots awaited them. The undergarments were soft but not what you would call "formfitting." The brown tunics were thick and comfortable. There were no socks but the boots reminded them of Uggs, suede on the outside with animal-fur lining on the inside.

After an hour or so had passed, Morsus returned and escorted them to a quaint dining area where Master Lumens sat in waiting. He stood upon their arrival. He brought his palms together and touched the tips of his index fingers to his forehead.

"You both looked refreshed," he said. "Please, have a seat."

Morsus exited as serving people came in with a variety of sumptuous dishes. Jack and Bowie's mouths started to water.

Bowie looked at Master Lumens to cue him if it was all right to dig in. Lumens caught on. "Help yourselves! You must be famished after the day's events."

Jack and Bowie tried not to stuff food in their faces, but it was as challenging as not thinking about pink elephants when someone says not to think about pink elephants. "Ez goocht," Bowie said thorough a mouthful of food.

Master Lumens interpreted for Bowie. "It's good? Yes, indeed."

Lumens let the boys eat for a few minutes without speaking. Jack noticed a map on the wall. The land mass pictured looked exactly like Atlantis which he was all too familiar with. It should have been more obvious, but then it hit Jack like a ton of bricks. "Are we in Atlantis?"

"Yes," Lumens calmly replied.

"You mean like the lost continent of Atlantis?" asked Bowie.

Apparently, you found it," said Lumens. Jack's heart raced. They were in Atlantis! Maybe he was hallucinating—but as hallucinations went, this one was going on far too long.

"Why are we here?" asked Jack.

"There is no short answer to your question," said Lumens.

"We're all ears," said Bowie.

"What?" Lumens looked confused.

"It's an expression where we come from," said Bowie. "It means we're paying attention and you don't need to rush the answer."

"Lumens looked amused. "It will suffice to say you are both here for a special purpose."

"Both? But the shell spoke to Jack," said Bowie.

"And Jack spoke to you," said Lumens.

"My grandmother said there was much at stake," said Jack.

"That is true, but it does not all rest on your shoulders," offered Lumens. "First things first, let me tell you a little bit about Atlantis."

# ATLANTIS 101

As the boys continued to eat, Master Lumens used the map of Atlantis to provide an overview. "There are six main territories. You are in Fronisi, here, which is considered more of a community than a territory." Lumens pointed to its location far north on the map.

"Southwest of Fronisi is Kentauros, home of the Centaurs—"

Bowie stopped him there. "Whoa, you mean there really are Centaurs?"

"Of course," said Lumens without hesitation.

"Like half man, half horse?" asked Bowie. "Isn't that a statue of one in the main hall there?"

"Centaurs are known as the Great Horse People because of their mastery of equestrian skills and preternatural connection with the animal," explained Lumens. "The statue to which you're referring is merely the artist's interpretation of that bond."

"No half man, half horse then, huh?" asked Bowie.

"I'm afraid not," said Lumens.

"Bummer!" Bowie was disappointed.

"Is the chimera also the artist's interpretation?" asked Jack.

"That is correct," confirmed Lumens.

"Well, in real life, they must still be butt ugly then!" concluded Bowie.

"Butt ugly," repeated Lumens. "A fitting description, I must admit." He continued his overview. "The Centaurs have always been the protectors of Fronisi. In fact, the military force here is comprised solely of Centaur soldiers. However, their homeland is here, southwest of Fronisi." Lumens pointed to it on the map. "They are the oldest race in Atlantis. Their existence predates written history."

"To the south of Kentauros is Laidir." Lumens pointed to the large landmass on the map. "Their origin is Celt."

"So that's why your guards thought I was Laidirian!" said Bowie.

"Precisely," said Lumens. "In fact, that may come in useful later." Bowie looked at Jack wondering what Lumens meant. Jack shrugged.

"At the southern end of Atlantis is Fens," continued Lumens. "Their people originated from Normandy. At one time, they were fierce conquerors but when they arrived here, they withdrew into their own territory, fortified their defenses and kept to themselves."

"Northeast of Fens is Andaar. Lumens pointed to the landmass on the map. "Originally they were Romans, and with so many territories within their empire, their people are comprised of many different races. The strength of Andaar comes from the diversity and unity of its people.

"Above Andaar is Skul. They were originally Vikings. There is no nice way of saying this, Skul is the enemy to everyone." Something pained him in saying it. He took pause as if dwelling on a distant memory.

Is everything all right?" asked Jack.

Master Lumens shook it off and continued his overview. He explained Atlantis had been a very advanced society dating back thousands of years before recorded history. But as travel by sea was limited, so too was knowledge of the outside world.

"Navigation improved greatly around 550 BC. At that time, Atlanteans began exploring far-reaching lands while maintaining anonymity," explained Lumens. "We became aware the world was filled with war and strife. Atlantis thus began to train in the art of war should we ever have to defend ourselves and we became quite skilled at it. Over the course of two-hundred years, Atlantis developed a formidable military presence.

"Around 350 BC, a division broke out between those who wanted to maintain Atlantis's segregation and those who wanted to integrate with the rest of the world. But both sides saw the inevitability of being discovered. Some, like my brother, Grigori, thought the best way to protect Atlantis was to mobilize our military force and conquer before being conquered. To that end, he sought first to unify Atlantis against potential enemies."

"Doesn't sound too bad," remarked Bowie.

Master Lumens gave Bowie a sideways glance. "Many thought that way, but there were also those opposed to being the aggressors, like myself, for no reason other than fear. And Grigori's ambitions far exceeded that of mere preservation."

"What happened then?" asked Jack.

"Grigori executed a plan to start a civil war with the intent of conquering all of Atlantis first and then plotting his conquest of the known world. But something happened which stopped his progression."

"What was it?" asked Jack.

Atlantis disappeared," said Lumens.

The boys looked at each other. Clearly, there was more to the story than a mere magic trick. "Where did it go?" asked Bowie.

"Information is not always useful. Knowledge often blinds us to the essence of truth. Destiny is found in the heart, not the mind," said Lumens.

Jack thought deeply about Lumens' comment. Bowie was not in as contemplative a mood. "No offense, but could you throw us a bone here?" Lumens considered the colloquialism.

Jack was trying to fit all the pieces together. Plato had written about Atlantis in his dialogs circa 350 BC, but the origin of the civilizations that currently populated the island continent came from different time periods much later chronologically. No other culture had proven or documented the existence of Atlantis. As Lumens alluded to, something must have happened that literally wiped it off the face of the earth, which is why it was considered a fictional place. Yet, here they were in Atlantis which was comprised of several different peoples.

"Master, Lumens?"

"Yes, Jack?"

"I'm not the only one who received a nautilus shell, am I?" said Jack.

Master Lumens smiled. "That is correct."

Bowie was a bit lost and turned to his friend. "Maybe you could explain it to me later." Jack nodded.

As if sensing the millions of questions the boys had, Master Lumens held up his hand, "All information will be revealed in due time. For now, let me continue." Lumens went back to the map.

"A century ago, Laidir was ruled by King Sanntach who wished to expand his territory. Kentauros was his first conquest. He underestimated the Centaurs and was soundly defeated. Laidir is currently ruled by King Broc and there's an uneasy peace between Laidir and Kentauros to this day. There are still occasional skirmishes along their border but neither truly wants war with the other."

Lumens pointed to the forest on the map which formed a natural border between Laidir and Kentauros on the west and Skul on the east. For Skul to attack Laidir or Kentauros, they'd have to go through the Forest of Quith which is fraught with many dangers in and of itself, not to mention difficult terrain. The forest has made it next to impossible to launch a major offensive.

"What about by ship?" questioned Jack.

Lumens pointed to the dark areas circumventing the coastline on the map. "The reefs are extremely treacherous, which would make a naval attack or sizable troop deployment difficult, if not impossible. Each territory has a navy of sorts, but few ships because there are a minimal number of places where they can be built and launched. Most ships are built on offshore islets. The continent is sprinkled with them but as you can imagine, they're susceptible to attacks from other ships. Among the territories, Skul has the most formidable navy with twenty ships. They constantly patrol the continent close to shore, which is why travel by sea is so hazardous."

Lumens pointed to Andaar. "Because of the distance and the Forest of Quith, relations between Kentauros and Andaar have been slow to develop. But the kings of each territory like and respect one another and are working to strengthen the bond between their regions. In fact, the Centaur king's son is currently enrolled at Strongthorne Academy in Andaar. His daughter will start at the academy this year. She'll be the second Centaur and first female to attend."

"Strongthorne Academy?" questioned Jack. "What do they teach there?"

"The academy is a school where young men, and now women, learn to become knights," said Lumens.

"Like armor and swords and jousting?" asked Bowie.

"Precisely," said Lumens.

"I wouldn't mind attending a school like that!" said Bowie.

"We'll get to that in a while," said Lumens. Jack didn't like the sound of that.

Diplomats from Andaar and Laidir have been working together to build a stronger relationship as well and they have an open trade agreement in place. However, Laidirians are proud to the point of arrogance. As a result, Laidirians are not well received by Andaarians."

"What about Fens?" asked Jack.

"It's ruled by King Cloyce and as I mentioned earlier, they keep to themselves." He traced an area with his finger. "The Forest of Quith runs southwest here, forming a border between Laidir and Fens. Neither side has established any sort of diplomatic ties. King Gi'tal of Kentauros has reached out to Fens, but to no avail. Recently, King Gnarus of Andaar has made some headway in terms of establishing an open dialog with Fens, but that's it. They are extremely distrusting and I can't say I blame them considering their own history."

Lumens lowered his voice. "There is a secret though I will entrust to you both which may lead to better relations in the future. The Fennish king's daughter has enrolled at Astoria Academy in Andaar. No one knows who she is except the mistresses of the academy and myself."

"From what you said about Fens, I'm surprised her father let her attend," said Jack.

"As strong as the gates are surrounding Solas, the capital of Fens, her will is stronger," said Lumens. "She didn't give him much choice."

"What is Astoria Academy?" asked Bowie.

"It is a school for young women who wish to deepen their connection to the earth and learn to heal as well as cultivate other such gifts."

"Tell us more about Andaar if you would," said Jack.

"Andaar is a great state, working for higher ideals. Its people are strong and truly seek peace. Because of the ongoing war with Skul though, they're disposition is one of aggressive conservancy rather than harmonious integration," said Lumens.

"Let me see if I've got this all down," said Jack. "Skul is at war with everyone. They're bad. No one likes Skul. Kentauros and Laidir don't really like each other but neither wants war with the other. Laidir and Andaar get along all right but Laidirians aren't well liked in Andaar. Kentauros and Andaar get along but because of the distance and danger of the forest, relations have been slow to develop. Fens keeps to itself and has no interest in anyone or anything outside of Fens. Andaar is a great state that wants peace but can't have it because of the ongoing war with Skul."

Bowie had a hard time tracking it all. "Maybe you can go through it again with me later." Jack nodded.

Lumens looked grave. Jack intuitively knew the reason. "Where is your brother now?"

Master Lumens held Jack in his gaze. "He rules Skul. At one point, we were as close as two brothers could me. Suffice to say that is no longer the case.

"Grigori is extremely gifted in both magic and martial abilities. As a youth, he had the gift of prophecy, though he lost much of that ability when his heart became closed. He still has prophetic dreams but their meaning and significance are often unclear.

"He blames me for many things, including the death of his wife, Arellia. That's another story for another time. Before she died though, she channeled the remainder of her life force into an *amanata* crystal. Should he ever be mortally wounded, he can ingest the crystal which will restore him to full health. It resides in a small pouch tied to his belt. He keeps it with him at all times.

"He had four sons, Luce, Nephalim, Darne and Ontul. I have not heard word of Luce and Nephalim for many years. It is possible they are dead. His other two—" Lumens shuttered.

Jack pressed gently. "What happened to them?"

"Grigori experimented with magic beyond his ability. His sons were transformed," said Lumens.

"Into what?" asked Bowie.

"Into creatures far less than human." Lumens left it at that.

Jack redirected the conversation. "Master Lumens, you said we were here for a purpose. What is it?"

"That is yet to be discovered," said Lumens.

Jack tried a work-around to the question. "How will we know we're on the right track?"

"When you no longer have to ask the question," replied Lumens.

"That's a bit vague but we'll go with it for now," confirmed Bowie.

Lumens bowed. "I am pleased."

"What year is this?" asked Jack.

"That is also a rather complicated question but Atlantis sees it as the year 206," answered Lumens.

"What about in terms of techne?" questioned Jack.

"What's techne?" asked Bowie.

"The origin of the world 'technology,'" answered Jack.

Bowie pointed his thumb at Jack as he addressed Lumens, "He's a smart one. Reads a lot."

"I think what you're asking is relative to where you are from, what time period are we in?" offered Lumens.

"That's right," agreed Jack.

"From what I know of your history, Atlantis is in what you would call the Middle Ages." said Lumens.

"Excellent!" Bowie said to Jack. "We could make a fortune here knowing what we know. Think of it, smart phones in Atlantis!"

"Do you know how to make a smart phone or a cell tower?" scrutinized Jack.

"Well, no, but we could explain it to—" Bowie caught himself. "I see where you're going with this. So, we start small then. Rubber bands!" Bowie turned to Master Lumens, "Do you have rubber trees in Atlantis?"

"You must not tell anyone where you are from and most importantly, you must not bring any advancements from your world into Atlantis at this time," warned Lumens. "Despite the good you would want to do, it would likely bring devastation, especially in terms of weaponry. Even the enemy lives by a steadfast code of honor—but advanced weapons would likely override it." Master Lumens addressed Bowie, "I believe you currently own such a weapon. With your permission, I would like to hold on to it for a while."

Bowie didn't catch on at first. Jack did. "He's talking about your gun." Bowie had kept the gun with one bullet in his Gortex jacket pocket when they were sailing. Terrim removed it from Bowie when they captured the boys. Not knowing what it was, he handed it over to Magistrate Morsus who in turn gave it to Master Lumens.

"Oh, right, yeah, no problem," said Bowie.

"How long will we need to be here to serve our purpose?" asked Jack.

"I can't answer that at this time."

"Will we ever return to where we came from then?" persisted Jack. Lumens remained silent.

"What's next for us?" wondered Bowie.

"You will be guests here for a few weeks and instructed on the customs and cultures of Atlantis." said Lumens.

"And then what?" asked Jack.

Lumens looked at each one of the boys in turn. "You will be enrolled at Strongthorne Academy. The new term starts in a few months. To fulfill your purpose here, you must first train to become knights."

"What?" questioned Jack.

"Excellent!" said Bowie.

"Master Lumens, we can't do that." Jack struggled to come up with reasons. "First of all, people will know we're not from here!"

"To maintain a level of equality, students are not allowed to discuss their background, family name or the like. For some students, that information can hardly be concealed but it is not to be discussed and there are plenty of students who will be unknown like yourselves."

Jack looked at Master Lumens with a sullen expression. "I don't have what it takes to become a knight."

Bowie chimed in, "Sure you do! You're smart as a whip, you've got good hand-eye coordination and all right, you're a bit soft in the muscle department, but nothing a little bit of scrapping around can't fix."

"Your friend thinks you can do it," said Lumens.

"He's an optimist," countered Jack. He had no idea what it all meant or why he had been chosen but he felt compelled to do what was being asked of him. He turned to Bowie for reassurance who gave it to him with a big thumbs up. Jack acquiesced. "I guess we're going to knight school."

"Great! Why don't we celebrate over dessert!" suggested Bowie.

# GRIGORI'S DREAM

It was mid-afternoon in the Forest of Quith but felt later under the canopy of dense foliage. Grigori lead a platoon along the path heading south. Next to him was his general Thorgills the Beater, magistrate to the Skullian town of Vile. Thorgills had earned his moniker from a strange method of torture he employed. He used a stick about four-feet long to beat prisoners to death in the town square. He avoided striking the head or breaking bones since severe pain could cause a person to lose consciousness. He literally prolonged the agony as long as he could, beating the person raw for hours if possible before summoning the executioner to finish the job.

Grigori and his troops approached a clearing. The path continued through it and up a small grade back into the dense foliage. The forest masked the approaching force comprised of almost a hundred Strongthorne students along with Galdus Slade, the dean of the academy. Of Mauretanian descent, Slade was dark skinned with fiery brown eyes and the seasoned mien of a formidable warrior. The students in his charge looked young, probably freshmen, but Grigori couldn't be sure. Both groups stopped upon seeing the other. No one lifted a weapon, waiting for their respective commander's orders.

Grigori and Slade looked at each other with the hate of sworn enemies. Slade spoke first. "We don't have to do this here and now." Though they outnumbered the Skullians more than two to one, his young students were not yet battle tested.

Grigori weighed the situation carefully but pride and hatred persuaded him more than common sense. He nodded at Thorgills.

Thorgills called out, "Battle formation!" His men pulled swords and awaited the call to charge.

The Strongthorne students were divided, roughly half in the clearing and the other half atop the ridge looking down on the clearing. From that second group emerged a lion and a leopard. Grigori looked at the big cats. He focused his attention on the lion whose eyes were ablaze and pierced Grigori's soul. Thorgills suddenly covered his left cheek with his hand as though he had been stung by a bee. The lion roared and the sound reverberated throughout the forest. Grigori was overcome by the feeling of defeat as well as the inescapable sensation of imminent death. He opened his mouth to scream but nothing came out.

Grigori awoke from his dream in a cold sweat and sat upright yelling. Two guards stormed into his bedchambers along with his sons Luce and Nephilim. "Father, are you all right?" asked Luce.

It took a few moments for Grigori to regain his bearings but he quickly shook it off for fear of exposing his vulnerability. "Just a dream." Luce dismissed the guards. He and his brother stayed. As soon as the doors to Grigori's bedchambers closed, his sons kneeled by the side of the bed.

"Was it one of your prophetic dreams?" asked Nephilim.

Grigori looked at his boys and hesitated. Though his sons had always been fiercely loyal and devoted to him, he didn't trust them entirely. They were ambitious, much like himself. "Thorgills and I were in the forest with troops and were confronted by a group of Strongthorne students. Slade was with them. There were two beasts in their ranks, big cats. They posed some sort of threat to us."

"What do you mean by *us*?" questioned Luce.

Grigori concealed the truth. "Skul, of course. I don't know how or why." He changed the subject. "When did you both arrive?"

"We met up at Swordbend Island three days ago and rowed into shore under cover of darkness last night," said Luce. "We took the backroads here and arrived before dawn."

"You're sure no one saw you?" questioned Grigori.

"We took all the necessary precautions," assured Nephilim. "I am certain we arrived undetected."

Grigori was pleased. "Very well. Give me a few minutes to dress and I will join you for breakfast." His sons bowed in turn and left his bedchamber.

Grigori walked to the window and looked out at the rising sun. His dream troubled him though there was nothing he could do about it in the moment.

He would be making several trips into the forest over the ensuing months to unfold his plan that would lead to him becoming ruler of Atlantis. But the dream suggested there may be opposition and it involved students at the academy. He walked to the door and opened it. "Summon Commander Videt," he said.

"Yes, my lord," confirmed the lead guard. Commander Videt was his intelligence officer who ran a network of spies throughout all the territories in Atlantis, including Andaar.

Grigori needed information and he needed it quickly.

# ROAD TRIP TO ANDAAR

In addition to history and cultural lessons to help the boys adapt to their new environment, they were also taught horsemanship, swordsmanship and archery. Such skills were necessary for basic survival in Atlantis. Of course, it would only be cursory instruction. The real training would come at Strongthorne Academy. Bowie was a natural with the sword and Jack was an excellent shot with a bow and arrow.

The trip to Andaar was meant to be discreet and the boys had to be protected, especially through the portion of the journey crossing the Forest of Quith. An escort of ten Centaur soldiers were assigned, including their original captors, Terrim and Scalt. Besides crossing the forest, it was still a dangerous journey as they would have to ride along the outskirts of Laidir. Tensions between Centaurs and Laidirians were high though there was less animosity in the more rural areas and it wasn't uncommon for Centaurs to travel the back roads of Laidir on their way to Andaar.

After several weeks of study, it was time for Jack and Bowie to go. As the boys mounted their horses to leave Fronisi, Master Lumens came out to bid them farewell. He first addressed Bowie. "I am confident you will enjoy knight school very much."

"I'm sure I will," responded Bowie. "Thank you for putting up with us."

"The pleasure was all ours," said Master Lumens. "Bowie, you must work hard to prevent your emotions from guiding you."

"That sounds impossible," said Bowie matter-of-factly.

Master Lumens laughed heartily then put his hand on Bowie's arm. "Do the best you can."

"Aye, I can always do my best." Bowie bowed to Master Lumens.

Lumens returned the bow then addressed Jack. "Don't forget the advice your grandmother gave you: just be yourself. But to be yourself, you have to discover who you really are. That's the real work."

Jack thought about it for a moment and then asked, "Are we ready for what's to come?"

"Great question," was all Master Lumens said and stepped away from the escort.

Bowie leaned over to Jack. "Wouldn't mind if he had a 'great answer' to follow it." Jack nodded in agreement.

Lumens addressed the soldiers. "Take care of these two. They're worth the trouble as you well may discover during your journey." Terrim and Scalt nodded in acknowledgement.

Lumens turned to the boys. "Jack, Bowie, we'll speak again but not for a time. I bid you good fortune at Strongthorne."

"Goodbye, Master Lumens," said Jack as he bowed from his mounted position. Master Lumens bowed back.

"Master Lumens?"

"Yes, Jack?"

"Much has happened to me, to us, this past month. Most of it still feels like a dream and little of it makes sense. But we do believe there's a reason for it all. We want you to know that."

Bowie added, "In other words, we trust you."

Lumens eyes softened. "Your trust means a great deal to me and I will do everything in my power to be worthy of it." Master Lumens bowed one last time to the boys. He didn't stay to watch them leave the compound.

***

The ride through Kentauros was uneventful. They were able to stop daily at inns for meals and rest. Having never ridden horses before coming to Atlantis, Jack and Bowie were both saddle-sore at the end of each day but otherwise they managed well enough. During the journey, they became friends with the soldiers and shared in songs and stories. When they crossed the border into Laidir, that's when things got dicey.

Locals scoffed at the sight of the Centaurs. Several inns and shops closed their doors to the group and merchant carts refused to do business with them. Many a night they set up tented camps on the rough terrain well outside of populated areas. Toward the southern end of Laidir, they approached an inn called the Drowned Rat—not the most inviting of names. Regardless, the innkeeper, Angus MacAllister, was mildly cordial to Centaur patrons and at the very least welcomed their money.

"Angus!" Terrim called out to the innkeeper. Angus came out and though only about five and a half feet tall, was built stout and strong. He didn't look unhappy to see them but he didn't look thrilled either.

"What have we got here? You ladies out for a tea party?" asked the innkeeper.

Terrim laughed. "I see your temperament has not improved with time, my old friend."

"Nor have your looks," Angus shot back. "And don't call me 'friend,' but if your coin is true, you could have the face of a chimera for all I care."

Scalt threw Angus a bag of coins. "We'll be leaving in the morning."

"Aye," said Angus. "Well, don't just sit on your high horses all day! Come down here with us common folk. Aileen has a batch of venison stew on the fire. That should feed this sorry looking lot and the beds have just been filled with fresh straw so you can get your beauty rest. You sure need it!"

"Your hospitality is always a tonic to a weary traveler," retorted Scalt.

"He reminds me of my uncle," Bowie said to Jack.

Angus overheard Bowie's accent and looked baffled. "What's a Laidirian doing with this horse lovin' lot?"

Terrim had a cover story prepared. "I caught him trying to ride off with my horse a few days back. I gave him the choice between losing his hand or becoming my servant for a time."

"Aye," said Bowie. "I was desperate to be with a woman and I didn't really care what she looked like. It's been so long I wasn't seeing straight. I didn't know it was his horse I was hitting on. I thought it might be his sister. You can see the family resemblance." Everyone stared at Bowie including Angus. Then Angus broke out into a laugh that echoed against the stratosphere. Jack and the other soldiers joined in. Even Terrim laughed, though he had just been gravely insulted.

"That will teach you to make friends with a Laidirian," scolded Angus.

"I'll think better of it next time," acknowledged Terrim.

"Douglas, Donnel, get your sorry butts out here!" yelled Angus to his two sons. "We've got some ladies here for tea. Tend to their horses while I make them some wee little sandwiches!"

The group feasted on an excellent stew, compliments of the innkeeper's wife. As evening approached, everyone retired to the main room which had a roaring fire going to ward off the night's chill. Douglas and Donnel brought out a recorder and harp respectively and played soothing tunes which aided in the digestion of the venison stew.

Two guards stood watch outside. The other soldiers inside kept their leather armor on and had their swords close by just in case.

Between the warmth of the fire and the music, Jack and Bowie began dosing off. The soldiers, while relaxed, remained alert. They never forgot they were in Laidir.

The guards rushed inside. "We've got company," said one guard.

Scalt asked, "How many and who are they?"

"Looks like a Laidirian goblin patrol. Sixteen horses, medium armor."

"Everyone keep your swords by your chairs. Be ready but don't look ready." He looked at the innkeeper and his family. "Downstairs is not a good place to be right now."

"You don't need to tell us twice." Angus hurried his family upstairs to hide out.

Terrim turned to Jack and Bowie. "Stay behind us. It may be fine or it could turn ugly. Depends on their mood."

The front door opened, letting in the brisk night air. Four Laidirian soldiers, wearing dented armor streaked with blood, walked in. The sergeant, a tall and broad man with jet black hair down to his shoulders, immediately locked eyes with Terrim. A fresh, bloodied gash ran across his right cheek.

"That explains the rancid smell. I thought ol' Angus might have been gutting a chimera," said the Laidirian sergeant. His three men laughed.

Terrim couldn't just ignore the jibe. "I pray your sword is sharper than your wit." The Centaurs all laughed.

"Aye, you can ask the goblins who found out the hard way tonight," said the sergeant.

"Looks like one of them left you a little something," said Terrim, pointing to the gash on the sergeant's face.

The sergeant touched his wound. "You mean this? One of the buggers got a bit too friendly but I set things straight."

"Come, join us. I'm sure there is enough stew for you and your men—"

The sergeant cut him off and got right in his face. Soldiers on both sides tensed up. "You're in Laidir!" said the sergeant. "You don't invite us to stay. We decide whether or not you and your men go!"

"But we were here first," said Bowie.

The sergeant looked at him. "Who are you and what are you doing with this lot?"

Bowie stuck to the earlier cover story. "Name's Bowie. They caught me trying to ride off with this one's horse. I thought it was sister at first. You can see the family resemblance." It had the same effect as it did earlier in the day. The Laidirians' laughter filled up the room. Jack playfully elbowed Terrim in the ribs. "That one never gets old," he said chuckling. Terrim did not return the chuckle.

"I gave him the choice of being my servant for a bit or losing a hand," said Terrim.

"Losing your hand would have been less painful than spending time with this lot," the sergeant said to Bowie.

"I know that now," responded Bowie, which spurred another round of laughter. Bowie took the sergeant aside and whispered to him. "Look, I owe this bloke another two weeks and he hasn't treated me half bad. Let me serve you and your men tonight. You'll get some extra attention and he gets to feel like a hero loaning me out to you as a gesture of friendship. Besides, we're leaving in the morning."

The sergeant thought about it for a while. Truth be told, he and his men were exhausted. Despite his dislike of Centaurs, he knew they had to be tough to travel so far into Laidir and the last thing he needed tonight was a fight ending in needless bloodshed. Bowie had also given him a way out that would help him save face.

The sergeant turned to Terrim. "I suppose if you'd loan out this lad for the night, we may all be able to get along."

Terrim accepted the deal. "He's all yours."

"If I were you next time, I'd cut off his hand—and stick it in his mouth!" the sergeant said to Terrim as he slapped Bowie on the back. He called out to his soldiers, "Come on, boys! Tonight, we'll play nice with the horsemen!" He extended his arm to Terrim. They embraced hands to elbows, the handshake of warriors. "Sergeant Garbhan at your service."

"Captain Terrim at your service."

The innkeeper and his family came out of hiding. As the evening progressed, stories were shared, music was played and food and drink were served to the contentment of the inn's warrior patrons.

In the morning, after a hearty breakfast of eggs, cheese, hard bread and a strong drink resembling coffee on steroids, the Centaurs along with Jack and Bowie prepared to depart the inn. But one last exchange of insults between the Laidirian and Centaur leaders was a necessary formality before continuing on their journey.

"Have a safe trip, you pansy kissing toads," said Sergeant Garbhan.

"I'd make you kiss my bum," said Terrim. "But your mom beat you to it!"
Everyone laughed.

When the Centaurs were out of earshot, Sergeant Garbhan turned to his men. "I hate to admit it, but I like that lot!"

The escort rode south along the Laidirian boarder without further incident.

***

The sun sat low in the sky as they approached the outskirts of the forest. "We'll camp here for the night," said Terrim. "I don't want to attempt crossing the forest in the dark. Get a fire going right away. And I want two guards on duty."

Scalt stepped up. "Let me take a quick gander to make sure there aren't any enemy troops or bandits close by."

"Good idea, but don't stray too far in," said Terrim.

Scalt proceeded into the forest. At the base of a tree about fifty yards in was a small cave with an opening just big enough to accommodate a man in a crouched position. On the floor of the cave, he noticed the faint glint of a metallic object.

He looked around one last time then removed his sword and set it close by before entering the cave. There was a sharp slope and it was nearly pitch black save for a pinhole of daylight poking through the forest canopy to the cave floor.

Scalt picked up the object, a dagger. The coat of arms on the handle was an eviscerated chimera. "Skul!" he said out loud. Four sets of red eyes opened around the periphery of the cave. Scalt suddenly realized his mistake—he had entered a goblin den and just woke up four of the creatures. With their excellent night vision, the goblins immediately recognized the unwanted visitor in their midst. The goblins hissed, ready to attack. Scalt yelled to cause a diversion and then bolted for the exit.

From the camp, the unmistakable shrill cries of goblins pierced the twilight sky. Terrim called out, "Goblins! Take up defensive positions!" Four of the Centaurs grabbed bows and arrows. Another four grabbed swords and shields and took up formation. Bowie grabbed a spear and positioned himself next to them.

From the edge of the forest, Scalt bolted forth toward the camp. Two deep bloody gashes could be seen running from his lower jaw to his neck. A few seconds behind him were four goblins in hot pursuit.

Jack and Bowie learned about goblins while in Fronisi but nothing prepared them for seeing the creatures in person. With their black skin, the goblins initially appeared as mere shadows in the twilight but as they got closer, their formidable size and ferocity could not be camouflaged. They were truly terrifying to behold! Each one stood close to seven feet tall though their posture was slightly hunched over like a velociraptor. Their musculature was lean yet proportional to their height. Their hands were similar in structure to human hands but with longer digits tipped with razor-sharp, one-inch claws. Their feet bore a similar shape to human feet but elongated and arched, clearly evolved for speed. And they were fast!

"We can't shoot without the risk of hitting him!" yelled one of the archers.

Another soldier called out, "He's not going to make it in time! They're gaining on—"

Before the guard finished his sentence, Jack grabbed two flaming branches from the fire and ran toward Scalt as fast as he could.

Bowie called out, "Jack, what are doing?" He didn't respond.

"Follow Jack and attack at will," commanded Terrim.

Bowie wasn't about to abandon his friend. He followed the others and was able to outrun them because he wasn't weighed down by armor as they were.

The goblins were so focused on their quarry, they failed to see what was unfolding in front of them. They were almost on top of Scalt. The lead goblin swiped at the fleeing soldier. The leather armor took the brunt of it, but the wretched claw still managed to catch exposed flesh along Scalt's rib cage causing another gash. The burst of adrenaline coursed through Scalt's legs and he actually gained a few feet of distance but then lost his footing and fell to the ground with a thud.

The goblins had their claws out and teeth bared, ready to pounce on their victim when suddenly they were blinded by firelight. Jack waved the flaming branches in front of their faces. He knew most forest creatures feared fire, at least where he was from. He hoped the same instinctual behavior applied in Atlantis. It was a gamble but he didn't have time to think about the outcome. Fortunately, his gamble paid off. The goblins reared back, putting their hands in front of their faces for protection.

Bowie plunged his spear into the goblin on the left, penetrating its heart and killing it instantly. The other goblins were disoriented, which gave the soldiers time to attack in full force, disposing of the other three.

"Secure a perimeter," commanded Terrim. "And get him back to our camp. Pull out the healing kit and start cleaning those wounds. Scalt, are you alright?" he asked concerned.

It stings a bit," Scalt said coyly. "My sword is fifty paces into the forest by the tree where their den was."

Terrim turned to two of his soldiers, "Grab torches and retrieve his sword. Be quick about it!" They complied.

"It was foolish of me," said Scalt, "walking straight into a goblin den. If they hadn't been sleeping, I'd be dead for sure."

"If it hadn't been for Jack's quick thinking, you'd be dead for sure," said Terrim.

Scalt turned to Jack. "It's true. I am grateful for your bravery. I owe you my life."

"You owe me nothing," said Jack. "It's an honor to be of service to one who risks his own life every day."

"Well said," said Terrim.

Bowie whispered to Jack, "Quite the poet, aren't we?"

"Shut it!" Jack whispered back.

Scalt turned to Terrim. "I retrieved this from the cave." He handed Terrim the Skullian dagger. Scalt became light-headed and nearly blacked out.

"Tend to him," said Terrim. "He's badly wounded."

"Yes, sir!" Two of the soldiers got under each of Scalt's arms and took him back to the camp.

Jack looked at Terrim. "Sir, you look concerned."

"It may be nothing, but goblins generally don't collect things."

"It could be a coincidence," offered Bowie.

"Perhaps," said Terrim.

They waited until morning before riding through the Forest of Quith. With such a large group, the chance of a daytime attack from goblins, chimera or any other forest predators was unlikely. Though the canopy of tree tops was dense, streaks of light managed to squeeze through. Still, great caution was exercised. There could still be bandits or others up to no good, not to mention enemy troops. Jack and Bowie rode in the middle with Scalt who was feeling better after having his wounds dressed and getting a good night's rest.

A few hours into the ride, the forest noticeably thinned. Scalt explained goblins were not known to inhabit this portion of the forest. By noon, they entered into a small clearing just in front of the tree line demarcating the forest's border.

"We will leave you here," said Terrim.

"We don't want to arouse any suspicion," added Scalt. "Two new students riding in with an escort from Fronisi would surely lift a few curious heads.

We'll wait an hour or so before riding into town to resupply our journey home and rest up."

It wasn't easy for Jack or Bowie to say good-bye to Terrim and Scalt. After Lumens pardoned the boys, they had become good friends with them.

Jack and Bowie dismounted and unloaded their packs from the horses. "Gentlemen, it's been a pleasure!" said Bowie.

"Likewise, Bowie," offered Terrim.

Scalt pointed forward. "The main road will take you straight to the academy. Farewell and good fortune to you both. You will learn much but the learning will be hard. The next time we meet, you will not be the same men we parted with today." Terrim and Scalt in turn placed their respective right hands over their hearts and then extended them palm up to the boys, a Fronisi gesture of welcome and good-bye, the "Aloha" of Atlantis as it were.

The boys returned the gesture. Jack spoke first, "We thank you and your men for providing us safe passage."

Terrim smiled. "Master Lumens believed the risk was worth it. We trust his judgment. After our journey with you, we trust it even more."

Scalt, still bandaged from the goblin attack, came forward. "What you did was brave beyond your years and I am forever grateful." He bowed to Jack who returned the bow. "And Bowie, I don't know if you're extremely brave or extremely reckless." The soldiers laughed. Scalt continued, "I suspect a little bit of both. But I do know this, you are a warrior." He bowed to Bowie who returned the gesture.

Bowie felt things were a getting a bit too serious, "Lads?"

"What is it?" asked Terrim.

"Thank you for not running your spears through us when we first met."

Terrim laughed. "You're very welcome! Keep that sense of humor, Bowie. You're going to need it for what's to come."

"Good luck and farewell," said Scalt. They would not see their friends again for a long while.

"I'm going to miss those guys," remarked Bowie.

"Me too," said Jack. "Come on, we don't want to be late for school."

# Welcome to Knight School

As they exited the forest, Jack and Bowie caught their first glimpse of Strongthorne Academy several miles off in the distance. The fortified castle was large enough to be a city unto itself. From their vantage point, they could make out the stone curtain walls connected by four watchtowers with crenellated tops serving as observation posts. On a central spire flew a flag with Strongthorne's coat of arms comprised of two bagwyn supporters, the shield featuring a green dragon on a maroon field with gold flanches, a phoenix perched on top of the helm and the academy's motto: *veritas quod victoria* (truth is victory). The castle was not as beautiful in design as the structures in Fronisi but impressive in its own right.

The castle was surrounded by three concentric circles of land, each comprised of a high stone wall. Each ring of land in turn was divided by a moat. There was a single passageway down the center but multiple draw bridges between the rings provided alternative avenues of ingress and egress.

To the east of the castle stood the town of Concordia filled with shops, inns and the dwellings of about two thousand citizens. South from the town and academy were acres of farmland. Between the farms and the forest was approximately a mile of uncultivated land.

The road to the academy was deceiving long. It took about an hour and a half to reach the entrance on foot. Jack and Bowie walked up to the entryway at the first ring circumventing the academy with student centuries posted on either side. Though just a few years older than Jack and Bowie, the armed guards looked very adult in their plate armor. Behind them stood an older student wearing leather armor and a handsome dark green cloak. Jack and Bowie felt very grubby in contrast. The older student came forth and bowed slightly upon their approach. "Good day to you both," he said. He held a scroll in his hands. "Are you new cadets to the academy?" he asked.

"Yes," answered Bowie.

Once the student confirmed Jack and Bowie were new students, his demeanor quickly changed to curt condescension. He was an upperclassman after all and they were just plebes, freshmen, scum, a.k.a. "dung huggers." Respect would have to be earned from now on. "Names?"

"Jack and Bowie," answered Jack nervously.

"Your name is Jacknbowie?"

"No," corrected Jack. "I'm Jack. And he's Bowie."

"Strange names. Can he talk for himself or is he a moron?" asked the upperclassman.

Bowie stepped aggressively toward the upperclassman. "Oh, I can talk but I'd rather show you—"

Jack held his hand in front of Bowie to stop him. The upperclassman put his hand on the pommel of his sword. The other two guards drew their swords ready to strike. From the walls, Jack caught a glimpse of two archers with their bowstrings pulled back ready to loose arrows into Bowie's chest. Without thinking about it, Jack stepped in front of his friend to shield him. The upperclassman looked at Bowie as if he were crazy. Bowie stared back. The standoff seemed to last a lifetime.

Bowie wanted to establish that he was no pushover and not someone to be taken lightly. He also knew he was a second away from getting killed. Bowie smiled which got the upperclassman smiling, then laughing. Bowie laughed back. Jack laughed out of sheer terror. The guards laughed and lowered their swords. The archers lowered their bows.

The upperclassman and Bowie embraced hand to elbow. "I'm Galler Straith, fourth year. Welcome to Strongthorne Academy!" He and Bowie released their grip then Galler did the same with Jack who was feeling a bit weak in the knees but managed to remain upright. "Continue on to the gatehouse. You'll be directed further from there."

"Thank you, Galler." said Bowie. "Come on, Jack."

As they continued on, Jack said under his breath, "Try not to get us killed at the next checkpoint."

"No promises," replied Bowie.

When Jack and Bowie were out of earshot, Galler turned to the guards next to him shaking his head. "Freshmen!" he commented, then got serious. "But keep an eye on that one," he said in reference to Bowie. "He shows no fear of death."

"What about the other one?" asked one of the guards.

"He doesn't look like much," said Galler.

"True," answered the guard, "but he stepped in front of his friend without hesitation."

"He looked scared," said Galler.

"As well he should," acknowledged the guard, "but he still did it."

In front of the gatehouse was a long registrar's table attended by several students in leather armor with green cloaks as well as a full complement of student guards also in leather armor sans cloaks. Similar to the first wall at the outer ring, archers stood at the ready on either side of the curtain walls.

Inside, upperclassmen engaged in archery and weapons sparring. Other classmates cheered their friends on. In the distance, a blacksmith's hammer was heard pounding the finishing touches on a bassinet.

Jack and Bowie approached one of the students at the table expecting another round of insults like the ones doled out by Galler. "Good day, gents," said the jovial student in greeting. "Names please?" Jack and Bowie looked at each other somewhat surprised.

"I'm Jack."

"And I'm Bowie." They each said their own names to avoid another "Jacknbowie" fiasco.

The student looked at his list and checked off both their names. "Ah, there you are! Welcome Jack and welcome Bowie to Strongthorne Academy! I'm Crenn Reggs, fourth year and new student ambassador," he said with a bit of relish.

"I must say you're a right bit nicer than the guard at the gate back there," said Bowie as he pointed to the first checkpoint.

"You mean Galler? He's a bit rough around the edges but once you get to know him, you'll probably like him less," said Crenn. "I'll take you on a brief tour of the castle and then to the freshman barracks, your new home for the next year, if you live that long," he said with an implacable smile though he wasn't joking in the slightest.

The tour started at the inner courtyard which contained the weapons training area dubbed "The Bone Yard" due to countless students breaking bones during training. Midway through the tour was the stadium at the north end within the castle walls which could house ten times the garrison for tournaments and other outdoor gatherings. After that, they toured the Great Hall where the entire student body, faculty and support staff dined. Tables could also be moved for indoor entertainment and gatherings.

The castle itself was built on top of bedrock. The architects had designed a "basement" layer carved out of the rocky foundation for storage that could hold enough food to sustain a siege for a full year, though no enemy had ever dared try. It also contained the dungeon filled with iron-barred cells, suspended cages, racks, shackles and devices intended to extract information from reluctant participants and/or just inflict good old-fashioned agonizing pain.

"Does the castle house prisoners?" asked Bowie.

"The town has its own dungeon," answered Crenn.

"Then what's this dungeon used for?" asked Jack.

"Let's just say you don't want to get detention," answered Crenn dryly.

They returned to the ground level and Crenn finished the tour by pointing out the various barracks. "Over there is where the seniors live. Next to them are the juniors, though they're off on active duty the first half of the year. Across the way is the sophomore barracks and next to the stables is where the freshmen reside."

"Next to the stables?" said Jack somewhat disgusted.

"Lovely," said Bowie. The image of four-post beds with warm and comfy sheets, down pillows and a roaring fireplace quickly dissolved.

"Well, not exactly," said Crenn. Jack and Bowie looked relieved.

Crenn continued with a smirk that was anything but subtle. "The freshman barracks is directly connected to the stables."

He wasn't kidding—the horses whinnied as the boys entered the barracks. The stables were on one side with nothing separating them from the freshmen's living quarters. And the smell was, well, "horsey" to say the least. Bowie wrinkled his nose a bit. Jack nearly passed out from the stench.

There were a hundred cots laid out in the room, two rows of fifty on either side. Each cot was nothing more than a wood frame with a flat board on top that stood a little over a foot above ground. The mattresses, if they could be called such, were course burlap sacks filled with two to three inches of straw. A folded woolen blanket was laid at the foot of each cot. Next to each cot stood a tall open box with a bar toward the top and a dozen crudely constructed hangers—those were the "closets." Next to the closets were wooden chests for other personal belongings.

In the middle of the room stood wrought iron fire pits to provide some warmth during cold weather. Jack looked warily at Crenn. "What if an ember catches a mattress on fire?"

"It happens from time to time. That's why we keep those buckets of water around." Crenn pointed to the buckets spread every twenty feet or so around the periphery of the room.

"The good news is since you're the first to arrive, you get first pick of the beds. Jack and Bowie immediately headed toward the far end of the barracks, as far away from the horse smell as they could get.

A wise choice," acknowledged Crenn.

Crenn left them to settle in and told them their *consilium* would check in with them later in the day and take them through "orientation." Neither Jack nor Bowie knew what a consilium was but Jack figured it had something to do with a counselor or advisor. They had no clue though as to what orientation would be like.

Their new classmates arrived piecemeal throughout the day and all had the same disappointed expression when they saw the rural décor of the freshman barracks and an even sourer expression when they smelled it. Bowie made a point of introducing himself to each new classmate as he walked in. Jack was still shy around new people but Bowie's friendliness was infectious and soon the two became the unofficial welcoming committee of the freshman class.

As boys that age often do, they bonded instantly. Because they were not allowed to talk about their backgrounds, they asked each other questions about the school itself, if anyone knew what the training would be like, and most importantly, what time meals were served. In total, there were a hundred new students/knights-in-training as it were in the freshman class, one for each dilapidated cot.

Among their new classmates was Gaul Delain, a snobby though good-natured boy with dark skin, well-manicured braids and an athletic build. Then there was Scurra Tarn, pale as a ghost with spiky reddish blond hair who was likely to become the class clown. There were also two brothers a year apart in age but starting the academy at the same time, Yor and Narro Skere. Each brother praised the other for his hunting prowess and each had a fair share of scars from their hunting expeditions to prove it.

One of the last freshmen to arrive was a small, mousy boy who made Jack look like a linebacker in comparison. The boys stared at the newcomer as he walked in and several whispered their doubt of him making it past the first week, let alone the first day. Always one to support the underdog, Bowie greeted him warmly. "Hello, I'm Bowie. Nice to make your acquaintance." He stuck out his arm to shake hands as warriors but the newbie didn't know what to do, clearly not up to speed on warrior etiquette. Bowie continued, "We've got a bed right here for you." Bowie took the boy's pack and led him to one of the two remaining open cots which was closest to the stables. "The smell is a bit ripe, but you'll get used to it!"

"Not likely!" said Scurra.

Bowie set down his pack on the cot. The boy looked around as if the slightest sound would send him into a panic. "I didn't get your name," said Bowie.

The boy started to speak but was barely audible. "Grrrr—"

"I'm sorry, I couldn't hear you," said Bowie compassionately.

"My name is Grob, Grob Mealy."

Bowie winced a bit. As kind as he was, he couldn't mask his real feelings. "Grob Mealy? That's a terrible name!"

"I know," said Grob.

Bowie patted him on the shoulder. "Come join us once you get settled in."

\*\*\*

After some more socializing, Jack and Bowie walked out of the barracks together to get some much-needed fresh air. A short distance away, four Centaurs on horseback caught their attention.

Two were adult men, regal in appearance. The other was a teenage boy, slightly older than Jack and Bowie with a brooding look more common among men five times his age. He was lean yet quite muscular.

The last in the party was a girl their own age with long black hair pulled back into a tight ponytail and light blue eyes. Her expression was fierce but tinted with nervousness. Bowie didn't know it yet but he had just experienced love at first sight. "She's a fine looking tart!" he exclaimed just loud enough for Jack to hear. He starred at her. She felt his energy and turned toward him, catching his eyes with her own. She didn't know it yet but she had also just experienced love at first sight. They stared at each other for a while. The younger male Centaur harrumphed a bit.

"I might leave out 'tart' when you meet her," mentioned Jack.

"What?" asked Bowie, still lost in the girl's eyes. "Oh, yeah, right. Good call."

Shaking himself out of it, brazen Bowie headed right up to the group of four. The two adult Centaurs looked like they could be brothers. The younger male Centaur put his hand on his sword pommel as Bowie approached. The eldest Centaur scolded him. "Jemm, that's uncalled for." The adolescent Centaur reluctantly removed his hand.

Bowie extended his arm to the eldest Centaur first. "I'm Bowie. It's a pleasure to meet you." Bowie's boldness delighted the elder Centaur. They shook hands to elbows.

"I'm Gi'tal," answered the Centaur. "This is my brother, Arma." Arma and Bowie greeted each other. "This is my son, Jemm." Bowie extended his arm but quickly withdrew it when he saw the hateful look in Jemm's eyes. "And this is my daughter, Shaunteera." Bowie bowed and she returned the gesture without them taking their eyes off each other. There was a palpable chemistry between them and Jemm didn't like it at all. Gi'tal and Arma exchanged a quick smile, having been teenagers themselves once.

The fact that Bowie sounded like a Laidirian and greeted them warmly was a great joy to the older Centaurs who truly wanted peace with their southern neighbors. They had no idea Bowie was actually from a place much farther away. Jemm was not so delighted. He cringed every time Bowie spoke.

Jack suddenly remembered their conversation with Master Lumens—this group was Centaur royalty and Shaunteera was a princess. Even though she would not talk about her background as was dictated by the school's guidelines, her equestrian skills would surly give her away if the Centaur entourage she arrived with hadn't already.

Jack bowed low. "Your highness, it's a pleasure to meet you and your family."

"What is your name, young man?" asked Gi'tal.

"It's Jack, your highness."

"Jack, I appreciate the respect, but while here at the academy, I would prefer it if you called me by my given name."

"Of course, your—of course, Gi'tal," corrected Jack.

He bowed to Arma, Jemm and Shaunteera. Jemm wasn't exactly friendly but didn't feel as threatened by Jack as his did Bowie.

"We have a long journey ahead of us and Shaunteera should get settled in," said Gi'tal.

"Are you starting as a student here?" Jack asked Shaunteera out of politeness though he already knew the answer.

"Yes! Do you have a problem with that?" challenged Shaunteera. Jack was taken back but Bowie just laughed.

"What's so funny?" Shaunteera asked Bowie.

"I think she means 'yes,'" Bowie said to Jack.

"You'll have to forgive my daughter," remarked Gi'tal. "She's the first girl—" Shaunteera cleared her throat.

Gi'tal corrected himself, "Excuse me, 'woman' to enter Strongthorne Academy. Don't misjudge her my new friends. She may be beautiful, but she is also deadly."

"Father!" Shaunteera blushed. Gi'tal and Arma laughed sweetly, albeit at her expense.

Gi'tal leaned down to Bowie and Jack. "I would consider it a personal favor if you both kept an eye on her for me."

"That won't be necessary, Father. I can take care of myself!" said Shaunteera scornfully.

"It's the ones who underestimate you who will need care," affirmed Arma. "And it never hurts to have friends."

"I give you my word," Bowie stated earnestly. Jemm leaned toward Bowie and not so quietly said, "If you harm my sister in any way, I will personally slit your throat."

Bowie was unintimidated by his new found foe. "Bring friends."

Gi'tal and Arma had another good laugh. "I like this one," said Arma. "Jemm, there's no reason why you and him can't get along."

Jemm starred down at Bowie. "I have the only two friends I'll ever need," he said as he patted his horse and put his hand on the hilt of his sword and began drawing it.

Arma walked his horse between them. "Nephew, enough! He's a plebeian!" Wait until he's trained for a while before you formally challenge him."

"You're right, Uncle. It would be dishonorable to challenge one who is so ... weak!"

"Bowie, weak?" interjected Jack. "Well, I wouldn't go that far."

Bowie didn't find the whole thing amusing and looked at Jemm cold and hard. "Why don't you and I go somewhere and I'll show you just how 'weak' I am."

"Arma turned to Bowie this time, "Save your energy for your training my young friend. You two will have plenty of time to get to know each other in the future."

"Can't wait," said Bowie.

"Nor can I," said Jemm.

It was likely the last time Bowie and Jemm would ever agree on anything.

# ORIENTATION

As is often the case with teenagers, once they felt comfortable with each other, the conversations got louder and the rough-housing began. Spontaneous wrestling matches ensued, along with the throwing of hay and general mayhem as it were. In a single moment, it all stopped.

It was as if an icy wind had blown through the barracks. All eyes turned toward the doorway. There stood a knight, tall and muscular dressed in boiled leather and an impeccable royal blue cloak. He was young, less than thirty years old, with long blond hair pulled back into a scalp-cracking ponytail. Sir Daran Stave was a knight of legend in Atlantis as well as an alumnus of Strongthorne Academy. He was recruited directly into the King's Guard upon graduation and was promoted to captain before his twenty-first birthday, the youngest soldier ever to earn that honor. In a time and place without cell phones, social media or cable TV, the students didn't recognize him from any picture. But his scar was as legendary as the man himself. It ran down the left side of his face from the middle of his forehead to the jawline. The fearless eye had not been damaged by the blow causing the scar but rather had likely starred down the assailant as the counterstrike finished him off.

"You're Sir Daran Stave," said one of the freshmen in total awe.

"'Sir Daran' will suffice," iterated the knight. Having their complete attention, he continued. "I am the new consilium for the freshman class." A wave of chatter rose among the students, a wave that quickly halted by the slight clearing of Sir Daran's throat. "Please stand in front of your cots." Sir Daran's scar pulsed a bit. "Now." The freshmen ran to the front of their cots and stood at attention.

"As your consilium, I will oversee your entire curriculum and personally train you in combat. By the end of the first year, should you survive, you will learn how to wield a sword and other weapons, and equally important, how to defend against a sword and other weapons. You will also learn advanced horsemanship as well as military strategy and tactics. However, combat alone does not make a knight. Your education will also include etiquette and protocol, mathematics, literature, physics, music, commerce, history and astronomy.

"If you make it through all four years here, you will become a knight of Andaar." The cadets smiled at this comment. "However, about half of you will likely not make it." They stopped smiling. "Not because we'll kick you out, although we may, but because you'll be dead."

Bowie turned to Jack and whispered, "Not exactly what you'd call a motivational speaker."

Sir Daran walked up and down the ranks. "Your past is not important to me and it will not be discussed. I don't care who your brother or your father is or was. I don't care if you come from wealth or poverty. In my eyes, you are all equally pathetic and worthless at this point. But hopefully, not for long. Not for long." He stopped in front of Bowie and sized him up. "Name?"

"Bowie, sir." Bowie's accent once again hinted of Laidir. Sir Daran was not a fan of Laidirians.

"Welcome, Bowie," said Sir Daran cordially as if welcoming a guest.

Bowie didn't trust it for one second but answered courteously, "Thank you, sir."

"You look a lot like a bandit I killed last year in the forest during a chimera hunt. I'm pretty sure he was Laidirian. A relative perhaps?" proposed Sir Daran.

"Wouldn't surprise me, sir," answered Bowie. "We were short one at the last family reunion." The boys laughed but stopped immediately as Sir Daran turned his head a fraction of an inch. Sir Daran almost laughed himself but thought better of it. These cadets were all too green and getting friendly might lead to them letting their guard down—and that could cost them their lives. But he liked Bowie right away. Bowie's joke was not disrespectful. Yet, to have the nerve to tell any joke while looking into the eyes of Sir Daran showed either a complete disregard for life or abundant mettle. Time would tell.

Sir Daran stepped away from Bowie and addressed all the boys as well as Shaunteera, "You will follow me through orientation. Our first stop is the barber shop."

In single file, the freshmen followed Sir Daran to a building with a pole out front painted with red and white stripes. As was common in medieval culture, barbers cut hair and trimmed beards as well as treated wounds and performed crude surgery when necessary. The barber shop also housed the infirmary. Jack noticed two upperclassmen running about holding buckets of tomatoes and laughing. "I don't like the look of that!" Jack said to Bowie. "What do you think they're up to?"

Bowie suspected dubious intent as well. "I suppose we'll find out soon enough."

The freshmen entered the barber shop which had hospital cots along each wall. The barber came out from the back room. The boys and Shaunteera collectively shuddered. The barber was not what you'd call handsome … "hideous" was probably a more accurate description. Grummel was a corpulent man with a ruddy complexion and an eye patch. He looked like a fat pirate who never used sunscreen. But what he lacked in aesthetic appeal, he more than made up for in joviality.

"Good day, students! I know I'm not much to look at but I'm quick with my sheers, swift with my razor and so-so as a doctor. The boys looked worried. Grummel laughed. "Don't fret! I've been patchin' up soldiers twice as long as you are old."

"Has anyone ever died under your care?" asked Grob.

Without skipping a beat, Grummel answered, "Of course they have! I'm a barber not a miracle worker!" He laughed out loud at his own joke. The freshmen weren't primed yet for Grummel's humor.

"All right, one of you take a seat right here and the rest of you stand in line," said Grummel. "This won't take long."

Gaul Delain sat on the splintery stool that could have passed as a torture device in its own right. Grummel stepped up behind him with shears in one hand and a sharp bronze razor in the other. Grummel asked Gaul, "How would you like it cut?" then winked at the others.

Not able to see Grummel was mocking him, Gaul answered, "Just a little off the length and cleaned up around the neck area, if you don't mind."

"Mind? Why, not at all!" With the speed of an attacking hawk, Grummel sheared off every last one of Gaul's braids and then followed through with his razor, producing a nearly bald scalp in under ten seconds. "Just as you asked, a little off the length and cleaned up around the neck. Next!"

One by one, the freshmen took turns getting their heads butchered. When it was Bowie's turn, he smiled at Grummel and asked to keep his ponytail. "Suuuure," Grummel said obligingly as he cut off Bowie's ponytail and handed it to him, which is exactly what he expected.

Bowie held up his lock of hair. "It will make a nice souvenir." Grummel laughed and slapped Bowie on the back, half-knocking him off the stool.

Within an hour, Grummel had reduced their heads into fuzzy bowling balls, including Shaunteera's.

"And what do you say to Grummel for his kindness?" asked Sir Daran.

"Thank you," they all said on cue.

"My pleasure!" said Grummel, followed by a hearty laugh.

"All right, single file. We're off to meet your brothers in arms," said Sir Daran.

As they filed out of the barber shop, Jack and Bowie had a funny feeling, as if hundreds of eyes were watching them. Halfway across the courtyard, Sir Daran brought them to a halt and took several steps away from the collective. He looked up and around, seemingly speaking to no one. "Brothers of the Strongthorne Academy, may I present to you the freshman class!" As he finished his sentence, the entire garrison of approximately two hundred students came out from behind turrets, posts and hay bales—each student holding tomatoes. Bowie looked at Jack, "Here we go."

There was no place to take cover. The assault commenced. The freshmen covered their heads and groins as best they could. But between the volume and velocity of tomatoes thrown, each freshman was covered from head to toe in tomato pulp. Poor Grob was simply overwhelmed and pummeled to the ground. Jack took several hits that knocked him off balance but he held his footing. Bowie stood like a statue.

After thirty seconds or so, the hail of tomatoes stopped. Grob looked up from the ground and slowly stood up. A tomato came out of nowhere and hit him square on the forehead, knocking him flat on his back.

Sir Daran looked up at the perpetrator with a hint of disdain. "Sorry!" claimed the upperclassman who threw the last tomato. He wasn't really sorry but when Sir Daran looked at you …

The upperclassmen disbanded. Sir Daran turned to the freshman class. "That went well." He continued toward the supply hall and motioned them to follow.

The quartermaster, Pickins, was a lean and shrewd man, some sixty years of age. He had two clerks helping him. Seeing the ornate clothing of the other students, Jack and Bowie thought at least they'd have something decent to wear. They were wrong. The freshman uniforms were functional but would definitely not win any fashion awards. They would come to learn the uniforms improved as they advanced to the next grade level.

"Step up, lad," said Pickins. Narro was first. Pickins grabbed him by the shoulders, turned him around, looked at his feet and said to one of his clerks, "Number five tunic and cloak, belt: 1 choot, boot size: 1 cam and a chigger."

Jack and Bowie recalled their briefing at Fronisi regarding measurements—a *choot* was approximately the length of one yard, a cam was one-quarter of a choot (approximately 9–10 inches) and a chigger was one-tenth of a cam, about an inch.

Narro moved aside to grab his supplies from the clerk while another student replaced him in front of Pickins. Narro was handed two tunics made of wool, one brown cloak made of thick wool treated with wax to provide added protection against the elements, one pair of leather boots, four pairs of thick woolen socks, three pairs of undergarments and a length of cord which acted as a belt.

By the end, each boy and Shaunteera held their new uniforms in their arms and were marched back outside. "Sir, what about armor?" asked one of the boys.

"When you've proven you're worth the effort, we'll get you armor," answered Sir Daran. "You'll have one hour to put away your supplies, clean yourselves up, dress and meet me in the Great Hall for dinner. Dismissed!"

"Yes, sir!" they said in unison and headed off to their barracks.

Shaunteera stayed back until all the boys left before addressing Sir Daran. "Sir, where should I clean and dress?"

Sir Daran appeared confused. "I take it you have your spot in the freshman barracks?"

"Yes, sir," she answered.

"And you know where the latrine is?" he asked.

"Yes, sir," she replied.

"Then what is your question?" he inquired.

"Sir, I'm a woman!" said Shaunteera.

"Really?" he said sarcastically. "I hadn't noticed. Especially with that haircut."

She felt for where her long hair used to be and grimaced a bit.

"There will be no special treatment because you're female," he said.

"I don't expect—"

He cut her off, "Yes, you do. I suggest if privacy is important to you, then you bathe before or after the rest of your classmates. And I'm sure you can always dress in the stable area if need be. You won't have to worry about anyone following you in there."

"Yes, sir." She knew better than to argue with him and turned to leave.

"Shaunteera," he called out. "Know this: you will get no more and no less than any freshmen here but you are all under my protection. Do you understand?"

"Yes, sir, no harm will come to me under your watch," she said.

"That's not what I said. You will get plenty harmed—ridiculed, jeered, bruised and bloodied—but I will not tolerate any harm coming to you because you're female."

"Yes, sir. Thank you, sir." She smiled at him. He didn't return it.

"Now get out of here. You're starting to annoy me." He waved her away.

"Yes, sir!" She headed off to the barracks at a brisk pace.

Sir Daran had the utmost respect for Shaunteera entering the academy but he'd never let her know that. Boy, girl, it didn't matter. She was a freshman and still pond scum until he trained her up a bit. Never let it be said Sir Daran wasn't an equal opportunity butt-kicker.

# ETIQUETTE AND PROTOCOL

The courtyard bell rang three times indicating five minutes before the start of each class period. No bell was rung after that because if class started and you were tardy, little was going to save you from detention in the dungeon. You'd better have an excuse nothing short of a life-threatening wound and even then, it was still up to the individual instructor. The bell rang four times when the class period ended and there were short breaks between classes. Most academic classes were held in the morning before the midday meal. The afternoons were reserved for combat training.

Jack and Bowie each had a parchment with their classes written down. Their first class was Etiquette and Protocol with Sir Gigas. Along with another twenty plus of the freshmen, they filed into the room and took their seats behind rustic desks and stools. At each desk was a place setting with a plate, napkin and goblet along with various forks, knives and spoons. At the front of the room was a larger desk, presumably for the instructor, also with a place setting. Propped up against the wall was a life-size mannequin dressed as a courtier. The boys didn't know what to make of it.

From behind a curtain at the front of the room entered a man the size of a tree. The boys were awestruck. "He's freakin' huge!" said Bowie a little too loudly.

The man stood just under seven feet tall and was muscular to scale. "Good day, boys," he said with a rather melodic voice betraying his gargantuan stature. "I am Sir Gigas, your instructor for Etiquette and Protocol."

A smart-alecky boy from the back of the room asked, "Are you going to teach us how to eat?" The other boys snickered.

"Actually, yes," answered Sir Gigas evenly. "As a student and alum of Strongthorne Academy, you will be expected and called upon to conduct yourselves with the utmost propriety and chivalry. You will need to learn the social graces. Uncouth manners or inappropriate behavior could sully a critical negotiation and may even put your life and the lives of your comrades in peril." He gave the boys a moment to take that in before continuing.

"Much in the way of diplomacy centers around dining. In front of you is a standard place setting for a banquet at the royal court of Andaar, albeit we're using cruder accouterments for practice."

The smart-alecky boy in the back of the room held up a butter knife and raised his other hand to ask a question.

"Yes?" acknowledged Sir Gigas.

"Is this supposed to be a knife? Doesn't look very sharp!" said the smart-alecky boy. The other students laughed, that is until Sir Gigas picked up the butter knife from his own place setting and threw it with such force and velocity that it ran through the palm of the boy's raised hand, pinning it to the back wall. The boy gasped in shock as blood trickled out from the wound.

Sir Gigas grabbed the napkin from his place setting and slowly walked over to the boy. "Excellent observation. In fact, that knife is intended to be dull. It's a butter knife. As the name implies, it's designed for spreading butter." Sir Gigas grabbed the knife handle and yanked the weapon free. He handed the boy his napkin to use as a bandage. "Better go to the barber and have that looked at."

"Yes sir," said the boy, wincing in pain with tears in his eyes. He was turning paler by the second. He stood up on wobbly legs and stumbled out of the classroom.

Sir Gigas headed back toward the front of the classroom as if nothing had happened. "As this lesson just taught us, while engaged in etiquette, it is important to remember that at all times you are still a soldier." His voice grew louder and his eyes got crazier. "That means a butter knife could become a throwing dagger. A spoon could be used as an eye gouge ..." Back at the front of the room, he picked up the plate and broke it in half on his desk leaving a razor-sharp edge. "Or a plate could become an axe!" With one swift motion, he beheaded the mannequin with the plate. The students gasped. Sir Gigas looked up seething with rage. "Any other questions?"

Bowie raised his hand. Horrified, all the boys looked at Bowie, then at Sir Gigas. Anticipating a sarcastic question, Sir Gigas grabbed the cutting knife from his place setting and readied it to throw. He looked at Bowie with fevered eyes. Bowie held up a tiny fork. "What's this used for?"

Sir Gigas was practically convulsing, then realized Bowie's question was sincere. He quickly shifted gears.

"Right. That one's for shellfish."

"Oh," commented Bowie. He looked around at the other students. "Shellfish."

The students wiped the sweat from their brows and together, survived the rest of class.

# MUSIC

After Etiquette and Protocol with Sir Gigas, the other academic classes were a breeze—or at the very least less violent. There was one more class before the midday meal, music. There were short stools strewn throughout the classroom with several unusual instruments leaning against the walls, including crumhorns and rebecs, shawms, zinks and lutes.

"I've never seen instruments like this! Well, except that one." Bowie pointed to a set of bagpipes.

"Some of them are pretty funky-looking. I feel like we're in a Dr. Seuss book!" whispered Jack.

A short, balding and rather pudgy man dressed in an ornate multi-colored tunic walked into the room with a sparkle in his eye. "Welcome, welcome!" he said rather animated. "I'm Sir Sranjali, your music teacher. Please, have a seat."

Each student took a stool and sat in loose rows. Sir Sranjali looked up at the ceiling as if scrutinizing one of the beams. The freshmen quickly learned this was his segue to a serious discussion. "Music is the manifestation of the heart and soul. Music can bring peace between enemies. Music can also incite war and rally the troops. Music is the pulse of the universe." He paused to let the profoundness of his message sink in. "But most of all, and never forget this, music is one of the best ways to impress the ladies." The boys looked at each other wondering if he said what he just said.

"Doesn't matter what you look like. Women love musicians! Trust me on this one," he said with a wink.

Bowie whispered to Jack, "I guess our world and Atlantis are more alike than we thought!"

Sir Sranjali encouraged the students to try out the different instruments to see which one they liked. Bowie picked up a lute and strummed it. He tried some guitar chords which didn't work but he made some adjustments and played an impromptu melody.

"Very good!" encouraged Sir Sranjali.

Most of the boys preferred instruments they could bang on but a few picked up the ones requiring more finesse. Despite Jack's genius level IQ, music was not his forte. However, he enjoyed singing so he figured he'd get something out of the class.

Sir Sranjali was a musical marvel. He went from student to student and taught them a few notes to practice on the respective instrument they had chosen. He could play them all. Then he gave each of the singers a range of notes and sang along with them. He had the voice of a nightingale.

After going around the room, he silenced everyone and conducted. First, he motioned the percussionists to start, then the woodwind instruments to join in using the notes he had taught them, then the string players, then finally, the singers. Though the melody was very rough around the edges, it was also brilliant and inspiring. They performed for a while then heard four bells indicating the end of class.

"Where did the time go?" said Sri Sranjali, thoroughly delighted by their progress. "All right then, best to get going. I can't let you take the instruments with you but you are always welcome to come to the classroom at any time and practice. In spring, a select few of you will be asked to perform at a school event. Doesn't that sound like fun, yes?" The students nodded.

"Off you go then," said Sir Sranjali. As the students filed out, he grabbed Bowie's arm. "You have a gift, young man. I could see it right away."

"Thank you, sir!" said Bowie.

"Don't thank me, it's your gift!" joked Sir Sranjali. "Off you go!"

"Sir," Bowie nodded and met Jack at the door.

Jack looked at his friend with a lifted brow. "I never thought I'd see the day when Bowie Blackwood was the teacher's pet!"

"You and me both!" conceded Bowie.

# PELL TRAINING

After lunch, the freshmen headed to the Bone Yard where several dozen pells stood. Pells were wooden posts set in the ground used to teach cadets how to execute sword strikes, the equivalent of a heavy bag for a boxer.

Sir Daran stood waiting for them along with an attendant next to a cart loaded with wooden training swords called *wasters*. "Good afternoon, boys," he said before noticing Shaunteera. "And girl," he added inertly.

"Good afternoon," responded the freshmen in unison.

Sir Daran grabbed a few of the wasters from the cart and handed them out to the students as he walked along their line. "Today, we begin your weapons training, starting with the sword. No doubt you've learned some rudimentary skills from your fathers or brothers or mothers for all I know. My advice is to forget everything you think you know. We're starting from scratch, right here, right now.

"You'll notice these swords are made of wood. Once you can show me you have enough competence not to accidentally cut off one of your own limbs or the limbs of a classmate, we will move you up to real swords." Sir Daran stopped in front of Gaul and handed him a waster. "Strike the pell," he commanded.

Gaul reared back and let out a battle cry as he struck the pell ferociously. Despite being made of wood, the wasters still had honed edges and his got stuck in the pell. In the added second it took Gaul to withdraw it, Sir Daran grabbed one of the wasters and struck him on his exposed flank, dropping him to the ground in a pained heap. "As I have just demonstrated," Sir Daran said stoically, "striking hard is just part of the technique. You will need to learn proper footwork and body positioning. And while it will certainly behoove you to strike hard enough to do damage, you'll need to avoid getting your weapon stuck in your opponent's armor or bone to avoid a counterstrike."

Sir Daran handed Bowie a waster. "Strike the pell," he commanded. Bowie unleashed a strike that broke the pell in two. "Of course, striking hard enough will sometimes do the job," noted Sir Daran. He pointed to the attendant, "Replace his pell with a thicker one." The attendant stared at the broken pell in shock—no freshman had ever broken one during training.

After some basic instruction from Sir Daran, the freshmen stood in front of their respective pells and delivered strikes as he called them out. Intermittently, he pulled individuals aside and commanded them to attack him. He easily blocked and counterstruck. No student escaped painful reminders as to why Sir Daran was a legendary swordsman.

Several of the freshmen, including Gaul and the Skere brothers, had received ample sword training from their own fathers. Shaunteera was even trained to wield two swords while riding on horseback—but no one came close to matching Sir Daran's virtuosity.

Halfway through the training, Jack arms felt like spaghetti. Despite his weakness though, he exhibited excellent skill. Often, he was able to defend himself with very little movement and once made contact, albeit a glancing blow to Sir Daran's thigh. But the consilium took note for it had been some time since anyone, let alone a freshman, had penetrated his defenses.

Poor Grob was one big welt by the end of the instruction. When it was time to move on to equestrian training, Bowie put his arm around Grob to give him support and half carry him. "You did great!" said Bowie encouragingly.

"Great?" questioned Grob. "I was terrible!"

"You're still alive," said Bowie. "I'd say that's great!" Grob smiled. Jack couldn't help smiling himself. Bowie was relentlessly optimistic and a natural leader. He knew in time, Bowie would make a great knight. He wasn't so sure about himself.

"I saw you got one in on Sir Daran," said Bowie impressed.

"Barely touched him," said Jack.

"Don't sell yourself short, Jack," scolded Bowie. "No one else got close, including me. Mark my words, there's a warrior in you!"

"Maybe," said Jack, "but it'll be hard to see him through all the bruises."

# The Challenge

Their first day of school was rough to say the least. The freshmen were riddled with bruises, welts, cuts and scrapes. The Skere brothers proudly displayed the more noteworthy wounds to one another likely to leave scars. Grob couldn't even lift his tunic over his head—it got stuck around his mouth and almost suffocated him save for two classmates who came to his aid. The rest of them could barely move but mustered up enough energy to bathe, dress and limp to the Grand Hall for the evening meal.

They walked into a cacophony of upperclassmen chatter. There were several tables in each section and each section was designated for the respective class year. The most dilapidated tables were assigned to the freshman class. No one harassed them though as the upperclassmen sympathetically remembered how they felt after their first day of combat training. Even the freshmen had earned a good meal and some semblance of peace for the moment.

Bowie conversed with Scurra as they walked toward their tables. Coming from the opposite direction was Kellen Aquilam, a senior cadet of great distinction and reputation in the academy and throughout Atlantis. In his time at Strongthorne, he had proven himself an exceptional scholar, warrior and leader. He had been entrusted with dozens of assignments which put his life in peril on more than one occasion. Kellen had killed half a dozen goblins during their attack on the entourage of the magistrate of Camber-Elan traveling through the Forest of Quith to celebrate the Festival of Parsis. On another occasion, he fended off three bandits while carrying a vital message to Anterra, killing two and sparing the remaining one sans right hand. Kellen also fought in the Battle of Cur and while wounded, managed to carry out three comrades to the healer before allowing himself to receive treatment.

And he spent the past summer in a coveted internship training with the Andaarian king's personal guard.

To his peers, Kellen was a loyal and compassionate friend. He was well liked and held in high regard by most of the other students, regardless of year. Of course, Bowie didn't know any of this when they accidentally bumped into each other. "Watch where you're going!" asserted Kellen.

"I was just about to say the same thing to you," retorted Bowie.

Jack whispered in Bowie's ear, "That's Kellen! You don't want to mess—"

Bowie waved his friend off.

The Great Hall went silent. Kellen was already walking ahead but turned around out of sheer surprise. "What did you say?" Kellen and his three friends in tow approached Bowie. The shortest in the group was a head taller than Bowie. Scurra scurried away.

Bowie held his ground. "I said I was just about to say the same thing to you!"

Kellen couldn't believe the arrogant attitude of this lowly freshman. He laughed a bit which triggered off laughter throughout the room. None of the freshmen were laughing, save for Bowie who rather seemed to enjoy himself. Kellen didn't know what to make of him. Was this plebeian mocking him or was he just plain crazy? By the accent, he assumed this student was Laidirian, which left a bad taste in his mouth to begin with. Nevertheless, he had to save face among his peers. He looked down at Bowie. "If you know what's good for you, you'll apologize and move on."

Bowie had no plans to back down. "That's funny."

"What's funny?" asked Kellen.

"I was just about to say the same thing to you, again!"

"Perhaps we should settle this another time," suggested Kellen, thinking his warning would be enough. He didn't know Bowie … yet.

"Do you want to do this before or after dinner?" asked Bowie. The room sounded off with a collective "Ooooooooooooh!"

"I do admire your spirit," Kellen said seriously, "but I'll still have to teach you a lesson. By the bylaws of Strongthorne Academy, I officially challenge you. Do you accept the challenge?"

"Of course!" said Bowie.

"I will record the challenge with Dean Slade. I'm sure Sir Daran will inform you of the particulars. Until then," said Kellen and walked on.

"Until then," replied Bowie, not understanding what he just agreed to.

Jack ushered Bowie to their sitting area. The freshmen all gathered round. "What's this challenge about?" asked Bowie. "I just wanted to go outside and get to it!"

Gaul answered, "That's not how things are done at Strongthorne. If a major disagreement or issue arises, a student may call for an official challenge to resolve it."

"Sounds kind of formal," said Bowie.

"It is," said Scurra. "You will meet in the stadium with all students and faculty in attendance for single combat. The victor is the last man standing and the one who drinks from the Chalice of Arbarium to officially end the challenge."

"What's the drink?" asked Bowie.

"What do you mean?" asked Grob.

"What do they put in the Chalice of Arboretum?"

"It's Arbarium," corrected Jack.

"Whatever," said Bowie.

"That's what you're concerned about?" asked Gaul.

"Well, yeah, I may not like it," said Bowie.

"You'd only have to take a sip," said Scurra.

"It better not be alcohol of any kind," Bowie stressed. "I'll never let a drop touch my lips!"

"I think it's some sort of fruit juice," said Narro.

"Good to know," said Bowie relieved. "So, that's it then?"

"No, that's not it then!" said Shaunteera. "Kellen is a master swordsman and a fierce warrior!"

"He'll pulverize you!" said Grob.

"I don't know about that!" said Bowie. "You saw me with a sword today. I was pretty good!"

Scurra rolled his eyes. "Are you kidding? Kellen is the best swordsman in the academy!"

"I like a challenge!" said Bowie. "Enough talk, let's eat!"

Everyone was more afraid than Bowie. That should have told Bowie something but he was thick when it came to practical fear.

The next day before weapons training started, Sir Daran approached Bowie. "I see you've been making friends already."

"You heard about the challenge then, sir?"

"It's become a topic of discussion," said Sir Daran. "The challenge is to take place on *dies Saturni* in the stadium, precisely one hour after breakfast."

"Why one hour?" asked Bowie.

"It's not good to fight on a full stomach. Anyway, you may pick one student as your attendant."

"What does he do?" wondered Bowie.

"He attends to you," answered Sir Daran. "Make sure he brings salve, bandages and smelling salts. You're going to need them."

Bowie leaned into Sir Daran. "Is there any wagering taking place on the event?"

"Always," Sir Daran whispered back.

"I wouldn't bet against me, sir," said Bowie and took his place next to his friends.

Sir Daran smiled to himself. Then he spent the next three days pre-pummeling Bowie to prepare him for the pummeling he was going to receive at the end of the week.

***

In the ensuing days prior to the challenge, Jack was a nervous wreck. He was deeply worried about his best friend. Despite Bowie's toughness, he wouldn't stand a chance against a seasoned warrior such as Kellen. While chances of death were slim, getting physically beaten to a bloody pulp and humiliated at the same time was very likely.

Bowie asked Jack to be his attendant for the challenge. Jack took his duty seriously and spent what little free time he had gathering information about Kellen's fighting style, trying to find weaknesses he could pass on to Bowie to give him any advantage whatsoever or at the very least, a better way to avoid severe pain. Unfortunately, Jack could find no apparent flaws in Kellen's martial ability.

Kellen joked around with his friends about the whole thing but regretted challenging an inexperienced freshman. He could have just let the incident go. But no, Bowie was too much in his face to forgive it. The only fear he really had was the freshman being a wildcard and unafraid when *he* should have been very afraid. Kellen's attendant, Frosser Glint, had done a little spying on his own, watching Bowie during weapons practice. "He's a natural fighter, I'll grant him that," he told Kellen, "but very rough around the edges. He goes for power every time. No finesse whatsoever. You'll make easy work of him. Four years from now, I might say something different but you should be able to take him in ten blows, fifteen tops."

Saturday arrived and after breakfast, the students and faculty gathered in the stadium for the challenge. Each class took their respective section in the stands, sans the junior class who were still abroad. Faculty took the front row.

Kellen looked calm, confident and regal to boot. As Glint helped him into his leather armor, he put on his game face and focused on the task at hand, beating the tar out of the plebeian whom had challenged his honor and reputation, not to mention his senior-class pride. He didn't bear hatred toward Bowie. In fact, he admired the younger boy for being so gutsy, but out of school, that kind of arrogance would surely get a student killed. He would teach Bowie a lesson for his own benefit.

On the other hand, Bowie looked like he did on any other day, content and nonplussed, though fairly banged up after several days of Sir Daran's school of accelerated combat. Jack helped him into his leather armor. "You know you don't have to do this," he offered.

"Yes, I do," said Bowie. "Don't worry about me. I've gone up against worse."

"No, you haven't!" insisted Jack.

Bowie turned to face his friend, his eyes filled with both sadness and ferocity. "Trust me, I have."

Sir Gantry Trenn, the sophomore class consilium, served as referee. He was middle-aged and thick around the middle with a fleshy, bearded face, but had the confident gait of a seasoned combatant with over two decades of warfare under his belt. He walked to the middle of the stadium holding two wasters and shields. "Brothers of Strongthorne Academy, there is a conflict between two of us. We will not allow this conflict to fester and separate us. We won't always agree. At times, we may disagree strongly with one another. But when the sword is raised against one of us, it is raised against all of us! If there is an unresolved conflict, there is weakness. If the sword strikes then, it wounds us all. We will resolve this conflict and be done with it. Bowie, Kellen, come forth."

Bowie and Kellen did as they were instructed. In addition to their leather armor, each wore soft-padded leather helmets, vambraces and greaves.

Sir Gantry spoke first to Kellen. "You bring this challenge forward?"

"Yes."

"Bowie, do you accept this challenge?"

"I do."

"The rules are simple. You fight until one of you can no longer fight. The other then drinks from the chalice and is declared victor. That is the end of the conflict. There will be no discussion of it to follow. There will be no further dispute. If any ill will is harbored afterward, the student will be expelled from the academy, never to return. Do you both agree to these terms?"

Both boys answered yes.

"Very well, take these." Sir Gantry handed each boy a waster and shield. "Go to your respective ends. When the horn sounds, the challenge begins. Good luck to you both, though one of you will be the luckier."

They each walked back to opposite sides of the stadium.

Jack made one last attempt. "There is no shame in not fighting him. You can lay down your sword."

"No," said Bowie.

"Your pride is going to get you hurt. I've seen Kellen fight. He's better than you! Please, don't do this," pleaded Jack.

Bowie could feel how much his friend cared about him and that's all he really needed. "I'll see you when it's over."

The seniors at the other end spoke words of encouragement to Kellen. Kellen took a few practice swings and defensive postures. That's when Jack noticed something. "Bowie, his left ankle is vulnerable. His defensive stances and counter moves leave it open by a fraction of an inch."

"Noted," said Bowie. He put on his game face which was anything but a game.

From across the field, Kellen caught Bowie's gaze. As a warrior, all his senses had been heightened through experience. He sensed a predatory energy from Bowie and for the briefest moment felt unnerved by the threat. He had faced goblins, thieves and enemy warriors with stoic resolve, but Bowie? The fear didn't sit well with Kellen. He knew he was far more skilled in the martial arts. But you never can fully predict what a wild animal will do when backed into a corner.

The horn sounded. Both stood without moving, then Bowie began a slow walk toward his opponent, matched by Kellen. Bowie broke into a canter. Kellen remained walking. Bowie was wasting vital energy. Jack didn't understand what his friend was doing. What was the rush? What was Bowie hoping to achieve? The sophomore and senior onlookers snickered among themselves. "This will be over in a few seconds," Jack overheard.

Dean Slade sat with the other teachers. Sir Glavin Stipes, the senior's consilium who looked like a mountain with arms and legs, turned to Sir Daran. "I'll wager a *ghip* your dung hugger doesn't even land one blow. Look at him! He'll be spent by the time he gets to Kellen."

"I'll take the wager," said Sir Daran. "Double if he lands the first blow?"

"Sure, why not!" laughed Sir Glavin.

Kellen kept up his slow, steady pace. Bowie broke out into a full run. His eyes lit up with fire and he let out a war cry that reverberated throughout the stadium. Kellen stopped. What was Bowie doing? Was he trying to finish him off in one charge? Pure insanity! Kellen would have no part of it. He shifted his weight lower and prepared to move right or left to deflect the force of Bowie's charge while counterstriking with a hard blow to Bowie's shoulder, hopefully ending this charade quickly.

Though it looked like Bowie was out of control, he noticed every minute detail of Kellen as he approached. Kellen's right foot made a slight move to the right as he pulled in his shield closer to his body by a fraction of an inch, also to the right. As Jack had pointed out, the left ankle was slightly vulnerable. But how to strike there without getting counterstruck?

Bowie predicted Kellen would shift right and strike with a hard forward blow. If he was wrong, he was toast. But Bowie calculated correctly. He knew Kellen was a more skilled fighter but he also knew the senior would look bad if it took a lot of effort to defeat a freshman. Kellen would try to end it quickly with a finishing blow instead of winning through finesse.

Bowie charged like a rhino. When he got within eight feet of his opponent, he launched himself horizontally. Kellen took a bigger step to the right than planned. Bowie shielded his head and body from a downward blow and was hoping for a shot at Kellen's left ankle. Cripple his opponent and maybe he'd have a chance. He streamlined his sword against his right side and positioned his shield so his weapon was even more obstructed from Kellen's view. While still in the air, he twisted his body so his back faced the ground as he made a cutting move at Kellen's left thigh. Kellen dropped his shield to block the blow right as Bowie angled the direction of his sword lower and landed a solid strike against Kellen's left shin. The leather of the vambrace prevented the bone from breaking but the strike was hard enough to break the skin, draw blood and cause a bruise that would take a full month afterward to heal. Had it been a real sword, Kellen's ankle would have been severed.

The snickering in the stadium stopped instantaneously. You could hear a pin drop from a mile away.

After delivering the blow, gravity kicked in and Bowie hit the muddy ground harder than expected. It knocked the wind out of him but he had struck first, temporarily stunning Kellen. Sir Daran quietly accepted his two ghip from Sir Glavin.

Kellen stumbled backward but recovered quickly. His shin hurt like hell. He could barely put weight on it. Bowie caught a lungful of air and stood up. He raised his shield and approached Kellen.

Kellen put the weight on his good leg. He was trained to ignore pain—and was glad of that training. He could lick his wound later but now he was ready to fight. Bowie attempted a thrust which Kellen easily deflected. He counter-fainted then landed a blow against Bowie's ribcage.

"That tickled a bit," taunted Bowie, though the pain was sharp. Then Kellen proceeded to show why he was Strongthorne's best swordsman. For the next ten minutes, he landed all of his blows while blocking all of Bowie's—but Bowie wouldn't go down. After twenty minutes, they both dropped their shields and double handed their swords. After thirty minutes, both were losing wind, but Kellen had been in real battles and knew how to pace himself. Bowie on the other hand went all out.

Kellen got a second wind and redoubled his attack, striking hard. Bowie quickly learned Kellen's patterns but by the time he was able to block two or three blows in a row, Kellen switched tactics and landed repeatedly before Bowie caught on again. Out of every ten blows Kellen landed, Bowie snuck in one or two, but none with any real force.

Blood was streaming from a cut on Bowie's forehead. His right eye and cheek were swollen. Out of frustration, he made an overcommitted lunge which Kellen readily anticipated. He blocked it easily and landed a solid blow against Bowie's shoulder and neck doubling him over. When Bowie tried to stand up, Kellen hit the side of Bowie's face with the flat of his sword, seemingly knocking him out.

Bowie laid there is a heap, face down. Jack grabbed the smelling salts and started to run to Bowie but Gaul held him back. "It's not officially over yet."

Kellen was not happy nor satisfied. He took no pleasure in defeating Bowie. Kellen removed his leather helmet and dropped it to the ground. He looked over at the chalice, his friends encouraging him to drink from it so he could be declared the victor. Kellen looked down at Bowie and walked over to him. Frosser Glint called out, "What are you doing?"

"I want to make sure he's okay," said Kellen.

"Drink from the chalice first!" insisted Frosser.

Bowie was facing away from Kellen. His eyes opened and he prepared.

Kellen bent down to check on Bowie. He gently pulled back Bowie's shoulder.

Bowie unfurled a right hook, the same right hook that had knocked out Eric Header, fourteen other boys and a drunk woman outside of a Scottish kilt shop (long story). Kellen Aquilam was just added to that list.

The collective gasp in the stadium would have been comical had it not been filled with sheer disbelief and shock. After a few seconds, the freshman class cheered with abandon, followed by the sophomore class. The faculty was stunned. The senior class was paralyzed.

Bowie got up, nose broken and blood running down his face. He limped toward the chalice. He picked up the vessel and was about to drink from it but turned to look at Kellen lying on the ground unconscious. He walked over to his opponent and bent down to check on him. Kellen came to, shaking the fog from his eyes.

Bowie spoke, "You soundly defeated me and the only reason why you didn't drink from the cup first was to check on me."

"That was my misfortune," said Kellen. "There are no second chances."

"Exactly," said Bowie. "In a real battle, you wouldn't have checked on me. You would have finished me off."

"True," considered Kellen.

"You did the honorable thing. I did not. You are the victor. Take a drink and let's be done with this," said Bowie.

"Help me up," said Kellen. Bowie complied. Kellen rubbed his sore jaw, took the chalice from Bowie and drained it. Sir Gantry came over and raised Kellen's hand into the air. "The victor!"

Everyone cheered. Kellen put his arm around Bowie's shoulder. "Is it time for lunch yet?" asked Bowie.

"You would do me a great honor to dine with me," said Kellen.

"I think we would do everyone a great honor if we bathed first!" Bowie said. Kellen laughed. Everyone laughed.

Bowie had just made his mark on Atlantis.

# PRANK

After the challenge between Kellen and Bowie earlier in the school year, the seniors greatly reduced the amount of razzing they would normally administer to the freshman class. The sophomores were another matter. Though the freshmen were quickly advancing in their combat training, the sophomores relentlessly pulled pranks on the dung huggers. On one occasion, they sawed through the legs of the benches in the Great Hall so when the freshmen sat down, the benches collapsed. Another time, they let out the horses into the freshman living area and since their mattresses were made of straw, the horses basically ate their beds.

The sophomores pulled a prank every two weeks or so. It would have been difficult for the freshmen to pinpoint the perpetrators had it not been for the sophomores always positioned close by and laughing the hardest when and where the pranks occurred. Jack and Bowie decided enough was enough and recruited the entire freshman class to get even.

While plotting one evening, Scurra walked in from the bathroom. "The funniest thing just happened. I was taking a bath and had my towel around my neck. I must have dozed off. The water level rose to the rim and I swallowed some which woke me up. It took me a minute to realize my towel had sunk to the bottom and clogged up the drain."

A devious smile formed on Jack's face. "You've got an idea, haven't you?" asked Bowie. All eyes zeroed in on Jack.

"What if we clogged up one of the drain pipes in the sophomore barracks?" suggested Jack.

One by one, they all caught on to what Jack was proposing. The plumbing for all barracks basically worked the same way. There was one inlet pipe that fed the sinks, baths and toilets and three separate drain pipes. An obstruction could "accidentally" clog up one of the drains so water would overflow into the living quarters.

If they clogged up the sewer outlet alone, it may be a lesson the sophomores would never forget. But on the remote chance they got caught or accused, which was just as good as getting caught, the last thing the freshmen wanted was to clean up raw sewage. Knowing Strongthorne justice, they would probably have to swap barracks with the sophomores until the cleanup was complete. The stench alone would take months to clear and the whole school would suffer as a result. But flooding the sophomores' living area would be revenge enough.

The freshmen spent the next couple of days on reconnaissance. Jack discovered blue prints in the library detailing the academy's plumbing system. Each inlet pipe broke off from a main pipe connected to the underground spring. They could temporarily block the inlet pipe into the sophomore barracks. They would then have to infiltrate the sophomore restroom and plug up the sink outlet which was the fastest flowing, then open up the inlet pipe again so the incoming water would start to buildup and overflow. However, all barracks were designed with an emergency drain in the middle of the living area should there ever be flooding. Leaky and partially collapsed roofs were not uncommon occurrences. The drain cover had a lid but was only opened if flooding actually occurred. They would have to seal the lid somehow. They would also have to consider one or more of the sophomores waking up while they were executing the prank. If that happened, their efforts would be foiled.

Grob was assigned to coax information out of Grummel. He told the barber he was having trouble sleeping and asked if there was anything he could prescribe. Grummel told him about the *somniculosus* shrub, a.k.a. "sleepy shrub," which grew wild throughout Atlantis. "For severe pain, you can drink a tea steeped from the leaves. But for insomnia, you can light the shrub on fire and breath in some of the smoke. You'll sleep like a baby!" Grummel gave him a few branches of the shrub. Perfect!

Each freshman played a role in the plan. A group of forty freshmen spent the next few weeks gradually loosening the floor boards under the sophomore bathroom area. Another ten foraged in the fields and harvested enough sleepy shrub to knock out a herd of elephants for a week. On the morning of the prank, another ten were assigned to mix the sleepy shrub into the kindling reserves used for the sophomore fire pits in the evening.

On the night of the prank, five of the freshmen would hide in close proximity to the sophomore inlet pipe. Once they temporarily shut off the pipe, another team of ten freshmen would make a quick entry into the sophomore bathroom through the loosened floor boards, clog up the sink drain and exit undetected. Another team of ten would stand watch around the academy—they had devised and practiced various signals to indicate a passing guard or other potential hazard. Fifteen would stay in the freshman quarters and pretend to be asleep, faking sounds of snoring, in case a guard or faculty member came by to check on them. That group was also responsible for arranging the pillows and blankets of every empty bed to make them appear as if they were being slept in.

Working to their advantage was the fact most of the guards were up top around the periphery of the castle. The academy was much more concerned about keeping enemies out then worrying about "enemies" within. Another advantage was there were always tasks and jobs going on day and night, less at night, but it wasn't uncommon to see students, attendants or stewards out on the grounds after dark.

There was a storm the evening of the prank which provided added cover. Fires would be lit for sure and the sound of the rain would potentially mask any unintentional noise caused by the freshmen.

After dinner, the five freshmen taking care of the inlet pipe made their way to their position and waited until approximately an hour after the main core of students had gone to bed. Narro made the sound of a common blue jay to signal the commencement of the prank. The first team shut off the inlet pipe to the sophomore barracks. The team slotted to plug up the sink drains then removed the loosened floorboards and entered making as little noise as possible. They jammed all kinds of things down the sinks—rocks, branches, leaves and pieces of fabric. They made some noise but the sleepy shrub did its work. Yor, who was on the infiltration team, entered the sophomore living quarters and sealed the emergency drain pipe with resin.

Once the drain for the sinks was thoroughly clogged, that group exited the building. Scurra noticed one of the freshmen missing so he tiptoed into the sophomore living area and found Yor sprawled out on the floor, sound asleep himself due to breathing in smoke from the sleepy shrub. Scurra held Yor's nose and mouth tight until he woke up and shook off the effects. They snuck out together and replaced the floor boards. Another bird call signaled the students to reopen the inlet pipe. Within a minute, the sinks overflowed.

Gradually, the freshmen returned to their barracks, but not all at once to avoid drawing attention. The freshmen warmed themselves by their own fire pits and sniggered amongst themselves. So far, so good. They had pulled it off. But would it work?

Eventually, the freshmen dozed off but were awakened by the sound of screaming sophomores. "The emergency drain won't open," one sophomore shouted. The freshmen went outside to watch the comedy of errors unfold. Sophomores were franticly trying to stop the flow of water while using buckets to bail out their quarters. The seniors and faculty came out to investigate the ruckus. Everyone laughed. Everyone but the sophomores.

Bowie looked at the other freshmen. "Job well done!" As they went back inside congratulating each other, Sir Daran sat on one of the cots, trimming an ingrown fingernail with his razor-sharp dagger. The freshmen froze in their tracks.

"Blue jays don't sing when it's raining," he said casually.

Jack and Bowie simultaneously said, "It was my idea."

"I'll see you both after breakfast," said Sir Daran. "Sleep well, if you can."

# Detention

"They had it coming," said Sir Daran. "They've goaded you all for quite some time. And an assault on the freshman class is an assault on me."

"I like the way you think, sir," said Bowie.

"Nonetheless, we can't encourage revenge and anarchy within our hallowed walls now, can we?" stressed Sir Daran.

"No, sir," they reluctantly agreed.

"Your secret will be safe with me," said Sir Daran.

"Thank you, sir!" said Jack.

"However, you will both serve detention."

Jack and Bowie dreaded the idea. Having toured the dungeon at the beginning of the school year, detention was quite an unpleasant consideration.

"I must say, I am quite impressed with your planning and strategy. You both showed great resourcefulness and leadership. It was exceptional teamwork," admitted Sir Daran.

"Jack was the real mastermind behind it all!" said Bowie, wanting to give his friend full credit.

"You're not doing me any favors," whispered Jack.

"I believe I detected the faint smell of sleepy shrub coming from the sophomore dorm, if I'm not mistaken," said Sir Daran.

"Yes sir," confirmed Jack.

"I've had a few injuries in my day and have been administered both the tea and the smoke," acknowledged Sir Daran. "Ingenious, yes. So, as a reward for your ingenuity, I'm going to let you decide what your detention should be—"

Jack and Bowie almost broke ranks and hugged him. "Thank you, sir!"

"—among the following choices," he finished.

"Oh," said Bowie.

"You have your choice between four hours on the rack, four hours in the pillory, twelve hours in the suspended coffin cage, two days in a cell without food or water or one afternoon helping the cook prepare dinner for the school."

Jack and Bowie looked at each other. Was he joking about the last option? They dared not ask.

Bowie spoke for them both. "Sir, I believe we'll take the last one."

"Are you sure?" asked Sir Daran.

"Yes, sir," said Bowie.

"Very well then. Report to Beurk after lunch to help prepare tonight's dinner."

"Thank you, sir," said Jack as they hurried out before Sir Daran could change his mind. But Jack stopped in the doorway. "Sir?"

"Yes?"

"Thank you for going easy on us," said Jack.

Sir Daran came as close to a laugh as they had ever seen though it better resembled a twisted smile. "I didn't."

***

As Jack and Bowie stepped into the kitchen that afternoon, they were hit hard by a rancid smell. Beurk, Strongthorne's cook, stood behind a large wooden table with blood up to his shoulders and all over his apron as he eviscerated a dead chimera. He basically looked like a giant blood clot with the added adornment of chunks of chimera guts strewn throughout his bristly beard. Beurk was a stout man with massive arms and hands the size of shields calloused over by countless knife cuts, cleaver gouges and burns. His hygiene in general left something to be desired and one questioned how such a man was in charge of something supposed to keep others healthy.

"Hello, boys! Just in time to help me with dinner," Beurk said good-naturedly. Chimera intestines sloshed around in a bucket below the butchering table. The smell was so unbearable, not even the flies could take it.

"Beurk," ventured Jack, "how old is that carcass?"

The cook scratched his head. "Oh, hmmm, let me see ... what's today?"

"*Dies Martis*," answered Jack.

"Dies Martis, already?" Beurk took a whiff of the spoiled carcass as if just noticing its less-than-savory odor for the first time. "Well, nothing some herbs and spices can't fix!" said Beurk cheerfully.

Bowie whispered to Jack, "I don't think there're enough herbs and spices in all of Atlantis to fix that smell!" The boys second-guessed whether half a day in the pillory would have been easier punishment.

"Don't be shy, boys! Grab an apron and cleaver from over there and let's get to it!" Beurk yanked out a three-foot length of bloody intestine. Jack ran out the door dry-heaving. Though Bowie had a rock-hard constitution, had he just won the lottery, he would gladly have forfeited his winnings to avoid another minute of the wafting putridity. "You get used to it," offered Beurk.

After an hour, the smell was still horrible but Jack and Bowie were able to clean and dress the chimera without throwing up or passing out. Beurk was impressed. "Not bad for plebes! Most first-timers would be in the infirmary by now!"

"What's for dinner?" asked Bowie.

"You're actually going to eat dinner after all this?" asked Jack.

"Sure, why not?" answered Bowie. Jack shook his head in disbelief.

"Don't know yet," answered Beurk. "Was thinking about chimera stew but I couldn't get enough vegetables, just peppers."

Jack walked over to one of the tables supporting a huge wheel of what appeared to be cheese. "What is this?" he asked.

"The best chider cheese in all of Atlantis!" said Beurk proudly. "I make it myself from the milk of the chider goat! Try some!"

Jack broke off a chunk and shared it with Bowie. It was pretty good. He spotted some open sacks of grain across the room. "What are those?"

"One is wheat and the other is corn," answered Beurk.

"Corn?" questioned Jack.

"That's right," confirmed Beurk. Jack's eyes lit up.

"I can see the wheels turning," said Bowie. "What are you thinking?"

Jack whispered, "Corn, peppers, cheese and shredded meat? Think about it!"

Bowie didn't catch on at first, then it hit him. "Right!"

Hours later, the dinner bell rang and the multitude of students and faculty gathered in the Great Hall to dine. The faculty was served first and the honor went to Beurk to serve them. Of course, he had cleaned up somewhat before serving the meal. He walked out proudly displaying a large platter piled high with corn chips smothered in melted chider cheese, shredded chimera meat and peppers. He laid the platter down in front of Dean Slade.

"What is this?" asked Dean Slade.

"Try it, my lord!" insisted Beurk.

It was the strangest dish Dean Slade had ever seen and not particularly appetizing looking, but seeing the pride in Beurk's eyes left him no choice but to graciously give it a taste. He grabbed a chip and lifted it up. The melted cheese was gooey and formed a string from the plate to the dean's mouth. The flavor of the corn chip with the cheese, meat and peppers was fantastic. Dean Slade was quite content. "Excellent, Beurk. You've outdone yourself!"

Beurk beamed with teary eyes. "Thank you, my lord. I'm so very pleased you like it! "

The other faculty members reached over and grabbed a portion. They all seemed to enjoy this strange new concoction. "What do you call this dish?" asked the dean.

"My lord, it's called *nachos*."

# GOBLINS

Jack stood watch atop the southwestern tower. As the watch commander on duty, it was his charge to monitor all activity around the castle, town and surrounding area. With a telescope, he could see several miles in every direction. Jack still feared heights, but knowing if he fell the possibility was greater of him dying than getting hurt was strangely comforting.

Most days, there was little of significance to see. With Concordia practically attached to the castle, the telescope caught a great deal of activity in and around the streets. It was not uncommon to spot a quarrel between a merchant and customer. And if the discussion got heated, Jack could order a message to the town magistrate so he could send a soldier or two to break up the conflict—though there would usually be too long a delay to prevent one of the parties from getting a broken nose.

On watch with him were the Skere brothers. But Jack was the watch commander, which meant he had seniority as well as the authority to call for full mobilization of the school should the situation arise. However, a minor scuffle in town hardly required intervention from the most elite group of warriors-in-training on the island continent.

Jack looked across the valley floor and scanned the tree line of the forest. He brought the telescope up to his eye and noticed peculiar movement among the foliage not indicative of wind. From the boundary of the forest broke a horse with a man slumped over the saddle. The rider was badly wounded with an arrow sticking out of his back. A few seconds later, a sandy blond-haired boy also on horseback broke from the tree line riding hard and looking back over his left shoulder which had two arrows protruding from it. About a hundred feet trailing, nine dark figures chased the rider at full bore.

That morning, Kellen and Bowie were sent together to deliver a message to the magistrate of Tammen, a small town about a half-day's ride from the academy requiring some travel through the less dangerous part of the forest. Jack's jaw dropped when he realized what he was seeing. Kellen was the wounded rider slumped over on the first horse. Bowie was the second rider, wounded in his shoulder, though he seemed unfazed. Jack figured Bowie was too pumped up with adrenaline to feel the pain. Chasing Bowie were ... "GOBLINS!"

"Say what?" questioned the Skere brothers.

Jack didn't hesitate. "Ring the bell five times! Alert the student liaison to direct the townspeople inside the gates of the castle ASAP. Kellen is seriously wounded and riding toward the castle. Bowie is behind him pursued by nine goblins!"

"Goblins?" said Narro.

"In broad daylight?" said Yor. "That's not what they do!"

"I'm the watch commander on duty. It's my call. Do it, now!" Jack went over to the rope—the quickest, albeit scariest way to descend the tower.

"Where are you going?" asked Yor.

"To meet them!" Jack donned the padded leather gloves for the quick descent, grabbed onto the rope and slid down. The gloves smoked right away from the friction but were thick enough to prevent rope burns.

Narro looked at Yor. "What do you think?"

Yor looked skeptical. He walked over to the telescope and casually put it to his eye. In view was exactly what Jack had described. He froze for a second then snapped out of it. "Ring the bell!"

Narro rang the bell five times, waited ten seconds then rang it again five times so there was no mistaking the signal, full mobilization of the school.

Halfway down the rope, Jack caught site of Shaunteera who had been sword sparring with a sophomore student but stopped when she heard the bell. "Shaunteera!" he yelled. "Grab your weapons and pick me up! Bowie's riding in with goblins on his back!" She could tell by Jack's tone he wasn't joking. She grabbed two swords, mounted her horse and road over to pick him up. He slid off the rope and onto the back of her horse. As soon as he landed, he grabbed her tight around the waist. Shaunteera kicked hard and they bolted off.

Crenn and Galler were on guard duty at the front gate. "Open the gate!" yelled Jack. The two seniors complied. Kellen's best friend Deyglenn Nills and a few of the other seniors were in the yard and stopped when they heard the orders. "Deyglenn, assemble an infantry company," commanded Jack. "Follow us!"

"What is it?" asked Deyglenn.

"Goblins!" answered Jack.

"In broad daylight?" one of the seniors commented. "Doesn't make any sense!"

"If Jack's wrong, it's his funeral," said Deyglenn and then sprang into action. He grabbed the short horn on his waste and blew it hard. From all around the castle, infantry students quickly armed themselves and assembled at the front gate.

Jack caught site of Hawk, the senior archery commander. "I need a company of archers ready in thirty seconds. Join Deyglenn at the front gate and follow us out as fast as you can!"

"Done!" Hawk yelled down to Burl, Strongthorne's blacksmith and armorer. "Bows and arrows for one company!" Burl nodded and ran into the armory to grab the needed weaponry. Hawk whistled to alert all archers within earshot to mobilize. Other students followed to help ready the troops. By the time Jack and Shaunteera reached the third gate, Deyglenn and Hawk were in formation and following on foot at a brisk pace.

From the port, Dean Slade and Sir Daran heard the bell ring five times. "Full mobilization?" asked Sir Daran.

"Scope!" commanded Dean Slade. His steward complied. "Who's on watch?" asked the dean.

"It's Jack, my lord," answered his steward.

Through the scope, Dean Slade couldn't believe what he was seeing. Bowie was on horseback and bleeding from two arrow wounds with nine goblins in hot pursuit. His horse was losing speed and the goblins were closing in. Jack and Shaunteera were heading straight toward him, while reinforcements were several hundred paces behind them. Dean Slade thought out loud, "Very bold, Jack."

"We'll ride out to help them but we won't get there in time to make any difference," said Sir Daran.

Bowie caught site of Jack and Shaunteera riding directly toward him. Jack shouted as loud as he could so both Shaunteera and Bowie could hear his plan. "Take me right up to Bowie and veer hard left after I dismount. I'll take the goblins on the right. Take out the ones on the left. Bowie, prepare to swing me around!"

Jack perched himself on the back of the horse, lifted his sword in his left hand and reached out his right hand toward Bowie. At breakneck speed,

Shaunteera passed within a few inches of Bowie's horse as Jack grabbed Bowie by the wrist and pivoted around. Jack swung his sword across the neckline of the five goblins closing in. The creatures continued running for a few seconds more until their bodies realized their heads had been removed.

From horseback, Sir Daran turned to Dean Slade. "He just fell five goblins with one strike. I'll bet that's a new record."

"It is. The old record was four," said Dean Slade.

"You know that for sure?" questioned Sir Daran.

"Of course," grumbled the dean. "I held it!"

The momentum spun Jack around so he landed in front of Bowie. Jack grabbed the reigns and pulled up hard. Bowie jumped off the back of the horse before it had fully stopped. "I'm going to help her," he said. He ran toward Shaunteera who was on a collision course with the four remaining goblins.

"Right behind you," said Jack as he dismounted.

Two goblins ran straight for Shaunteera with two more trailing a few paces behind. She pulled out both swords and held them low in each hand. Both goblins prepared to strike with their claws. At the last second, Shaunteera dug her knees into her horse and yelled "Head down!" Her horse lowered its head and Shaunteera lowered herself against her horse's back. The goblins swung but missed Shaunteera and her horse by less than an inch. In the same moment, she swung upward with her swords, mortally wounding both goblins. She regained her grip on the right sword but her left sword was wrenched out of her hand, stuck in the goblin's torso. The two remaining goblins closed in fast. She turned her horse into the goblin on her right and swung downward, splitting its head open. The goblin on the left knocked her off her horse. Shaunteera hit the ground hard but managed to roll forward acrobatically. The goblin wasted no time and swung at Shaunteera who was still jarred from the impact.

She dodged two blows but the goblin knocked her sword away with the third one. He raised his claws over his head to make a downward strike and finish her off but before he could hit his target, Bowie's sword point came through the goblin's chest cavity, killing it instantly. The goblin crumpled on top of Shaunteera who let out a disgusted gasp. "Bleeech!"

"I don't know, Shaunteera, he's just not your type," remarked Bowie.

"Get him off me, please!" she protested.

Jack ran up to them with his sword drawn. "You two okay?"

"Shaunteera has a new boyfriend," said Bowie.

"He's not her type," commented Jack.

"That's what I told her!" confirmed Bowie.

"GET HIM OFF ME NOW!" grunted Shaunteera.

Jack and Bowie got on one side of the goblin and rolled it off, then helped Shaunteera up.

Before they could collect themselves, a group of twenty goblins broke from the sanctuary of the forest and charged them.

"I thought we were missing a few," quipped Bowie.

"There're too many of them," observed Jack. Despite their training, the odds were against them surviving an onslaught of twenty raging goblins.

As the faster goblins came within ten paces, the three braced for impact with swords drawn. A *whoosh* emanated from behind the trio as a hundred arrows found their goblin targets. Fifty of the infantrymen ran in front to shield the trio. The additional infantry took on the remainder of the goblin hoard but not before Hawk and his archers let loose another round of arrows cutting down all but four of them which were then easily dispatched.

"Ach, why did you have to spoil all the fun?" said Bowie. "We could have taken them!"

Hawk just shook his head. "Freshmen."

As Dean Slade and Sir Daran rode onto the scene, more goblins lingering by the edge of the tree line blended back into the forest like shadows falling into a dark pit.

"Good work," commanded Dean Slade. He turned to Hawk and Deyglenn, "Keep your men out here for a while. Patrol the forest's edge to see if there are any more goblins close by."

"You'll probably want to see the barber," Dean Slade said pointing to the arrows sticking out of Bowie's shoulder.

Bowie winced as his adrenaline rush dissipated and the pain began to throb. "Come to think of it, my lord, they are a bit ouchy."

"My lord?" said Jack.

The dean was already ahead of him. "I know, Jack. Goblins don't use weapons and certainly not bows and arrows." He looked at the arrows sticking out of Bowie's shoulder. "The goblins didn't do this though. These are Skullian arrows."

"We were saddling back up after a short break and before Kellen could mount his horse, an arrow hit him in the back," acknowledged Bowie. "I noticed some movement in the brush and made out two archers. I shielded Kellen and took two in the shoulder. I charged them which they weren't expecting and took 'em out. When I got Kellen onto his horse, I heard the screech of goblins. Couldn't tell how many. Sounded like a lot of them. I slapped Kellen's horse, mounted mine as quick as I could and high-tailed it out of there!"

"Well done, Bowie."

"Thank you, my lord."

Dean Slade turned to Jack. "Tell me why you initiated full mobilization."

"I didn't know what we were dealing with and thought it best to do too much than too little," said Jack. "I saw Kellen badly wounded riding toward the castle. I knew he'd get help as soon as he rode in so there was nothing more to do there. I called out a company each of infantry and archers because I didn't know if there were more goblins coming."

"A click of goblins usually doesn't exceed ten," said the dean. "Calling out two companies may be considered overkill and would take longer to mobilize compared to a few squads."

"True, my lord, but they were exhibiting unusual behavior, chasing their quarry in broad daylight in an area where they're not known to dwell. My gut told me there might be more," said Jack. "Which there were."

"And why did you ride ahead when there were so many of them? Why not wait for the reinforcements?" questioned the dean.

"The goblins would have caught up to Bowie. I thought it best to take the fight to them, even up the odds and buy some time until the reinforcements arrived, which they did," said Jack.

"And where did you learn to wield a sword like that?" asked Dean Slade.

"From Sir Daran, my lord," said Jack.

Dean Slade gave Sir Daran an approving nod, then turned back to Jack. "You did well. When we get back to the castle, I want to sit down with you and discuss what happened in more detail."

Jack bowed. "Yes, my lord."

Goblin attacks in broad daylight outside of the forest were next to unheard of and never in such large numbers. Was it a mere coincidence Skullian archers were in the same vicinity? Though intelligent creatures, goblins were still wild animals. Had the goblins then acted on their own or was someone behind this whole thing? If it was a person, that person would have to possess formidable dark powers.

# A Warrior's Resolve

Strongthorne students were regularly assigned to town patrol which was basically a security detail the academy provided to Concordia as a courtesy. They worked with the magistrate and local guards to keep the peace.

Freshmen like Jack and Bowie were assigned morning shifts. Evening shifts went to upperclassmen because that's generally when more serious trouble started, mainly at the local pubs. For the most part, town patrol provided an opportunity to bond with the townsfolk and propagate good relations with the merchants, many of whom provided supplies to the school. Being on patrol was a welcome task as it often meant free food and beverages for the patrollers. While the students were not "officially" allowed to accept gifts, the rule was rarely enforced due to a lack of evidence as the bribes were mostly consumable and delicious.

A special treat included checking in with Marilee Bowers who ran the best bakery in town. Mrs. Bowers was a delightfully plump widow who made one question whether profits from her bakery were reinvested in the business or eaten. From being a baker most of her life, her hands and arms were extremely strong. Her hugs were on par with the constrictive force of an adult anaconda. Bowie was her favorite student from the academy and Jack was not far behind. She always had mouth-watering pastries warm from the oven to feed them.

As typical during an extended spell of mild weather, trade increased so a lot more "oots" (out-of-towners) visited Concordia than usual. The extra business was good for the merchants and town coffers but it also meant libations flowed more abundantly, especially at the Goblin's Brow pub where a fight often started at the drop of a hat. Anyone entering the town had to check their weapons at the armory but it was nearly impossible to confiscate concealed weapons like daggers.

As was common, traders from Skul, claiming of course they were from somewhere else, converged at the Goblin's Brow. The place smelled like a wet chimera which was somehow comforting to Skullians. It was late morning and a group of four traders had finished their business early. They were partaking in several rounds of hardberry grog, an especially potent brew made from the fermented fruit of hardberry shrubs that grew wild throughout Atlantis. The more they drank, the louder they became. One of the traders, a nasty looking man with a jagged scar running across his forehead, yelled at a patron to stop looking at him or he'd smash his head into the ground. His cohorts all laughed while he headed out back to use the outhouse.

Jack and Bowie caught ear of the threat as they walked by the pub. "We should notify the magistrate," suggested Jack.

"Let's see what's going on first," said Bowie.

They walked into the pub to the terrified expressions of the customers staring back at them. In the corner, they saw three rather bulky men drinking up a storm. The clear leader was the man who had a genetically implanted sneer, dark disheveled hair and a thick brow that rivaled early cavemen. He was a good head taller than Bowie. His eyes were cold and menacing. He was the first to speak upon seeing Jack and Bowie enter the establishment. "Well, look what we have here—students from the cottage academy!" he slapped the back of one of his comrades and they all laughed.

Bowie looked over at Jim the bartender who had a fresh black eye. He knew the leader had given it to him. "Where did you get that shiner?"

Jim looked down at the floor. "Uh, I was just being clumsy. I tripped over a case of grog in the storeroom and hit one of the shelves."

Bowie knew it was a lie but didn't want to get Jim into more hot water with the ruffians. He casually approached the leader who was no ordinary trader by the look of him. "Cottage academy? That's cute!" said Bowie. "Look, we're not here to interfere with your drinking." He didn't want Jim to lose out on the business.

"Smart of you," the man said condescendingly. One of the patrons ran out the door.

"Just keep it down a bit if you don't mind," said Bowie and turned to leave.

The man almost capitulated but his drunken self couldn't resist the urge to taunt Bowie. "I'll be as loud as I want to be!" he shouted.

Bowie approached the man again holding his hand to his ear as if he didn't hear him. "What was that?"

The man shouted louder, "I said I'll be as loud as I want to be!" Jack slowly reached for a throwing knife sheathed in his belt.

Bowie got within inches of the man's face. "Now I heard you but I don't think Jim heard you." The man turned to the bartender to repeat his drunken decree. Realizing his mistake of taking his eyes off his enemy a split second too late, he turned back just in time to meet Bowie's patented right hook.

The man dropped like a sack a mud. His two friends were completely stunned for a moment before springing into action. The closest one went after him but Bowie feinted a punch and then followed through with a kick to the gut, doubling the man over. Bowie followed through with a forearm strike to the neck knocking him out cold. The third man grabbed a bottle at the bar and broke it to attack Bowie with the sharp edges. As soon as he raised his arm to strike, Jack's throwing knife pierced the man's wrist and pinned his arm to a wood support beam, taking him out of commission.

In all the chaos, Bowie didn't see the fourth man coming back from the outhouse with a dagger drawn. He turned to see the weapon reared back to stab him—but the weapon never arrived at its intended target as the man wielding it was struck through the heart by Jack's sword. He was dead before he hit the ground.

Bowie looked at Jack with gratitude for saving his life. Jack smiled until the full impact of what he had done hit him like a ton of bricks—he had just killed a man. A moment later, a half dozen of the town's guards arrived with the patron who exited earlier.

The guards were led by Captain Honnol who knew the boys. He immediately had the ruffians apprehended. One guard knelt by the fourth man, going through the compulsory motion of taking the man's pulse to confirm what he knew would be the absence of one. He looked up at the captain. "He's gone, sir."

"He came at me from behind. Jack got to him first," said Bowie.

The captain looked at Jack and sensed what he was going through. He pulled him aside. "It's never easy killing a man, especially the first time. You did what you had to do," said Captain Honnol. "You saved your friend. Justice was served."

"Justice?" questioned Jack. "How can there be justice when there's no chance for redemption?"

The captain was a battle-hardened soldier but also compassionate. "I know what you're feeling. We all do," he said as he looked at each of his guards in turn. "But you will accept it and move on."

"How do you know?" asked Jack.

"Because you're a warrior," said the captain. He patted Jack on his shoulder and turned to his men. "Take them to the dungeon."

Bowie addressed the captain, "I have a feeling these men are from Skul."

"My suspicion as well. Don't worry, we'll find out," the captain said menacingly.

Jack and Bowie headed back to the castle. Jack wanted to be alone and spent the rest of the afternoon contemplating what had transpired.

Later that day, Dean Slade summoned Jack to discuss the incident. "They were Skullians," he confirmed. "Probably spies though they haven't admitted to it yet. But they will," he added. He looked at Jack intensely, trying to assess his young student's condition after taking the life of another human being. "Are you all right?"

Jack would never forget the feeling of plunging his sword into the man's flesh and feeling the life force leave his body. He also realized he hadn't hesitated. An enemy meant to kill his friend. He could live with killing a man easier than Bowie dying due to his inaction. He also knew being a "warrior" as the captain had called him, wouldn't always be so cut and dry as the situation presented itself at the pub. But if he truly chose to travel the warrior's path, he could never hesitate in doing what he had to do to uphold his beliefs, his honor, the honor of those for whom he fought or the lives of those he defended. His resolve to follow the warrior's path was a turning point for Jack. That's what becoming a knight meant.

"I'm all right, my lord," answered Jack. And he meant it.

# Survival Training

After several months of training, the freshmen had collectively become quite competent in combat and were thus assigned a field trip to teach them intensive survival skills. They would learn how to find potable water, forage for food, hunt and trap game, make fire, build shelters, create weapons and tools, identify medicinal herbs, administer first aid and more.

It was the sole privilege of Dean Slade to lead this two-week curriculum, taking the students into the wilderness with nothing more than the clothes on their backs, swords and shields. Twenty students were also allowed to bring bows and arrows. However, the students were not allowed to use their weapons during the survival training itself, but as soldiers, they had to be prepared in a moment's notice should they be called to arms or otherwise engage the enemy.

The freshmen gathered in the courtyard wearing their regular uniforms and cloaks. Dean Slade arrived dressed exactly like them. "As you can see, we're all starting off on the same foot here, down to our very undergarments." The students chuckled. "By the end of this field trip, you will learn crucial skills that will help you stay alive individually and collectively in a survival situation. Your training starts now."

Before they even left the castle gates, Dean Slade proceeded to teach them how to use natural landmarks and the sun to navigate. From there, they proceeded out in a westerly direction. He advised them along the way to collect grasses to use as make-shift mattress material and insulation, and flint for making fire and weapons.

As they hiked, Dean Slade pointed out edible flora, like wild berries which were plentiful throughout Atlantis. There were also tubers which tasted terrible but were starchy and nourishing nonetheless. And yes, there were plenty of bugs that made good protein "appetizers" as Dean Slade called them.

About two hours before sunset, they set up camp by a cluster of large boulders. Close by was a creek with fresh water. Dean Slade showed them how to build a fire from scratch. He also instructed them on constructing simple animal traps using twigs, rocks and vines. He had each student build a trap and then distribute it within a fifty-yard radius of their camp.

The grasses they collected were used to sleep on as well as stuff into their shirts and pants to ward off the night's chill. It was a bit itchy, but better to scratch than freeze. Before turning in for the night, Dean Slade instructed them on using astronomy to establish their position and distance traveled.

The next morning, they were awakened at sunrise by the chorus of various species of birds competing to welcome in the new day. The first order of business was breakfast. Out of the hundred animal traps set, twelve produced game—four rats, four birds, two rabbits, one ground squirrel and one giant toad. Tempting as it was to use their swords, Dean Slade showed them how to properly dress their game using tools made from flint. They cooked their catch on sticks over the fire and though it all looked awful, meat was meat and they devoured their share of the bounty as if they hadn't eaten in a month. Teenagers ...

By the end of day three, they were beginning to feel like seasoned survivalists living off the fat of the land. Granted, they smelled bad and looked disheveled but they were all in the same pigpen so-to-speak so no one really cared. However, three days of eating wild berries, tubers and paltry game wasn't doing much in the way of filling up their stomachs. Hence, their next stop was a visit to the best hunters and trappers in Andaar, the Crimm brothers.

During early morning of day four, they hiked through a small patch of woods. It opened into a meadow and about half a mile in, a small hut stood with a column of smoke trailing from its mud chimney. "Gather around," said Dean Slade. "We're going to play our annual game with the brothers and sneak up on them undetected."

"How many times have you been successful, my lord?" asked Scurra.

"Never," admitted the dean. "They have a sixth sense about them, which is one of the things that makes them so good at what they do. Anyway, they're probably making breakfast so they may be distracted. Let's give it a go!"

They spread out and got down on their bellies. As the dean stealthily crawled forward, the students followed. It took about an hour to get within fifty feet of the hut. Confident they had eluded detection, the dean motioned for all of them to stand up. He called out, "Brothers, I think we have finally caught you unawares!"

"Are you sure about that, my lord?" came a voice from behind the group. They turned to find Enoch and Reuben Crimm who had been following them the whole time.

Enoch was short but broad of chest with wild chestnut-colored hair. His brother was basketball-player tall, proportionately muscular with long blond hair and perpetually scrutinizing eyes.

Dressed in patched-up tunics and breeches, they resembled castaways on a deserted island but better fed. Their grungy look though was deceiving. Both were exceptional soldiers and had survived numerous battles while serving as knights in the Andaarian army. After a decade of devoted service and with the king's permission, they retired to live as they now did, one with the earth.

"Son of a chimera!" cursed Dean Slade.

Enoch spoke, "It's your own fault, my lord. You taught us the skills we now possess when we were freshmen."

"I'd say you've improved on them since your time at the academy," countered Dean Slade.

"Modesty forbids me to argue with my lord," retorted Enoch. Reuben just smiled. He didn't speak. He never spoke.

The dean approached the brothers who bowed before taking turns embracing him. "You look well!" he said to the brothers.

"As do you, my lord! So, who have you brought us today?" asked Enoch.

"A new group of freshmen eagerly waiting to learn what skills you are willing to teach them!" answered the dean. The freshmen bowed.

"Welcome to our humble abode!" said Enoch.

"Thank you, sirs!" the freshmen said collectively. Enoch detected Bowie's accent out of the group and approached him.

"You must be Bowie," said Enoch.

Bowie nodded. "Aye, sir, that's me!"

Then he turned to Jack. "And you're Jack."

Jack was amazed. "Yes, sir, but how did you know?"

"You're left-handed. From the story I heard, it was a left-handed student who took five goblin heads with one swing." He turned to Dean Slade. "Five? Isn't that a new record?" he gibed, knowing Dean Slade held the previous record and enjoyed rubbing a little salt in the wound of his old principal.

Enoch continued his assessment. "Four others in this group are left-handed but you stayed closest to Bowie when you started crawling toward our hut—"

"Excuse me, sir," Gaul interrupted and pointed at their hut. An inordinate amount of smoke was pouring out the chimney. Flames blew out the canvas-covered windows and licked the roof which went up in a blaze rather quickly.

Enoch addressed the students. "Rule number one, never use an excessive amount of straw to insulate your shelter. Rule number two, never leave a fire unattended, especially in a shelter made with an excessive amount of straw insulation."

The boys set up camp and spent the next two days helping the Crimm brothers build a new hut out of mud bricks and tree branches. Following the construction project, the brothers took out groups of ten freshmen at a time, teaching them how to track and hunt game. They learned how to build pit traps, and twice, came back with good-sized chimera. They were also taught to use make-shift camouflage to approach game without being detected as well as lure prey into position so it could be killed swiftly.

As a bonus, the Crimm brothers provided instruction in rough terrain and night combat. Sir Reuben was tireless, taking on each student in turn over and over again. He took a liking to Bowie who shared a similarly bold and unrelenting fighting style.

Jack became quite the ninja, learning how to control his breathing and blend in with his surroundings. He learned the art of silent movement and within a few days was able to sneak up on the brothers undetected.

Everyone's skills improved greatly during that time, including Grob's. During one combat simulation, Grob *killed* two other students, although he *died* in the process—after outmaneuvering the first student and dealing a mortal blow, he and the second student struck each other simultaneously with their tree-branch practice swords. "Why didn't you retreat when you saw you were outnumbered?" asked Dean Slade.

"Because I'm a Strongthorne warrior," said Grob. "We don't run. We fight!" he declared to the cheers of his classmates.

The students thanked their hosts at the end of their stay by preparing a huge feast of roasted chimera and foraged vegetables in their honor. They took turns sharing what they had learned from the brothers, singing songs, playing drums fashioned from hollowed-out tree trunks and animal skins, and dancing with abandon as only a group of unbathed survivalists can.

\*\*\*

The next day, Dean Slade and the students bid the Crimm brothers farewell and headed west into the Forest of Quith to put their newly acquired survival skills to the ultimate test.

Once they traversed the perimeter of the forest, light of day yielded to the darkness perpetuated by massive trees and dense flora. "Be ready for anything," said the dean who was in a heightened state of awareness. Within minutes, they heard the distant screech of a goblin. "They already know we're here," he said, "but they shouldn't bother us considering our numbers." The students huddled closer together just the same. They traveled north and planned to head back east toward Andaar in two days' time.

There was plenty of material from which to make shelters and traps. They also made spears out of strong branches and hunted for dinner in groups of ten, never straying far from the main group. They were able to kill several rodents and snakes as well as set up traps for what they hoped would be the next day's meal. They lit a central fire in the evening but also built smaller fires around the periphery of the camp to ward off any brazen predators. Six students per shift were assigned to guard-duty and positioned themselves accordingly.

Throughout the night, they heard all kinds of unsettling sounds that made sleeping difficult. When morning came, they checked on the traps. They acquired more rodents and gathered edible vegetation for breakfast, then packed up their camp, put out the fires and continued on.

During late afternoon, they crossed a ridge that sloped down into a sizable clearing—a rare find in the forest. When about half of the students were in the clearing, Dean Slade who was on point perked up his ears and stopped in his tracks. The students followed suit and stood still as statues. An opposing group of soldiers entered the clearing from the opposite side, talking loudly and laughing. The majority were infantrymen, forty of them, accompanied by six archers. They wore leather armor and there was no coat-of-arms on their shields to identify whether they were friends or foes.

The soldiers looked very surprised when they noticed the Strongthorne troops. Dean Slade took note of it. Why were these soldiers behaving so nonchalantly while traveling through the most dangerous part of Atlantis? Neither side spoke a word, trying to gauge the other. Then two men came forward and Dean Slade recognized them immediately—Grigori, ruler of Skul, and Thorgills the Beater, one of Grigori's top generals and magistrate to the Skullian town of Vile. A few of the students recognized them as well and the news spread like wildfire.

Upon seeing his old adversary, Grigori called out, "Skullians, battle formation!" His men immediately drew swords and positioned themselves. The six archers nocked arrows.

Dean Slade didn't move his eyes from the Skullians. "Strongthorne, ready arms!" The students next to the dean drew their swords and closed ranks.

"We don't have to do this now," offered Dean Slade. He was concerned for his freshman students who were well-trained but not yet battle tested. A temporary truce would spare blood on both sides.

Grigori laughed. "But you outnumber us two to one!" He pretended to be concerned, "But if you're worried about your boys, I'd be willing to call a truce," he said and let his offer sink in for a moment before provocatively adding, "provided you lay down your weapons and leave the forest at once."

Dean Slade looked at his students before responding to Grigori. "'Boys' you say? All I see are Strongthorne men!" The students banged their swords on their shields and cheered.

Jack and Bowie stood atop the ridge above the clearing with the other half of the freshmen. Grigori noticed the two boys standing there among the others. A jolt ran through his body as he flashed back to the lion and leopard from his dream. "Wait a minute," he mumbled.

"What did you say?" asked Dean Slade. He saw abject fear in Grigori's eyes.

"Wait a minute," Grigori said again but not loud enough for Thorgills to hear.

Thorgills turned to his men and yelled, "The chimera will have a feast of carrion tonight when we're through here!" His men banged their swords on their shields in response.

Jack turned to Bowie, "They're about to attack and my guess is their archers will try to take out Dean Slade before their infantry charges."

"I know what to do," replied Bowie.

Jack continued, "I'll command our archers to let loose a volley on their exposed archers."

"I'll form wedges to pick up the enemies who get through the first line," said Bowie.

"We'll follow around you on each side," said Jack.

As if in a trance, Grigori said "Stop," but it was barely a whisper.

Bowie yelled down the hill to his classmates on either side of the dean, "Tortoise formation on Dean Slade—"

Concurrently, Thorgills yelled "Attack!" As Jack anticipated, the Skullian archers let loose their arrows all aimed at Dean Slade but Strongthorne's tortoise formation, basically a protective shell of shields, deflected them all.

Thirty of the Skullian infantrymen followed with a frontal charge in wedge formation. Ten stayed back with Grigori and Thorgills.

A second later on Jack's command, twenty Strongthorne arrows took out the six Skullian archers unawares.

Bowie called out to his classmates around him. "Twenty infantry, wedge formation on me! Ten each, form wedge formations right and left. Gaul, head up the right. Scurra, take the left. Attack!" Bowie bellowed an infectious war cry and ran down the hill at the head of the larger wedge formation with the smaller wedge formations on either side following suit.

Jack called out to the archers, "Leave your shields but keep swords on. Ten archers each on the wings. I'll take the left wing, Yor, take the right. Flank the enemy and take 'em out when you have a clear shot. Go!" The archers formed up and headed down the slope.

The Skullian infantry charge was almost upon the students. "Hold firm!" yelled Dean Slade. The students braced themselves.

About twenty feet from impact, the Skullian commander leading the charge called out, "Shift left, half line!" The Skullians made a precision maneuver keeping the wedge but adjusting to the left so their point would hit halfway down the right side of the Strongthorne wedge, a weaker position.

Jack called out, "Bowie, they're shifting!"

Bowie called an audible. "Gaul, close ranks but keep formation." He didn't have time to explain but once the Skullians penetrated Strongthorne's right flank, they'd get sandwiched between his and Gaul's respective wedge formations.

Shields met shields in a deafening collision. The Skullian soldiers hit Strongthorne's right flank hard, knocking them back and separating out the students positioned farthest down the line, including Grob. But as the point of the Skullian wedge penetrated the first Strongthorne line, they were met by Bowie and Gaul's formations.

Anticipating the soldiers hanging back with Grigori and Thorgills would soon make a second charge, Jack called out orders, "Archers, aim at their troops in the rear. Loose!"

By the time they noticed the arrows coming straight at them, it was too late. *Thunk!* Two of the Skullian soldiers in the rear dropped instantly. Another two were hit in their extremities crippling them.

Grigori was still off kilter by the recognition of the two Strongthorne freshmen from his dream but he'd have to worry about that later and called for the second charge with him and Thorgills part of it. Jack commanded Yor to go wide and fire upon the secondary charge at an angle since their focus would be forward.

The fighting was fierce. Several students were wounded but quickly relieved by others. The remaining Skullian soldiers in the second charge were caught off guard by another wave of arrows, this time coming from the sides. Two more dropped and two more were injured but kept charging. Grigori and Thorgills though remained unharmed.

The second wave of Skullian infantry was significantly weakened by the Strongthorne archers and had little impact. Dean Slade took on Grigori and they fought ferociously. Thorgills plowed through the students swiftly. Though not killing any of them, he wounded several. Bowie saw what was happening and ran at Thorgills.

Meanwhile, Grob who had been separated after the first wave of Skullian infantry hit their line, suddenly found himself pitted against two enemy soldiers. He could easily have retreated—but that's not what Strongthorne warriors did. He fainted an attack on the first soldier and redirected it at the other one, striking his arm which forced the soldier to drop his shield. The soldier was able to deflect the second strike but Grob got underneath his guard on the third strike and penetrated the other's leather armor protecting the solar plexus. It took him a half second to remove his sword from the man's gut, which was a half second too long. The other soldier recovered from the faint and thrust his sword into Grob's side.

Grob's eyes went wide and he dropped his shield. But not his sword. As the Skullian soldier twisted his blade, Grob thrust his sword through the enemy's throat, severing his spinal cord and killing him instantly.

Bowie was fully engaged with Thorgills, clashing swords in mortal combat. His martial skills had greatly improved during the school year. Bowie pretended to stumble which prompted Thorgills to throw a powerful yet wild swing. Bowie felt the *whoosh* of Thorgills' sword as he ducked underneath it. He countered with his own swing meant to take off Thorgills' head.

Thorgills snapped his head back, but not enough. The tip of Bowie's sword sliced open a gash on Thorgills' cheek below his left eye. He put his hand on his face and pulled it back to see his own blood.

The Skullians were losing but Dean Slade did not want to risk the lives of his students any more than he had to. During a brief pause while battling Grigori, he offered a truce, "We can stop this now."

Grigori was still shaken. "Agreed! We will fight no further this day."

"It is so," acknowledged the dean.

Respectively, Grigori and Dean Slade called out orders for their troops to cease fighting. Once a mutual truce was called, each side was able to tend to their wounded without further incident. Such was the code of warriors.

Thorgills was filled with hate toward Bowie. He wanted to continue the fight but to disobey the truce would bring dishonor to himself and was punishable by death.

"That's gonna leave a mark!" Bowie quipped as he pointed to the gash on Thorgills' cheek.

"We'll finish this another time!" said Thorgills. "I'm sure of it!"

"I look forward to it," said Bowie. They parted ways and each attended to their comrades.

The Skullians suffered heavy losses, with half of their force dead and several badly wounded. About a third of the Strongthorne students were injured, a handful seriously. The first-aid skills they learned during survival training were put into action.

Jack joined Bowie. "I saw what you did to Thorgills. I don't think you two will become BFFs now."

"Probably not," agreed Bowie. "Hey, nice job out there!"

"Likewise," said Jack.

Dean Slade approached them both. "This could have gone a lot worse had it not been for you two. Your strategic execution in the face of danger was exceptional. You did Strongthorne great honor."

Thank you, my lord," they said.

"Dean, over here!" Scurra called out.

Dean Slade, Jack and Bowie turned to see Scurra kneeling on the ground next to Grob.

"No!" yelled Bowie and ran over, followed by the dean and Jack.

There on the ground lay Grob with the two dead Skullian soldiers close to him. Scurra put his fingers on Grob's carotid artery trying to find a pulse and shook his head. "He's gone."

Dean Slade looked at the scene and was able to ascertain what happened. "During the first charge, he must have gotten separated from the line and faced these two soldiers alone."

"He should have retreated and regrouped with the second line," said Scurra.

"Grob never retreated from anything," said Bowie.

Four enemy soldiers came by to retrieve the two whom Grob had killed. One of the soldiers paused for a moment and looked down at Grob with a sad expression. "He reminds me of my son. Brave, that one was and one hell of a fighter for his size. You trained him well," he directed at Dean Slade.

"Please give my condolences to the families of your fallen comrades," replied Dean Slade. The two adversaries bowed to one another. When one believes in the cause for which one fights and sees the enemy in the same light, mutual respect can exist.

As the Skullians departed, Shaunteera, Gaul and the Skere brothers rushed over. They fought back tears when they saw Grob. Jack felt the terrible loss of their friend as well. There was a bit of Grob in all of them. When Jack started at the academy, he never thought he could endure the training. When he felt like quitting, he looked at Grob who was always more beat up and in worse shape than he was. But as Bowie mentioned, Grob never retreated from anything, he never quit. This scrawny boy through determination, inner strength and a little help from his friends and teachers had become a formidable warrior. Grob was a symbol of what Strongthorne could do for all of them if they had the heart.

Despite the shock of losing Grob, Jack was plagued by another uneasy feeling. He pulled Dean Slade aside. "My lord, I'm troubled by this. Why would Grigori and his top general be this far into the forest? Where would they be heading with a relatively small number of soldiers?"

"I share your concern, Jack," acknowledged the dean.

"Did you notice anything strange about them when they appeared in the clearing?" asked Jack.

Dean Slade thought for a moment. "Yes, the first soldiers who came through were caught off guard, as if they weren't paying attention."

"Or worried about running into danger," added Jack.

"They should have been, but they weren't," surmised Dean Slade. 'What are you suggesting?"

"I can't put it together yet," admitted Jack, "but I think Grigori's appearance this far south has something to do with the goblin incident several months ago. I think we should send a message to Master Lumens about it."

"Agreed," said Dean Slade. He suddenly recalled something else, "At first, Grigori was eager to fight but right before we engaged in battle, he hesitated."

"Hesitated?" questioned Jack.

Then Dean Slade remembered clearly. "Grigori looked stricken and said to 'stop.' He didn't want to go through with the battle. It was Thorgills who launched the attack."

"Why do you think that was?" asked Jack.

"I cannot say for certain but something seemed to catch his eye at the ridge there that shook him up." Dean Slade pointed to the spot.

"That's where Bowie and I were standing when we first saw the Skullian troops," said Jack.

Dean Slade shifted gears. "Jack, I want you to handle triage and departure. We'll tend to our wounded and make litters for those who can't walk on their own. We're heading straight east to get out of the forest as soon as possible.

"Yes, my lord." He turned to execute the dean's orders and then paused. "My lord, what should be do with, um—"

"Cover Grob as best you can," said Dean Slade. "We'll take his body out on a litter and when we're a comfortable distance away from the forest, we'll give him a warrior's departure."

Many dead Skullians were laid side-by-side in a long rows and left at the edge of the clearing. The remaining Skullians departed abruptly. Dean Slade didn't know whether they would be coming back for their fallen soldiers or not. If they left them though, they would surely get scavenged by chimera and goblins alike. Skullian soldiers though weren't his business.

Within an hour, Strongthorne's wounded had been treated and the litters constructed. A blanket of sorts made from leaves and twine was wrapped around Grob's body before being placed on a litter. The traveling was slow and it took a full six hours to reach the edge of the forest. They continued another half mile into the valley before stopping to set up camp. The students were exhausted but none were too tired to help build the funeral pyre for Grob.

When it was completed, every student who could still stand formed a semicircle around the pyre. Dean Slade spoke a few words. "Today, I am filled with both pride and sorrow. You all fought courageously and beyond what would be expected of you at this stage in your training. I do not hesitate in saying you all have what it takes to become knights of Andaar. In the heat of battle, you followed orders, maintained discipline and executed both skill and ferocity. While this was but a first test, it was a difficult one and you passed valiantly. I must also commend Jack and Bowie for their leadership. Many lives were saved by their actions.

"Alas, it is with great sadness one of our own did not make it through this conflict." Dean Slade paused a moment. He personally took responsibility for every student who died during their time at the academy and bore the weight of that burden. He also knew death was unavoidable and for warriors, it would often come sooner than later. He accepted this though it didn't make the pill any easier to swallow.

"When Grob Mealy started at the academy, I must admit I didn't think he'd make it past the first week." The students chuckled remembering the boy who almost suffocated himself while doffing his tunic after their first day of combat training.

"He seemed so small, so frail. But I underestimated him. He had great heart and an iron will. And he had all of you as his classmates and friends. You embraced him and made his success your own. There is a saying: a chain is as strong as its weakest link. I say a chain is as strong as all its links!" The students huzzahed.

Dean Slade continued, "Grob became a formidable warrior. He lived and died bravely."

"And he took two enemies with him on the way out!" shouted one of the freshmen. The classmates huzzahed in agreement.

Dean Slade turned to Bowie. "Would you do the honor?"

"Yes, my lord." Bowie took a torch and lit the pyre.

"May our hearts be filled with his memory and may his journey back to the source of all creation be swift," concluded Dean Slade.

The students said their silent good-byes to Grob and stood in reverence as the flames consumed the vessel that once contained his soul, a soul that was now free.

While they would mourn his death, they would also celebrate his life. As Dean Slade eulogized, Grob has lived and died bravely. For a warrior, there was no better way.

# JUNIOR CLASS RETURNS

The students from the academy stood in formation at the dock along with the faculty to await the arrival of the *Delphinus II* carrying the junior class back from their naval training. Half a dozen wagons stood by to transport any wounded from the ship back to the infirmary. There were always wounded.

*Delphinus II* had been out six months with no word of her whereabouts. However, the ship had been spotted at a distance during guard duty the evening before and the time of arrival was estimated for the following morning.

As the fog cleared, the ship could be seen rounding Matsya Point. The junior class consilium and ship's captain Sir Maris Tempesto stood at the bow. He was of average height, built lean and strong with fair skin eroded from years at sea. He had the countenance of a carefree swashbuckler though his eyes sparkled with wisdom far beyond his young age. When within earshot of the harbor, he called out, "Fair winds and calm seas grace our arrival."

"And so your return is welcomed," answered back Dean Slade. This seemingly genteel dialog was actually a coded exchange between the dean and captain to establish that the ship was not under the control of or being used as a decoy by the enemy. Though standing at ease, the Strongthorne students were fully armed in case of such an event.

The three-masted naus powered by both sail and oars had been through the ringer with numerous burn marks dotting the hull caused by enemy fire arrows. The mainmast and mizzenmast also showed signs of charring. The sails looked like patchwork quilts, no doubt from countless repairs administered throughout their sea duty. Though beat up, the *Delphinus II* had a majesty about her. She had valiantly endured numerous missions and battles—one of which was fought two days earlier.

Once the ship was secured to the dock, the gangplank was lowered. About a dozen wounded students were immediately escorted off the ship by their classmates, mostly on stretchers.

Grummel performed triage on the lot with a squad of student medics assisting. He first examined a student with a bandaged head. He looked into the boy's eyes, felt around his neck and inspected the bandage. "He'll live," he said and winked at the barely conscious boy. As the barber went down the line, Dean Slade followed him, connecting with each student whether conscious or not. But those able came to attention as much as their wounds would allow, followed by "My lord" when it came their turn in front of the dean.

Another junior suffered a chest wound. Blood soaked through the bandages. The barber lifted the boy's eyelids and looked into his blank eyes. He listened to the boy's breathing and gently felt around the wound. He turned to Dean Slade with a grave expression. "I have limited resources to help him. We'll need to summon one of the senior healers from Astoria right away if he's to have a chance."

Dean Slade turned to Kellen. "Ride to Astoria with haste and inform the head mistress of our need. Take your squad with you."

"Yes, my lord." Kellen motioned to the members of his squad. They mounted their horses quickly and headed off to Astoria.

The wounded took absolute priority and once the wagons were in route, the more festive welcome commenced. Sir Maris approached the dean and bowed as the rest of the junior class disembarked. "My lord."

Dean Slade returned the bow then opened his arms and hugged the junior class consilium. "It is good to see you, my old friend." He looked at the wagons. "By the looks of it, the last battle was recent, was it not?"

"Aye, my lord. Two suns back. A Skullian frigate was scouting the waters nearby, no doubt anticipating our return. Very sleek and very fast. She could have easily outmaneuvered us. We exchanged fire arrows and were able to lose her in the fog."

"How many souls?" asked Dean Slade.

"We lost six, my lord," answered Sir Maris. "Three during an earlier battle four months back around the cape, two during a mid-winter storm and one during the battle two days ago." He then proceeded to name the fallen. Save for the freshmen, the deceased were well-known by the other students. As the names were called out, grief quickly found its way to their friends.

"All buried at sea, my lord," said Sir Maris. "May they rest in peace."

The dean motioned to his steward who snapped to attention, "My lord?"

"I will write their families this afternoon. See to it the letters are delivered as soon as possible."

"It will be done, my lord," answered his steward.

Dean Slade lowered his voice to Sir Maris. "More students than I can count have lost their lives and yet each one is a fresh stab to my heart."

"Aye, my lord. We have that in common," acknowledged Sir Maris.

"Come, the castle awaits you with good food, good friends and a warm hearth," said Dean Slade.

"A finer welcome could not be wished for," said Sir Maris. He embraced each consilium in turn then greeted the many students he knew. He stopped in front of Shaunteera, Bowie and Jack who bowed respectfully. "We traded goods with a Laidirian merchant ship a few months back and heard a story about three Strongthorne freshmen who had taken on a pack of goblins. "You must be Shaunteera," the consilium easily deduced.

"Sir," she said. Maris knew her father but refrained from mentioning it.

"And if I remember the tale correctly, one of you saved Kellen's life and took two arrows in the shoulder. 'Bowie' I believe it was?"

"That would be me, sir," acknowledged Bowie.

"How's the shoulder?" asked Sir Maris.

"Totally healed, sir, and ready for more arrows," answered Bowie. Everyone laughed.

"Excellent!" said Sir Maris. He moved in front of Jack.

"Sir," Jack said.

"Five goblins in one swing? Can that be true, Jack?" asked Sir Maris.

"I had help, sir," Jack said modestly, which got another laugh out of everyone.

Sir Maris looked at Bowie and Shaunteera. "Indeed!" Then he turned to Sir Daran. "Not bad. Not bad at all." Sir Daran shrugged a bit.

Dean Slade approached the juniors who each held a duffle bag filled with their limited belongings. "Juniors, welcome back to land!"

"My lord!" they answered in unison.

"Come! You must have tales to tell and we are eager to hear them!"

"My lord!" they responded.

Dean Slade nodded at a few seniors who took up guard duty in front of the gangplank. The sophomores and seniors dropped out of formation to connect with their junior friends.

Out of a long-standing tradition, the freshmen carried the juniors' duffle bags back to the academy for them. Introductions were made, new bonds of friendship formed and fueled by the spirit of camaraderie, one couldn't help but feel emboldened to take on any challenge. For several of Andaar's finest soldiers-in-training, the greatest challenge was yet to come ... the opposite sex.

# Astoria Academy

The entire student body assembled in the Great Hall. Dean Slade entered with the faculty in tow and stepped to the front. "Tomorrow we will be graced by visitors." A cloud of chatter arose as the students speculated who the visitors would be. "We will be hosting Astoria Academy."

Several of the older boys cheered. Most of the freshmen looked scared. Bowie noticed his classmate Brone Glaggins looking particularly traumatized. "What's wrong?" he asked.

"Girls are coming!" said Brone.

"So?" questioned Bowie.

"They're *girls*!" Brone exited to get some fresh air.

Dean Slade continued, "That means baths for everyone tomorrow morning." The room collectively groaned. "And you'll need to don your cleanest uniforms as well." More groans. "We'll be preparing the grounds for their arrival all of today. I want this place spotless!" The students let loose a barrage of gripes.

Sir Gigas stood up, pulled a spoon from his pocket and held it up menacingly. "Does anyone have a problem with that?" The room fell silent. Sir Gigas sat down.

Dean Slade resumed, "And I don't need to remind you that you will all conduct yourselves with the utmost decorum and chivalry. Our guests deserve nothing less. Don't forget we have a dungeon here."

Jack noticed Shaunteera looked mortified but his observation was interrupted by Bowie. "All right, women! Now we're talking! Hey, maybe I'll serenade them with a tune on the bagpipes," he suggested cheerfully.

"Not if you want them to stay," chided Jack. "Better stick with the lute."

\*\*\*

The students from Astoria Academy arrived by armed escort the following afternoon. The procession was led by the principle and vice principle of the academy, Lady Hesper and Lady Kiran respectively, both riding Akhal Teke horses whose golden coats shimmered in the sunlight. The majesty of the horses was the perfect complement to the women who rode them. Lady Hesper was middle-aged and fair-skinned with handsome features. Her energy and physique were that of a woman half her age. Lady Kiran was much darker in complexion, strikingly beautiful and ten years Lady Hesper's junior. They, along with their students, wore Astoria's traditional leaf-green diaphanous robes over dark green tunics.

The Stongthorne garrison stood in formation in the courtyard awaiting their guests. Dean Slade spoke as his consilia helped the ladies dismount. "Lady Hesper, Lady Kiran, your beauty and presence warm the very earth we stand upon as well as our hearts." He bowed his head and remained prostrate. Moved by his poetic welcome, the Astoria students let out a collective "Ahhh."

"Careful girls," warned Lady Hesper. "Don't be so easily charmed by the words of such a man." She concealed the slightest grin as she approached the dean. "But don't be so quick to deny such words when they resonate of obvious truth."

"Good lady," said Dean Slade, "if your wit was a sword, I would be dead before the duo began."

"Alas, I'm a healer not a necromancer!" she proclaimed. "We'd best call a truce so we may proceed without further injury to your person!"

Dean Slade laughed out loud, then took Lady Hesper's hand and kissed it. He addressed the entire Astoria group, "On behalf of the faculty and students of Strongthorne Academy, we welcome you to our humble home. Our student representatives will escort you to your respective quarters. No doubt you have had a long journey. We have refreshments waiting for you. Lady Hesper, Lady Kiran, Sir Glavan and Sir Daran will escort you to your private quarters."

Kellen and Deyglenn came forth. "Ladies of the fourth year, you are a breath of fresh air and spring itself is enhanced by your arrival. Would you be so kind as to follow me and my brother-at-arms." The senior Astoria students tittered and stepped forth.

The junior representatives came out next with their welcome. Not quite as eloquent as Kellen's, but still worthy of a titter. The sophomore representatives followed with a stiff, albeit polite, welcome. Then it was Jack and Bowie's turn.

Bowie walked right up to the freshman girls. "Right, then, so how many of you are from out of town?" The girls didn't get it at first until Jack snickered to indicate Bowie was joking. They all giggled and Bowie continued as if he were annoyed, "Come on, then, we haven't got all day. I've seen plow horses move faster than you lot." Like he did with almost everyone he met, he put the girls at ease right away. He extended his elbows in escort. About half a dozen girls grabbed each arm and the rest followed. He introduced himself, asked their names and made light jokes as he led them to their quarters. Jack was about to join them when he noticed one of the girls kneeling down and fiddling with her sandal strap.

She was petit in stature with short brown hair and delicate features but also had a strong presence. When Jack looked into her luminous green eyes, something stirred in him he had never felt before. A year earlier, he would have stumbled on his words but he had been through a lot and his warrior training had given him a strength and resiliency that had not only saved his life but also made it possible to talk to the opposite sex without sounding like a complete idiot.

"Let me help you with that," he offered.

"You're most kind. The strap broke just over the last hill."

"Let me see if I can fix it." Jack jimmy rigged the strap.

"You did it!" she said delighted.

"It'll hold for a little while but our blacksmith and armorer is excellent with leather. I'm sure he can fix it permanently. May I escort you there? I'm Jack, by the way." He bowed slightly and extended his elbow.

She gave him a smile that could have melted the North Pole. "I'm Kate," she said and took his arm. "Lead the way, if you please." Jack escorted her to the armory.

Numerous activities were planned for the guests during their visit, including demonstrations of jousting, melee battle and archery. Though the martial displays were more or less demonstrations, it didn't stop tempers from flaring up as the boys wanted to show off in front of their guests. The demos turned into less-than-cordial competitions at times. More boys ended up in the dungeon for detention during the three-day visit from Astoria Academy compared to an average month during the regular school year.

Each class put on their own demonstrations. With her superb equestrian skills, Shaunteera dominated the joust. In melee battle, Bowie showed great strength and prowess by pushing back four attackers with the shove of his shield, then systematically striking each one with a *fatal* blow. With bow and arrow, none could best Jack, not even the Skere brothers. Each brother hit the bull's-eye within a finger's width of dead center. Jack's arrow landed dead center to the applause of the spectators, especially Kate.

The Astoria students also had a chance to show off their wares so to speak. Trained in magical protection, they demonstrated their ability to cast protective spells. Some of the senior students from each academy ran a battle simulation. A group of three swordsmen were outnumbered by an opposing group of ten pikemen. One of the female students cast a protective spell around the three soldiers to repel the pike attacks. The spell held for about a minute before another student cast her spell to continue the effect.

The demonstration was quite impressive. Depending on the number of casters, a larger group of soldiers could be protected at one time within close range or a smaller group at a greater distance. Of course in actual battle, the casters would have to be protected as well as they would be vulnerable while casting. With precision and awareness, the combination of protective spells and coordinated attacks could be extremely effective against an enemy force, though it hadn't been tested in real battle. It was an idea though that Dean Slade and Lady Hester had been discussing for a while.

Drawing on their natural connection to the earth mother, the Astoria students were also skilled healers utilizing herbalism, spells and touch. A graduate from Astoria Academy was highly revered for her medical expertise. Minor wounds were in ready supply at Strongthorne. A clinic was set up where Astoria students applied their craft to the Strongthorne students. Cuts sealed up and bruises faded. While they couldn't entirely heal more severe wounds, they were able to reduce pain and expedite the healing process. Many of the Astoria students were also exceptional singers and dancers and those demonstrations seemed to be the favorites among the Strongthorne warriors.

During breaks between demonstrations, the students from both academies were allowed to intermingle, albeit under strict supervision. Friendships quickly formed as well as crushes. After the melee competition, ten women circumvented Bowie as he demonstrated different sword techniques. He then let the girls attack him with wasters. He'd allowed them to get in a strike every now and again, which got them all giggling.

"He's such a show-off," Shaunteera said to Jack as they watched from the periphery.

"But a likable show-off at that," said Jack.

"Sometimes," she conceded.

A beautiful blond-haired, blue-eyed Astoria student ran up to Shaunteera and bear-hugged her, taking her off guard and almost knocking her over. "Oh, sister, where have you been hiding! You were magnificent during the joust!"

Shaunteera tried to shrug off the girl who was stronger than she appeared. "Sis, no hugging, okay?"

"You don't want to wrinkle her armor," Jack added sarcastically. "Hey, wait a minute, sis? As in sister?"

The girl let go and hooked Shaunteera's arm in her own. Shaunteera was too tired to fight off the affection and begrudgingly allowed it. "Actually twin sisters," said the girl. She was tall and lithe and oozed sweetness. "She didn't tell you about me? Oh, that's so like her!" she said, not the least bit hurt. "I'm Lexi." She curtsied to Jack who bowed in return.

"I'm Jack."

"So you're Jack!" she said delighted. "Of course, she's written me all about you and Bowie and her other friends.

"Really?" Jack looked at Shaunteera who avoided his gaze.

Lexi turned to her sister. "I can see why father and uncle are so proud of you!" Her comment genuinely touched Shaunteera. "And I'm proud of you!" she added.

Shaunteera loved her sister dearly but could hardly keep up with Lexi's level of insufferable optimism. Besides, she had worked so hard to establish herself among a school of all-male students, she didn't want to reveal even a tiny modicum of softness or vulnerability. "Come on, Lexi, you can help me brush down my horse. Jack, we'll see you later."

"Looking forward to it!" said Jack.

Shaunteera sneered at him, knowing she was going to get a good razzing later for keeping her sister a secret.

Jack felt a presence as if he was being watched. He turned to find Kate standing alone and looking at him. He drew upon all his warrior training to quell the butterflies in his stomach and assert his boldness. "Hi," he was able to muster. Hey, it was better than nothing.

"The strap is holding," she said.

"The what?" Jack was confused.

"On my sandal," she said. "Remember?"

"Yes, of course!" Jack regained his composure. "I'm glad Burl was able to fix it."

"I enjoyed watching you today," She said and then blushed. "During the archery."

Jack blushed himself. "I'm glad you enjoyed it."

"Is it hard to learn? Archery?" She asked.

"It's easy to get started," said Jack.

"Would you teach me?" she asked.

When he first met Kate, he was able not to sound like a complete idiot. That grace period was over. "Uh, yeah, sure, I'd like to, um, let's, oh here!" Jack suddenly realized his bow was slung around his shoulder and that he was carrying a full quiver. *Remain calm* he silently admonished himself. "Let me show you. We'll use that hay bale over there as a target."

He handed her the bow and nocked an arrow for her. He then stood behind her to help steady the bow. Like him, she was left-handed. He was so close to her, he could feel the warmth of her skin and smell the floral fragrance of her garland.

"As you pull back the arrow, see the center of your target and adjust for the trajectory. At this distance, it won't be much." He put his hands gently on hers for guidance. The skin on her arms turned to goose bumps. "Now, breathe out slowly and at the end of your breath, release the string."

Kate did as Jack instructed. The arrow hit high on the haystack.

"Hey, that was great!" said Jack. "You're a natural archer!"

"I don't know about that," she said. "Maybe you're just a good teacher."

Jack was totally out of his element but at the same time felt surprisingly comfortable around Kate. "Would you like to visit the southwestern tower? There's quite a view from up there."

"I would love to," she said enthusiastically.

Jack and Kate talked the whole time about this and that, nothing special, which made it all special. They talked as if they had known each other their whole lives. Master Lumens would later suggest they may have known each other over several lifetimes.

\*\*\*

The night before the Astoria students were scheduled to return home, the students from both academies assembled in the Great Hall for an evening of entertainment. The Strongthorne students first treated the girls to a play based on Atlantis' history. Of course, the boys also played the rolls of the female characters, which was good for many laughs. At the conclusion of the play, the girls applauded loudly as the actors took their bows. While they were setting up for a musical act, Scurra came out to perform some standup comedy.

"It's been a real pleasure having the ladies from the Astoria Academy here, am I right?" All of the Strongthorne students in the room applauded. "You are all so beautiful inside and out but we had no idea how tough you were—you ate Beurk's food for three days and you're still standing. Maybe you healed each other's stomachs after the meals." Everyone laughed. Everyone, except Beurk.

"I see Sir Gigas is in the room tonight. You know, Sir Gigas was always big, even as a baby. Do you know what his mother said when he was first born? Ahhhhhhhhhhhh!" Everyone laughed. Everyone but Sir Gigas, who quietly pulled a fork out of his pocket to throw at Scurra. Dean Slade motioned him to put it away.

"As you know, we train hard and of course, the Strongthorne seniors have trained the hardest and longest of anyone here. Not the most chivalrous though as one would think. Someone from town once asked me about the senior class. I said I thought they could use some." Everyone laughed. Everyone but the senior class.

"And then there's Dean Slade." The crowd collectively went silent sensing that Scurra, who had been treading on thin ice, was about to break through it. Scurra might have been a joker, but he wasn't an idiot. "I'm sorry, that's all I have time for tonight." Everyone laughed, especially Dean Slade. "And now we have a song performed by a group who calls themselves *The Rolling Bones*. Take it away, boys."

Bowie had picked the song "Thunderstruck" from his all-time favorite rock band, AC/DC. He rearranged the music to work with medieval instruments and rewrote the lyrics so they applied to Atlantis. He was concerned at first not wanting to bring in anything from his world that might corrupt Atlantis as Master Lumens had warned. But Bowie reasoned there was no way rock-n-roll would lead to mass destruction of a civilization. Time would tell …

Adapted from the original version, Bowie launched right in with a rapid-fire lute solo. Then he sang lead vocals with backup from the band.

*I was caught*
*In the middle of an attack*
*I looked round*
*And I knew there was no turning back*
*My mind raced*
*And I thought what could I do*
*And I knew*
*There'd be help, help from you*
*Sound of war drums*
*Beating in my heart*
*The thunder of marching*
*Battle 'bout to start*
*You've been*

*Thunderstruck*

Save Jack and Bowie, no one had ever heard that kind of music before. Initially, everyone looked horrified. Then a foot started thumping in rhythm. The sixth row of Astorian girls swayed to the beat. Dean Slade involuntarily tapped his knee with his hand. Sir Sranjali beamed with pride.

*Walked down the path*
*Broke the limit, we hit the town*
*Wounded from battle, yeah battle, needed to rest some*
*We met some girls*
*Some Astorians who healed us in no time*
*Casting their spells*
*Soothing our welts*
*Yeah, yeah, their beauty was so fine*
*I was shaking from the joy*
*Thanks for healing this old boy*
*Yeah, them ladies were so kind*
*We were*
*Thunderstruck*

By the second stanza, everyone was into the song. The students and faculty clapped and stomped to the music. Rock-n-roll was there to stay.

*I was shaking from the joy*
*Thanks for healing this old boy*

Everyone got up from their seats and rocked out. When the word "Thunderstruck" came up in the song, everyone sang it.

*Thunderstruck, Thunderstruck, Thunderstruck, Thunderstruck*
*It's alright, we're doin' fine*
*It's alright, we're doin' fine, fine, fine*
*Thunderstruck, yeah, yeah, yeah*
*Thunderstruck, Thunderstruck*
*Thunderstruck, baby, baby*
*Thunderstruck, you've been Thunderstruck*
*Thunderstruck, Thunderstruck*
*You've been Thunderstruck*

When the song ended, there was a deafening silence. No one knew quite what to do or how to respond. Lady Hesper let out the Atlantis equivalent of a "whoop" and everyone else joined in whooping, clapping and cheering.

\*\*\*

After breakfast the next morning, the visitors made their final preparations for departure. There were many tears. Several of the students from both academies had known each other for years. When war was a constant and death at an early age a real possibility, bonds of friendship and romance formed fast. At least two dozen girls bid Bowie farewell. Within the three-day visit, he had acquired quite the harem of groupies.

Jack helped Kate secure her pack to the luggage wagon. They had grown close during their time together and promised to write each other regularly.

Teary-eyed, Lexi hugged Shaunteera and kissed her on the cheek. "I will miss you, sister."

Shaunteera waved her off. "Yeah, okay."

One of the senior students from Astoria counted her classmates to make sure all were accounted for and nodded to Lady Hesper when confirmed. Sir Daran helped Lady Kiran onto her horse. Definitely some chemistry there.

Dean Slade assisted Lady Hesper onto her horse. "Our time together has been too short," he said.

"An indication that the visit was a good one." Lady Hesper bowed her head to the dean.

"I swear in these three days alone, you've grown even more beautiful," he teased.

Lady Hesper raised an eyebrow. "Time to go, ladies. The snakes are out and they're starting to bite."

Suddenly, one of the junior class students from Strongthorne pointed up to the sky. "Is that a rain cloud?" There was no rain cloud. It was merely a ploy to get the faculty from both schools to look up while several of the students kissed.

"My mistake. Sorry," said the junior.

Dean Slade looked up at one of the walls where Sir Gantry stood with a parchment and quill writing down names. "Call out those who've committed the crime of kissing," said Dean Slade. So much for fooling the faculty.

Sir Gantry read off the list, which included about two dozen boys including Gaul, Scurra and both Skere brothers, but not Bowie. And then he read "Jack Pepper." Jack blushed. Kate blushed. All of his classmates razzed him with a collective "Ooooooh Jack!"

"And Sir Daran!" Sir Gantry added. Everyone looked over where Sir Daran was standing by Lady Kiran on horseback. Lady Kiran's face went unmistakably red. Sir Daran shrugged it off.

"The boys, and *consilium*, just mentioned are on clean-up duty. Naturally, they are to blame for this act. The girls are innocent," Dean Slade said to Lady Hesper.

"Not as innocent as I'd wish," she remarked.

"My cadre will meet you past the fields to escort you the rest of the way. Farewell and good fortune until the prom."

"Did I overhear the dean say 'prom?'" questioned Bowie. Jack nodded.

What Jack and Bowie didn't know was that one had to prove his worth before asking a date to the prom. For that privilege, they would have to embark on a quest and successfully complete it, let alone survive it.

# PROM QUEST

A yearling fawn nibbled on a small clump of grass sprouting around the periphery of a large, craggy boulder just outside the forest. The wind shifted and the fawn snapped its head up. An acrid scent intermingled with the earthen waft of the meadow grasses. A mature deer would have taken flight at once having developed an acute sense of predatory awareness.

The fawn caught notice of a tiny slithering motion appearing at the bottom edge of the boulder. It appeared to be a small snake or lizard undulating through the grass.

Curiosity overtook the fawn as it approached the bolder. It gently craned its neck to catch a glimpse of—a bellowing roar froze the fawn in its tracks. Using the boulder as cover and its serpent-like tail to lure the fawn into distraction, the predator ambushed its prey with lightning speed. Before the fawn could run, a large maw of razor-sharp teeth clamped down on its neck with unyielding pressure and swift penetration. The vertebrae shattered killing the prey instantly as the predator tore out a chunk of flesh leaving a small thread of sinew holding the remainder of the fawn's head to its body.

The talon of the chimera gripped the fawn's body with crushing force, shattering more vertebrae and rupturing the abdomen. The chimera crunched down on its prey, tearing and swallowing huge chunks of flesh with each bite, bones and all. Almost halfway through its meal, a small wriggling motion caught the chimera's attention at the bottom edge of the same boulder where it had lured its prey moments earlier. The chimera approached the writhing movement, its own tail darting side to side like a rattlesnake about to strike. As a predator, its approach was much bolder than that of the fawn's. Its senses suggested more prey, even if it amounted to a mere morsel.

The wriggling motion disappeared around the boulder. As the chimera peered around the stone obstacle, a bellowing roar temporarily froze the chimera. But this roar came from a Scottish teen clad in leather armor donning a sword and shield. Bowie swung at the vial beast with all his might— and missed completely as the chimera reflexively ducked out of the way. The sword struck the boulder and the ensuing vibration shook the sword right out of Bowie's hand. "Ahh!" There was no time to complete an explicative as the chimera racked Bowie with his talon. Bowie managed to raise his shield just enough to prevent the claws from resectioning his torso, but still knocked him to the ground after a ten-foot flight through the misty air.

With two quick bounds, the chimera was on top of Bowie, pinning him down. The beast hovered over his next meal, breathing hard into Bowie's face. "Ach! You've got to brush your teeth, man!"

The chimera reared its head back before going in for the kill. In that same moment, the blade of another sword sliced down on the beast's neck, severing the spinal cord and killing it instantly. The chimera fell off to one side but not before dousing Bowie in warm, sticky blood.

"Nice of you to show up," said Bowie.

Jack wiped the blood from his blade on the meadow grass. "Hey, it was a team effort all along."

"Team effort? You get to be the decoy next time," countered Bowie. Jack helped Bowie up who futility attempted to wipe the dirt and blood from his armor and clothes.

Jack pointed to the chimera with his sword. "By the looks of him, I'd say he's a young adult."

"Good enough! We completed our prom quest," said Bowie.

"Not quite," said Jack.

"What do you mean?" asked Bowie.

"We have to kill a chimera—"

"Check!" interrupted Bowie.

"And deliver it back to the academy," finished Jack.

"I forgot about that part." Bowie frowned. "How do we get it back?"

"Nothing in the rules says we can't gut it first," offered Jack.

"Thanks to Beurk, we know how to do that," said Bowie.

"That will cut down the weight by about twenty percent," said Jack.

"What about the other eighty percent?" asked Bowie.

"We'll assemble a makeshift sled and then use a hundred percent of *our* weight to tow it," said Jack.

"Are you going to ask Kate to the prom?"

Jack smiled. "Yup!"

"I haven't seen you look this happy since, well, I don't think I've ever seen you look this happy." said Bowie.

"Yup!" replied Jack. "Hey, what about you? Who are you going to ask?"

"Don't know yet. I don't even know if I'll go to the prom," said Bowie.

"What? There were plenty of Astoria girls who were interested in you! Why would you take on a quest and not go?" asked Jack.

"I couldn't let you have all the fun, could I?"

Jack shook his head. "You're my best friend but you're insane!"

"And you're my best friend. So what does that make you?" countered Bowie.

"Touché," said Jack.

The boys spent the rest of the afternoon field dressing the chimera and building a sled out of tree branches tied together with vines. With an eight-to ten-hour journey ahead of them dragging the dead weight of a chimera carcass, they decided to make camp for the night and built a large fire to ward off any predators, including other chimera, who might take an interest in their prize.

The next morning, they proceeded to roll the chimera onto the sled and drag the beast back to the academy some five miles away.

They arrived at the academy early evening. As they crossed the threshold of the main gate into the castle, they caught sight of several other slain chimeras, no doubt from other prom quests. Impressively, the Skere brothers had brought down a full-grown adult male chimera. To get the beast back to the academy, they bartered supplies with a passing merchant for a tow— ingenious in its simplicity. The brothers were sharing the story of their hunt with a group of students and showing off new scars earned during the quest. Yor had a fresh gash across his right cheek and Narro had a rather deep gouge to his left thigh. The pain of their wounds though only seemed to animate their spirit.

Scurra and Gaul looked pretty beat up after hauling their chimera the distance of three miles via makeshift stretcher. It was a baby chimera but they still satisfied the criteria of the prom quest.

Sir Daran checked off names of those completing their quests. Beurk was in his bliss, counting the inventory of new meat. None of the chimera would go to waste. The hides would be used for clothing and armor, the flesh for stews and jerky—even the bones would be used to make tools and other items.

Jack and Bowie dropped off their kill to a group of students whose detention was processing the chimeras. "We already gutted it," said Bowie. The detentionees were thrilled to hear it.

Dean Slade approached the two boys. "Well done! I look forward to hearing about the hunt."

They bowed slightly. "Thank you, my lord!"

"There's some hot food and drink waiting for you in the Great Hall," offered the dean.

"Excellent, my lord," said Bowie. "We'll head there now!"

Dean Slade cleared his throat.

The boys paused for a moment then looked at themselves objectively. From head to toe, they were caked in chimera blood and guts, dirt, grime, sweat and who knows what else.

"Perhaps a quick spritz and change of clothes are in order," said Jack.

"Good idea," agreed Dean Slade.

# Prom Date

Out of the two hundred and seventy cadets who took on prom quests, seven were severely injured, thirty-three suffered substantial wounds that required treatment and another twenty-eight just plain failed to fulfill their quests. That left two hundred and two cadets who were allowed to invite dates to the prom. Out of the invitations sent, twenty-six cadets received polite refusals despite their risking their lives in completing quests. Women ...

As planned, Jack sent an invitation to Kate. Her acceptance arrived two weeks later. Jack was thrilled—and more nervous than when he was actually hunting chimera.

Bowie on the other hand hadn't invited anyone. There were plenty of Astoria coeds who would have jumped at the chance to go to the prom with him. The girls thought he was bold, brave and "super cute," not to mention that he played a mean lute. Sir Sranjali was right, chicks dug musicians.

Despite Bowie's Astoria groupie fan base, he was reluctant to ask any of them out. Jack knew why though he didn't press the issue—Bowie wanted to ask Shaunteera but couldn't work up the nerve to do it. And may never. Bowie and Shaunteera argued and nitpicked each other constantly, a sure sign to their peers that they liked each other.

Throughout the school year, Bowie had repeatedly come to Shaunteera's aid. She vocally rebuked his interference but allowed it just the same. And then there were those moments when they weren't at war with each other—a look here, shared laugh there, pat on the shoulder ... but no one who didn't want to risk getting a beating from Bowie or Shaunteera ever brought it up. They unwittingly gravitated toward each other not as opposites attracting but rather as similar souls looking for a mutual place to harmoniously reside. But such poetry didn't do much in the way of bringing two hard-headed stubborn goats like them together.

Even though Jack and Bowie talked about almost everything, Bowie never talked about Shaunteera with any sort of affection or warmth. Jack could also tell Shaunteera liked Bowie though she didn't provide a lot of outward signs. She was a Centaur after all and a combative nature was standard issue. The problem was how to get Bowie to ask Shaunteera to the prom.

Bowie had completed the quest and there was no rule against asking out a female cadet from Strongthorne Academy since there had never been one before Shaunteera. Despite no rule to prevent it, Jack knew Bowie would never risk Shaunteera's rejection. Besides, Shaunteera was too Centaur-proud to ever admit she would like to be asked to the prom by Bowie.

Jack took on the challenge. He would have to work on both of them but he couldn't do it alone. He conferred with his freshman cohorts to devise a plan. A group of them would ask Bowie for some extracurricular help sword training and then plant some seeds about Shaunteera's softer side, though none of them personally could admit to experiencing it. Jack would ask Shaunteera for some equestrian tips and plant a few seeds about Bowie's good qualities. Bowie readily accepted the invitation to help his classmates train with swords as did Shaunteera with helping Jack with his horsemanship.

The freshmen assigned to work on Bowie consisted of Scurra, Gaul, the Skere brothers and a few others. Initially the plan fell nicely into place though every time a classmate paused to bring up Shaunteera, Bowie whacked them hard with his waster and derailed their intentions. It would take many bruises and lacerations for his friends to get out a handful of flatteries about her. After an hour, they took a much-needed water break and sat around in a circle. Each one in the group looked at the other and then all eyes fell on Scurra to start. "I feel bad for Shaunteera," he said.

Bowie's ears perked up. "Why?"

Scurra did his best to look troubled. "You know, with the prom coming up and all."

"Why would you feel bad for her?" asked Bowie.

Scurra hesitated. He didn't really have an answer for him. Gaul chimed in. "Well, it's just that most of us got to go on prom quests and because she's the first female student here, she really didn't get a chance to prove herself. You know how she's always trying to prove herself."

"Aye," admitted Bowie. "I suppose she might feel a bit left out, but what can we do about it?"

"If one of us asked her," Yor blurted out, "she'd get to go."

"It would almost be as good as going on a quest itself," Narro chimed in.

They were all smiling a little too much. Bowie took note of it and they noted Bowie noting it. They quickly switched to more somber expressions. Bowie noted that as well and eyed them suspiciously. "Did Shaunteera put you up to this?" he asked.

"Of course not!" said Scurra. "We didn't mean *you* should ask her. It just happens the rest of us have dates already."

"And you don't, yet," Yor threw in too quickly.

Bowie shook it off. "Even if I did ask her out, mind you as a generous favor to a fellow cadet, she'd never say yes. She's pretty stubborn and way too proud," said Bowie.

"We know the type," said Gaul as he stared straight at Bowie.

"I saw her crying the other day," said Scurra in a last-ditch resort. None of them had ever seen her cry so they all looked at him suspiciously.

"Yeah, that's right," said Gaul quickly thinking up a complete fabrication. "We were in town last week collecting food stuffs for Beurk. The grocer had a large bouquet of nemesia in a vase. You know how beautiful the nemesia are this time of year, right?" He looked for some buy-in from his classmates.

They were a bit slow coming to the table, then all at once, they sounded off to play along with Gaul's story. "Oh, yeah, those nemesia are really something," uttered Narro.

Yor made an extra effort, "They have a languid fluidity reflected in the diaphanous effervescence of their pedals." That caught everyone's attention.

"Well done," said Narro sotto voce to his brother.

Gaul continued. "Anyway, Shaunteera walked over to the vase and just stared at the flowers. After a few seconds, she turned to the grocer and said 'They're lovely.'"

Bowie looked skeptical. "She said 'They're lovely?' That would be a stretch for her!"

Narro forgot Gaul was telling a lie and questioned him. "I thought you said she was crying!" That earned him a quick elbow in the ribs from his brother. "Oh, sorry."

"Yeah, what about the crying?" asked Bowie.

"Well, maybe 'crying' is a bit exaggerated," said Gaul.

"Not anymore exaggerated than the rest of the story," Scurra said under his breath to no one in particular.

Gaul resumed. "But her eyes looked watery!"

"Maybe she had allergies!" said Narro, which earned him another elbow in the ribs. "Oh, sorry."

Bowie waved the whole thing off. "Come on, let's practice some more." Bowie picked up his waster and walked to the center of the pitch.

His classmates got beaten up for the second time that afternoon. Hopefully, Jack was making better progress.

***

Shaunteera gave pointers to Jack on his riding. After an hour or so, they cantered out into the field to let their horses cool down. "So, the prom's coming up soon," Jack unceremoniously brought up.

"So?" Shaunteera shot back.

"I just thought you'd be happy to see your sister again," offered Jack. "Kellen invited her and she accepted." Shaunteera made a sound something between a moan and a groan. Jack's plan was going miserably.

"You don't like your sister?" asked Jack.

"Of course, I do!" she said defensively. "It's just that, well, she and I are very different. She loves all that oopy goopy stuff, like proms and all that."

"I don't blame you," agreed Jack. "It's all a bunch of pomp and circumstance."

"Then why did you go on a quest if you didn't want to go to the prom?" asked Shaunteera.

Jack stuttered, "I, well, uh, that's uh, I thought it could be kind of fun, you know, they'll be food and dancing."

"You get food every day! You risked your life then for dancing?" questioned Shaunteera. "I'd rather practice sword fighting in the mud than go dancing."

Jack was about to blow it completely, then abruptly switched tactics. "I just feel bad for Bowie."

"Why?" Shaunteera asked a little too curiously.

"He took on the quest just to, you know, take on a quest. There wasn't anyone he really wanted to ask to the prom, per say," lobbed Jack.

For a fleeting nano-second, Shaunteera looked happy Bowie didn't have a date yet—then her expression soured. "Those girls from Astoria were fawning all over him," she scornfully remarked. "I'm sure any one of them would gladly accept his invitation."

"Yeah, but you know Bowie, he waited too long to ask one of them and now it's too late to get an invitation out and a response in time." Jack looked at Shaunteera to glean the faintest hint of her interest. She was gleanless. Jack had nothing to lose. "Hey, maybe you could go with him?"

Shaunteera stopped her horse dead in its tracks. "Me? No way! Bowie is the last person in Atlantis I'd go with to the prom."

"I just meant as a friend, helping out a fellow cadet. Just think how embarrassed he'll feel having completed the quest and then not actually going to the prom. You don't want him to look foolish, do you?" Jack said weakly.

"That's not my problem!" asserted Shaunteera. "Besides, I could never stop him from looking foolish! He has a gift for doing that all on his own."

Jack winced at his utter failure to make progress. "Come on, we all need to help each other out," he said desperately.

Shaunteera looked him squarely in the eye. "I will fight alongside him. I will offer him my sword and shield as a comrade in arms. But I will never go with him to the prom." Shaunteera started to gallop back to the academy. After she had gained some distance between her and Jack, she shouted, "It's not like he'd ask me anyway."

"Bingo!" Jack said to himself. That was just the opening he was looking for though he had no idea how to exploit it.

Shaunteera was seriously miffed. Why had Jack grilled her about Bowie and the prom? The whole thing was stupid. Proms were for silly girls like her sister who were into dressing up and attracting boys' attention.

Bowie annoyed her to no end. Sure, he was a heck of a good fighter and they had already shared many trials and tribulations together. And yes, he had saved her from that goblin even with two arrows in his shoulder, and yes, he was funny and smart and loyal and dare she say it that he wasn't half bad looking. But he was also loud and brash and quick to temper and ... Bowie! It was a thorn in her side to always be thinking about him!

She rode into the courtyard and dismounted in front of where the boys were practicing sword fighting. Bowie was in the process of tenderizing Scurra. When he saw Shaunteera, he got annoyed. The guys kept talking about her and even suggested he ask her to the prom. No way would he ask her!

Shaunteera was stubborn, opinionated, quick to temper ... who could put up with someone like that? Granted, she was a heck of a fighter and he trusted her implicitly. And she had her moments, albeit few and far between, when she was warm and sweet. She also had a sharp wit and an even better laugh. And when she took off her armor, literally and figuratively, she wasn't half bad looking. But take her to the prom? He'd rather have his feet boiled in oil first. He was tired thinking about her all the time.

"Coming back from a ride out in the country?" asked Bowie.

"It's none of your business what I was doing!" she retorted.

"What's gotten into you?" asked Bowie. "I'm just making a bit of polite conversation."

Shaunteera scoffed. "Polite conversation? You wouldn't know a polite conversation if it came right up and bit you on the—"

Bowie interrupted her mid-explicative by pointing the tip of his waster at her. "Careful girl, your next word may be your last!"

Veiled threat or not, she snatched Scurra's practice sword from his hand and attacked Bowie full force while her classmates stood by helplessly watching.

Bowie was caught off guard by the ferocity of her attack. She threw three successive blows which he narrowly dodged. Bowie's counteroffensive though was equally fierce. He threw five strikes, landing one across her left thigh. It stung like hell but only made her more furious.

She counterattacked even more aggressively. Bowie lost his footing and fell backwards. As he lay on his back, she closed in for the finishing blow— which wouldn't kill him using a waster but would absolutely hurt a great deal. She straddled Bowie and came down with a straight strike to his head. He dodged it and kicked her leg out from under her, causing her to fall on top of him. Swords were no good at this close a range so he pulled out a dagger from his boot and held it against her throat. A concealed backup weapon—she'd have to remember that in the future.

Jack rode up and dismounted. He and the other boys stood around the battling duo with stricken expressions. This is not what they had planned at all—they were going to soften up Bowie while Jack softened up Shaunteera. Instead, the two people whom they had tried to get on a date together were locked in virtual mortal combat. Then something happened none of them expected.

"Would you like to go to the prom with me?" asked Bowie.

The jaws of those witnessing the invitation dropped halfway to the ground until Shaunteera answered, "Yes, that would be nice." Then their jaws dropped the rest of the way to the ground. Bowie and Shaunteera got up and dusted themselves off.

"All right then," said Bowie.

"I look forward to it," answered Shaunteera.

"If she curtsies," said Scurra, "I swear to the Beyond I'll jump off the southwestern tower." Shaunteera shot him a dirty look.

Those who didn't believe in a higher power instantly changed their minds that day because it was nothing short of a miracle that Bowie and Shaunteera were going to the prom together.

# PROM

The procession from Astoria Academy arrived the morning of the prom. Jack and Bowie sat on a low wall in the courtyard watching.

"See those wagons behind them?" Jack pointed to endless line of large wagons trailing the Astoria students.

"You mean the grain wagons?" asked Bowie.

"Those aren't grain wagons," corrected Jack. "They're gown wagons."

"All of them?" Bowie couldn't believe it.

Jack reconsidered. "Well, not all of them. I'm sure a few are for make-up and accessories."

"Ach!" remarked Bowie.

Jack saw Kate in the group and immediately went over to her without saying another word to Bowie.

"Good-bye then," Bowie said to himself as he stood alone watching Jack half walk/half float over to his Astorian sweetheart.

Hugging was not permitted so Jack bowed to Kate as she curtsied to him. "It is good to see you again," he said, barely able to contain his excitement. He was so smitten, he forgot himself for a moment. "I was totally *psyched* when you accepted my invitation."

"Psyched? What does that mean? I've never heard that expression before," she said.

*Master Lumens is going to kill me*, Jack thought to himself. He got hold of his senses and tried to cover his faux pas. "I meant extremely happy, um, yeah."

She blushed. "You risked your life to invite me. Didn't seem right to refuse." She lowered her voice, "Truth be told, I would have accepted your invitation even if you hadn't slain a chimera."

"*Now* you tell me!" teased Jack. "We were advised, actually commanded, not to usurp your time when you arrived to give you a chance to rest and prepare for the evening. May I escort you to your chambers?'

"I'd be psyched," she said.

*Master Lumens is <u>definitely</u> going to kill me,* concluded Jack.

Shaunteera was practicing sword fighting when she nearly got upended by a hug. "Sister! It is so good to see you again!" gushed Lexi.

Shaunteera pushed her off. "Yeah, okay, you too."

"Kellen asked me to the prom," explained Lexi. "He seemed very nice when I met him and I've heard he's a good soldier."

"He's an exceptional soldier," confirmed Shaunteera. "Rumor has it he's being considered for the King's Guard."

"I just hope he's a good dancer!" giggled Lexi. "I really wish you were going to the prom tonight."

"Actually, I am going. Bowie asked me," said Shaunteera, though she regretted it as soon as the words left her mouth.

Lexi squealed with delight and clapped her hands together which attracted the attention of everyone within a thousand-yard radius. "That's wonderful!" She hugged Shaunteera. 'He's so brave and handsome and funny. I'm not surprised you like him!"

Shaunteera sneered. "Who said I like him?"

Lexi looked her sister dead in the eye. "If you didn't like him, *you* would have said 'no' when he asked you!"

Shaunteera was busted and she hated it, but Lexi was kind enough not to rub it in and changed the subject. "What are you going to wear?"

"Just my uniform," answered Shaunteera.

For the first time in Shaunteera's recollection, Lexi looked unhappy. "Oh, no, no, no! Sister, that will not do! But I can fix it!" Then she was happy again. "Girls!" Lexi called out to her classmates. A dozen Astoria students ran over immediately upon her summons.

Shaunteera looked terrified and started backing up. "No, I'm fine! You don't need to help me!"

Lexi's classmates circled Shaunteera, closing off any exit. She took a defensive posture but then realized there were just too many of them. The Astoria students converged on Shaunteera, overpowered her and carted her away for a complete prom make-over.

***

The boys anxiously awaited their dates in the Great Hall. The girls were supposed to arrive shortly after the courtyard bell was rung. They were fashionably late. Finally, Lady Hesper and Lady Kiran arrived in satin and lace gowns, clearly vogue by Atlantis standards. Dean Slade and Sir Daran walked forward to greet their female chaperone counterparts. "You both are a sight to behold. I feel as though I'm a cadet again," said the dean.

Lady Hesper and Lady Kiran curtsied gracefully. "You are too kind," said Lady Hesper. "I only wish I were as beautiful as when I was a student," she lowered her voice, "the first time you asked me to the prom."

"Trust me when I say time has only added wisdom and wit," offered the dean.

She blushed a bit. Then she turned to her students trailing her. All looked beautiful in their dresses and styled hair. "May I present the women of Astoria Academy. We celebrate the brave men who risked life and limb to share in this evening's festivities!"

Sir Daran took a step forward. "Seeing you all reminds us why risking our lives was well worth it." He nodded his head, signaling the cadets to seek out their dates.

The freshmen who completed their prom quests were upgraded with "dress" tunics and cloaks for the occasion—definitely a step up from their drab day-to-day uniforms. Kate looked gorgeous and it took every ounce of Jack's self-control not to ogle.

Bowie approached them and asked, "Have you seen Shaunteera?"

"I have," answered Kate. From behind a cluster of girls, Shaunteera appeared looking absolutely stunning. Though relatively short since it had been shaved off at the beginning of the school year, her hair was styled perfectly and adorned with a gold and sapphire-crusted hair clip. Her dress was designed with layers of diaphanous turquoise organza which highlighted her eyes. Her sister had brought a few extra dresses to choose from and this one looked perfect on Shaunteera. Her hands, though calloused from warrior training, had survived a manicure and two coats of nail polish. The empire waistband on the dress was adorned with gold beads and fit snuggly. She wore elegant leather sandals, also decorated with gold beads. She looked a bit uncomfortable—but not as uncomfortable as the boys from Strongthorne who were looking at her. It had taken several months for the male students to accept her as one of their own. They almost forgot she was a woman. Almost ...

Her own gang of friends, including Scurra, Gaul and the Skere brothers were taken back as well. "Chimera's breath!" commented Scurra, which was the equivalent of saying *Holy sh—!* "That can't be Shaunteera!"

An annoying sophomore walked up to Shaunteera and whispered something offensive in her ear, judging by her expression. She hit the boy in the stomach and pushed him to the floor, then continued walking toward her friends as if nothing had happened.

"Yup," confirmed Scurra, "that's our Shaunteera."

Bowie gulped twice. Seeing her as she looked tonight, he didn't have much chance to keep up his defenses. "You are quite the sight!" he said.

She didn't know how to take Bowie's comment at first as she was so used to exchanging insults with him. She furrowed her brow.

Bowie corrected himself. "What I meant to say was I don't think I've ever seen any woman look more beautiful than you do right now!" Bowie could be opinionated and obstinate but he also knew the truth and was inclined to speak it.

She smiled warmly as she took his arm. "Thank you, Bowie. You're looking rather handsome yourself."

"You just noticed?" he said. They both laughed. Mouths agape, their friends watched as Bowie and Shaunteera walked ahead. Without looking back, Shaunteera said, "You can close your mouths now." Their friends complied.

Jack refocused on Kate. "I don't agree with him."

"About what?" asked Kate.

"He said he'd never seen any woman look more beautiful. I have." He looked into her eyes and didn't look away.

She held his gaze and then said, "You are so full of it!"

"Too sappy?" asked Jack. "I thought the delivery was quite convincing."

"Men!" She rolled her eyes. Of course, Jack meant what he said and she knew it but sometimes humor is more romantic than romance.

A minute later, five bells rang, which meant full mobilization of all troops. Everyone stopped in their tracks.

One of the Strongthorne guards rushed in with a messenger to speak with Dean Slade. "My lord, we just got word that Shost Town is under attack from Skullian troops." The messenger estimated two battalions of the enemy but only three squads of Andaarian soldiers defending.

"Shost runs very close to the forest. They could have more soldiers in waiting," said Sir Daran.

"Strongthorne!" called out Dean Slade.

The Strongthorne students snapped to attention. "My lord!"

"Shost is under attack. We will ride out at once to engage the enemy. Those on guard duty or otherwise detained will remain at the academy. In my absence, Sir Maris is in command. Prepare for battle!"

"Ready the horses for our cavalry and wagons for the rest of the troops," commanded Sir Daran to the stable master.

"Ready weapons and light armor," commanded Sir Glavin to Burl.

Dean Slade turned to his guests. "Ladies, please accept our apologies. Duty calls."

Lady Hesper came forth. "No apology is necessary, my lord. We will prepare for the arrival of the wounded, pray there be few, if any. What else can we do to help?"

"Sir Maris will let you know. Your assistance is most welcomed," said Dean Slade. "We should be back by morning."

"We'll be ready," acknowledged Sir Maris.

Bowie took one last look at Shaunteera. "It was fun while it lasted."

"Be careful out there tonight. I've *almost* started to get use to you," said Shaunteera.

"Aye, be careful yourself, because I don't think I'll ever get use to you!" countered Bowie. "But I'd like to give it some time and see if my mind changes." He winked at her. She elbowed him in the gut. Bowie was assigned to the infantry and Shaunteera to the cavalry. They parted ways to prepare.

Jack held Kate's hand. "I have to go."

"Me too," said Kate. "We will make preparations for the injured. Please do not be one of them."

"I'll do my best." Jack turned to exit then paused. "These few moments were more than worth it."

"Worth what?"

"The chimera," said Jack.

"Being compared to a chimera, how romantic!" she said sarcastically.

Jack enjoyed a good laugh until Bowie grabbed him by the back of his tunic collar. "Come on, Romeo!"

"Who's Romeo?" asked Kate.

"Never mind!" said Jack as Bowie dragged him off to the armory.

The Astorian women changed back into their regular uniforms and worked with Grummel to prepare the infirmary. Once their preparations were complete, they rested for a few hours. The bell rang twice just after dawn, indicating the return of the Strongthorne troops.

Three hundred troops came through the open gates, twenty-seven of them assisted by other students due to injuries and two covered with sheets on one of the wagons. They walked slowly and looked battle weary. Jack and Bowie held Shaunteera between them. She had a bloody bandage around her leg. She looked pale and barely conscious. Lexi rushed out to meet them. "What happened to her?"

"She's stable," said Bowie. "As Sir Daran anticipated, the Skullians had an additional company of infantry waiting in ambush just inside the forest. But they lost the advantage of surprise and we were able to rout them. Your sister exchanged blows with an enemy footman and took a deep cut to her thigh. He fared worse."

"She lost a lot of blood," added Jack. "Bowie slowed the bleeding though by applying pressure while I bandaged her up. She refused to take one of the wagons back. Stubborn gal, if you can imagine."

Lexi looked worried. 'Sister, are you all right?'

"Luuvva you, seeester," spoke the barely conscious Shaunteera.

"Did she just say 'Love you, sister?'" asked Lexi.

"I think she did. She's in worse shape than I thought!" said Bowie.

Jemm, who had been on guard duty, rushed over once he saw Shaunteera was injured. "Lexi and I will take her from here." He turned to Jack and said, "Thank you."

"I just wrapped up her leg. It was really Bowie who saved her from bleeding out."

Jemm didn't know what to say and *thank you* would have been far too much of a stretch considering how much he despised Bowie. Yet, Bowie saved his sister's life once again. He looked at Bowie and nodded his approval, a gesture that would be as close to affection as their relationship would ever allow.

A few other students came out with litters and helped transport Shaunteera and the other injured students to the infirmary. Lexi was already applying healing spells to her sister's leg, indicated by a faint blue glow emanating from her hands.

Bowie turned to Jack. "Did you see that? I think Jemm likes me!"

"I wouldn't go that far," said Jack. "But that nod was bordering on civility."

Bowie suddenly looked concerned. "Do you think she'll be all right?"

"I do," said Jack. "With all the Astorians around, she should be up and walking around in no time. Let's clean ourselves up and then we'll go see her."

"How are you?" asked Bowie.

"I'm okay," said Jack and put his hand on Bowie's shoulder. "Thank you."

Kate saw Jack and ran up to him.

Before turning his attention to her, he asked Bowie, "How about you?"

Bowie smiled. "I was born for this!" he said, then went to help unload his injured classmates from the wagons.

Jack's armor was covered in blood but it wasn't his own. "Are you hurt at all?" Kate asked concerned.

"It's good to see you," was all he said.

She touched his face gently and said nothing.

All the injured were tended to. The two students killed were both sophomores. Pyres were set up and their bodies burned per the funeral ritual of Andaarian warriors.

***

The next day, save for the guards on duty, all of the Strongthorne students came out to bid their female counterparts farewell. Few words were spoken, but there was more intimacy in their departure than ever before.

Dean Slade addressed the women. "We owe you a debt of gratitude," and bowed low to show his respect.

"It is us who are indebted to you," said Lady Hesper. "We are honored to aid such men—and women," she added as Shaunteera on crutches came into view, "who risk everything to protect us all." She bowed low to Dean Slade.

Flanked by an armed escort, the women of Astoria rode off as the sun reached its zenith in the deep blue sky of Atlantis.

# War Games

As the school year came to a close, Strongthorne Academy held its annual war games among the students. The games were designed to spur some good-natured competition and provide each class with the opportunity to show off their prowess in the art of war. The prize for winning was pride and bragging rights which effectively outshined any plaque or trophy.

Each respective class year, identified on the field of battle by a colored gambeson, was pitted against the other three. The seniors wore red, the juniors blue, the sophomores yellow and the freshmen green. Like modern-day war games, real weapons were replaced with training weapons so no one actually died during battle. That was the theory anyway. Despite using wasters and non-lethal arrowheads dusted with colored chalk, "good natured competition" still got a bit gruesome with plenty of welts, bruises and lacerations, broken bones and concussions. No student in the history of the academy had ever died during the war games. At least that's the story the faculty claimed and they were sticking to it.

The consilia acted as judges but for the most part, the students were expected to act honorably. If a limb was struck, the student acted as if maimed. If what would be considered a lethal blow with a regular weapon connected, the student receiving the blow *died* and could no longer participate. Once dead, the student tied a black scarf around his neck identifying he was dead and then left the designated battlefield to await the conclusion.

The rules were simple: all participants entered onto the battlefield. Once each class was positioned in their respective quadrant, Dean Slade would blow the horn to begin the battle. Once the battle commenced, any student who left the battlefield for whatever reason was considered deceased. The last survivor or survivors of a given class still standing secured the win for their class. Dean Slade would blow the horn again to officially conclude the war games and declare the winner.

Year after year, the senior class consistently dominated the games. Even though their numbers were often smaller than the other classes due to attrition in the line of duty, they were by far the most strategic, best trained and fiercest fighters. Once, a junior class had taken the prize but that had been decades earlier and was mainly attributed to many of the seniors that year contracting food poisoning thanks to spoiled chimera eaten the night before. A freshmen or sophomore class had never won the war games—or even come close.

The morning of the games was cool and a layer of low fog clung to the ground like an old blanket. The Great Hall was practically silent at breakfast as the students mentally prepared. After a simple breakfast of porridge and eggs, the students went back to their respective barracks and donned their leather armor and colored gambesons.

Each class was allowed ten archers and each archer was given three arrows. However, archers were allowed to pick up arrows fired or dropped from other classes during the games. The rest of the troops were considered infantry and armed themselves with wasters and shields. No horses were allowed in the war games so as not to put those noble beasts at unnecessary risk of injury— the same concern did not apply to the students.

Kellen reviewed last-minute strategy with his classmates in the senior barracks. "There are fifty-four of us, sixty-three juniors, seventy-six sophomores and ninety-nine freshmen. We'll start in a classic wedge formation, archers on the inside. We can make a quick switch to tortoise formation should any of the groups attempt a long-range volley with arrows. And you know they will. It's tradition at this point. My gut is telling me to watch out for the freshmen—"

"The dung huggers won't be a problem," interrupted a senior.

Kellen stared down his naïve classmate. "Those dung huggers took on a Skullian platoon led by Grigori and Thorgills in their very first battle and only lost one man."

"And that core group of freshmen has Bowie, Jack, Yor and Narro, Scurra and Gaul," added Deyglenn.

They're as skilled as any soldiers I've ever seen."

"Let's not forget Shaunteera," another senior added. They all groaned thinking about how tough she was.

"She won't be on horseback," commented Kellen. "Thank God for that! But don't underestimate her on the ground. There's but a handful of us who could take her one-on-one in single combat."

"Aye!" they said collectively.

Kellen continued, "My feeling is the freshmen will have some tricks up their sleeves. I trust Bowie as far as I can throw him."

"But he saved your life!" chimed in another senior.

"I trust him as a friend and fellow warrior," said Kellen, "but as an enemy today? No."

"Jack's the one we have to watch for," added the senior infantryman Flogar Grons. "He's an expert tactician. He's been working with Dean Slade to form numerous battle strategies. Did you hear about the battle of Torn last month? Andaarian troops were outnumbered two to one but were still able to rout the enemy quickly."

"How?" asked another senior.

"Jack had been studying weather patterns and surmised the low fog, like today, would provide concealment for the troops. He suggested two companies of archers flank the Skullians using the fog to gain position. He had a decoy infantry battalion draw attention to a center point with good cover. When the sun came up, the fog cleared in minutes. Once the attack began, the Skullian archers failed to take out the decoy group. Andaarian archers countered and wiped them out. Then while trying to avoid the barrage of arrows, the Skullian infantry charged straight at the decoy battalion which retreated back to a pike defensive position. Arrows cut off their retreat and the pikemen cut off their advance," finished Grons.

"Brilliant!" said one of the seniors.

"All right, so we know what we're up against then," acknowledged Kellen. "But this is going to be a straight-up attack. Hold to our formations, watch for any flanking maneuvers and listen for my commands." Kellen was confident they would win but during his planning, he failed to make one key observation: neither Jack nor Bowie was in the Great Hall during breakfast.

The students headed out to the battlefield, a partitioned area outside of the castle. Each class took their positions against one side of the square-shaped area. The freshmen took the far south position, juniors the west, sophomores the east and the seniors positioned themselves north. Once in position, each class started banging their swords against their shields, shouting, raising their fists—your basic war-game warmup.

The townspeople positioned themselves along the eastern perimeter of the battlefield to watch, some selling food and trinkets. One forward-thinking vendor was already selling nachos. Despite the Andaarian quest for peace and harmony, watching students beat each other senseless was considered good entertainment.

The consilia walked out onto the battlefield and took various positions to best judge the fighting, followed by Dean Slade who carried the ceremonial horn. The townspeople went silent. The students went silent.

A small tower stood at the edge of the battlefield. An announcer, followed by his assistant, climbed up the ladder and positioned himself in front of a large conical amplifying device resembling a huge megaphone. He cleared his throat, grabbed a flagon of water from his assistant and took a swig, gargled a bit and spat it out before speaking into the device with the flourish of a professional announcer. "Ladies and gentlemen, boys and girls, let's get ready to battlllllllllllllle!" The crowd went wild with cheering and clapping. He then introduced each class in turn who answered back with a resounding huzzah. The crowd cheered each class though more hands were occupied with wagering than applauding.

"Dean Slade, the field is yours," said the announcer with a bow.

One of the seniors ran up to Kellen, "The freshmen only have nine archers!"

"Just nine?" questioned Kellen.

Dean Slade looked at each class and in turn asked, "Are you ready?" Each class responded with another huzzah. He then said with an air of pride for those young warriors for whom he had devoted his life to forging, "Let the games begin!" and blew his horn.

Each class immediately assembled into a wedge formation and converged on the middle point toward the other classes—first walking, then trotting, then running at full bore. At the front of the freshman class, Scurra held the point position. On either side was Gaul and Shaunteera.

The announcer relayed the action. "No messing around today as each class has formed solid wedge formations to get this melee going. They're moving cautiously, now they're picking up the pace and now they're going at an all-out run!"

About a hundred feet before impact, the freshman, sophomore and junior classes stopped and their respective archers positioned themselves.

The announcer resumed, "The three classes have halted their approach to let loose a volley of arrows at the seniors, trying to weaken the strongest class. We've seen this tactic time and time again—but wait!"

The sophomore and junior-class archers each let loose a volley on the senior class. The senior-class infantry closed ranks and shielded themselves with a quick switch to tortoise formation just as Kellen had planned.

The announcer's voice went up an octave, "Thunder and lightning! The freshman class let loose their arrows on the exposed junior archers and it looks like they've taken them all out. All the junior archers are dead!" Money exchanged hands in the audience.

No one expected the freshman class to let loose their arrows on the junior class instead, aiming primarily for their archers and effectively eliminating them. Before the juniors could rally, the sophomore and senior classes had resumed a frontal wedge attack. The freshman class shifted their wedge and aimed the point at the side of the junior-class wedge, just like the Skullians had done to them in the forest, which was also unexpected. The result was that only half of the junior-class infantry was able to confront the full number of freshman infantry on their right flank. With their archers out of commission, the juniors were also fighting sophomores at their tip and the seniors on their left flank. Meanwhile, the seniors' left flank clashed with the sophomore's right flank. With no threat from the freshman class on their right flank, the sophomore archers came out from behind the wedge and tried to circle around the senior class.

The senior-class archers formed an extended V behind their infantrymen to ward off attacks from the other classes attempting to outflank them. The sophomore archers took out one of the senior archers before they were mowed down by the remaining senior archers facing them. Meanwhile, the freshman archers maneuvered behind the juniors to take on the senior archers.

The Skere brothers took out four senior archers but not before seven of their own freshman archers were taken out in the exchange. "Focus on the brothers!" yelled Kellen. Five archers against two was overwhelming. However, the Skere brothers managed to take out four more senior archers before putting on the black scarves themselves. The sole senior archer remaining retreated behind his infantry.

The ground fighting was fierce. Having been outmaneuvered by the freshmen and then forced to face the other classes at their weakest points, almost all of the juniors were taken out in a matter of minutes. The seniors then faced the sophomores on their left flank and the freshmen on their right flank. The sophomores had already lost a third of their infantry. So had the freshmen, but with more students to begin with, their numbers gave them an advantage. The seniors though had only lost five infantrymen but once all the juniors were dispatched, the freshmen reformed a wedge and attacked the senior's right flank.

The freshmen's core infantry group of fighters, Scurra, Gaul and Shaunteera worked so effectively as a unit that they took out three times their number of the enemy. Kellen saw this and ordered the remainder of the senior class to tighten their formation to block blows and push back encroaching troops. From this fortified defensive position, the other three classes were forced to duke it out with each other.

The announcer chimed in. "The freshmen are really making a go of it this year! Their archers are all gone but not before taking out most of the senior archers. And now the seniors have tightened their ranks in a defensive position!" More money changed hands in the crowd.

The juniors were the first to get killed off in their entirety. As the chief strategist for the seniors, Kellen was impressed with the freshmen's strategy—their maneuvers dramatically weakened the second strongest class. Still, Kellen had a bad feeling he was missing something.

With the juniors out of the picture and the seniors in a defensive holding position, the freshmen went head-to-head against the sophomores and seemed to be equally matched. However, after a few exchanges of force, the freshmen momentarily opened up their line which allowed one or two sophomores at a time to fall through. The freshmen then re-closed the line and finished off the trapped sophomores. After this happened twice, the sophomores were more cautious.

"I wonder what they'll do next," Kellen said to his surrounding classmates. As soon as he finished his question, the freshmen turned toward the seniors and ran directly at them. Before Kellen could speak, six of the freshmen formed a ramp with their shields just in front of the seniors. Several other freshmen used the ramp to project themselves over the senior frontline and smash into the center of the formation. The six plebes who formed the ramp ran to the sides, which drew some of the seniors, thus weakening their front. The remaining sophomores clashed head-on with the seniors while the freshmen who had penetrated their center fought outward to weaken them. Jumping into the center of the seniors was a suicide move but with the sophomores attacking at the same time from the outside, the seniors were in a temporary pickle.

Then Kellen had a brilliant idea. "Eagle formation around the sophomores!" The seniors pulled back and reformed behind the sophomores in a half circle effectively containing them. Instead of following the seniors, the freshmen focused on the sophomores. Now the sophomores were being attacked in front by the freshmen and behind by the seniors. In short order, the sophomores were annihilated. As soon as the last sophomore went down, the freshmen moved to outflank the seniors. The seniors attempted another eagle formation around the freshmen. The freshmen reacted by breaking up their formation and attacking the seniors individually. Kellen saw that tactic as a fatal mistake because even though the freshmen outnumbered the seniors, the seniors had the advantage by staying in formation. He assumed they had just run out of strategies.

The freshmen still had the quantity advantage and held their own fairly well for a while. Kellen called out for the seniors to cluster around the toughest remaining freshmen—Scurra, Gaul and Shaunteera. The remaining senior archer picked off freshmen one at a time. The freshmen were losing ground. Shaunteera let out a battle cry and fought her way through several seniors to square off with Kellen. Her attack was fierce and for the first few blows, he could only defend himself. But Kellen was more skilled and quickly turned the tables on Shaunteera. She parried a crosscut but slipped on a stone in front of her. That mistake was all it took for Kellen to finish her off. The remaining seniors overwhelmed Scurra and Gaul shortly thereafter.

The announcer broadcasted, "That was a close one with Shaunteera giving Kellen a heck of a fight but alas as far as I can see from my vantage point, seven seniors are left and no one else from any other class." Cheers went up from the audience. More money changed hands.

The remaining seniors congratulated each other. The battle was a lot tougher than any one of them had anticipated. They walked toward the exit point together but then spread out as one adjusted a strap or tended to a wound or wiped the sweat from his brow. Three of the seniors ahead of the others crossed the battlefield boundary thus officially ending their participation in the war games. The wind picked up for a moment and Kellen stopped in his tracks. Something wasn't right. Their strategy had been sound in taking out the toughest of the freshmen, Narro and Yor, Scurra, Gaul, Shaunteera, Jack and Bowie ... wait a minute! Nine archers? "Seniors, halt!" Kellen called out. "Regroup!" The ones who had already left the battlefield tried to return but were held back by Sir Daran. They had crossed the boundary line and thus were considered dead.

Seemingly out of nowhere, a voice with a distinctive Scottish lilt was heard saying, "Took you long enough!" Bowie stood up from his prone position under concealment of the low fog, camouflaged with twigs and grasses over his green gambeson. He quickly dispatched the archer with his waster and after three additional moves, took out the other two senior infantrymen.

Kellen pulled out his own waster and charged Bowie just as a blunt-tipped arrow left a chalk mark in his back that surely would have pierced his heart had it been a real one. Kellen turned and saw Jack, the tenth freshman archer, also camouflaged standing behind him by fifty paces. The freshmen made no mistake with their last maneuver. They tricked Kellen into believing they were out of options. He never considered low fog and makeshift camouflage were concealing two of Strongthorne's finest warriors who also happened to be freshmen. Of course, Jack and Bowie had come out to the battlefield and taken covered positions long before the battle began. Though sneaky, it wasn't against the rules.

The announcer was speechless. A lot of money changed hands among the townspeople. Having lost another bet to the freshman consilia, Sir Glavin reluctantly handed Sir Daran a healthy handful of coins.

Dean Slade walked out onto the battlefield and joined Jack and Bowie. "I declare the freshman class winners of this year's war games!" He blew the horn.

One of the sophomores yelled at Jack and Bowie. "You sons of a chimera, you cheated! You have no honor!"

"Shut it, crumb!" retorted Bowie. "We followed the rules—"

"For once," interjected Jack.

Bowie continued, "—and won. Trust me, it wouldn't have taken trickery to beat you lot! I might be the son of chimera but you fought like a goblin's grandmom!"

The crowd collectively went "Oooooooooh." No one had ever met a goblin's grandmother nor did anyone know if such a thing existed, but regardless, comparing someone to a "goblin's grandmom" was considered a grave insult in Atlantis.

The sophomore class cleared the benches and charged Bowie. The freshman class came to his aid. Out of sheer frustration, the juniors attacked both the sophomores and freshmen. Kellen and the other seniors watched the spectacle unfold in front of them for a few moments as the three classes went at each other. The seniors looked at Kellen. "What the heck," he said and then let out a battle cry as he led the seniors in an attack against the other three classes.

Not to be left out, the consilia joined their respective students and battled each other. The crowd cheered and more money changed hands. The announcer could barely keep up with the blow-by-blow action.

The fighting went on for quite a while and only stopped once everyone had let off a good head of steam. Seven of the students were carried off the field in stretchers because of their injuries but nothing life-threatening. After a generous amount of salves, poultices and fresh bandages were applied, the students all gathered in the Great Hall for a well-deserved feast of nachos.

The freshmen won the bragging rights for the evening. Bowie took to his lute while Jack made up verses about the different students and faculty during the war games. While the other classes weren't too happy about losing, the war games were over, the freshmen had won and the songs were funny.

Each class was no longer the enemy of the other.

# Ambush

Three weeks after the war games, a messenger arrived early evening with an invitation from King Gnarus of Andaar. His majesty requested the presence of Jack, Bowie, and a handful of their classmates to celebrate their war games victory at his castle in Libertas. Sir Daran thought it odd because the king had never invited the winners of the war games to a celebration before. Then again, the freshmen had never won the war games before. He wanted to question the messenger but he had taken off as quickly as he had appeared.

It would take almost two full days to get to Libertas riding at a comfortable pace. The boys and Shaunteera prepared that night. Along with Sir Daran and a squad of senior students led by Kellen, they left after an early breakfast the next morning.

As the group exited the last portcullis of the castle, a figure in shadow watched from the edge of the forest with a telescope. The figure spoke briefly with two goblin messengers and handed one of them a note.

The first day of travel for the Strongthorne convoy was uneventful. The weather was fair and they set up camp after covering more than half their journey. The following morning, they continued on toward Libertas.

Sir Daran instructed the group to ride at a normal pace. After an hour though, he rode next to Kellen and spoke quietly. A few minutes later, they halted for their first break of the day. While they nibbled on chimera jerky, Sir Daran sat down next to the freshmen. Jack and Bowie looked at him intently. They had come to understand his nuances and sensed something was up.

"We're being followed, aren't we?" asked Jack. Sir Daran nodded slightly.

Shaunteera looked startled, "Followed?"

"Scurra, say something sarcastic to Shaunteera," said Jack. "Shaunteera, hit him in the arm like you're upset with him. The rest of us will laugh." Jack wanted anyone spying on them from a distance to think they were unaware of being followed. The freshmen did as they were told. Meanwhile, Kellen casually walked among his squad informing each senior of Sir Daran's suspicion.

"It's not a large number," said Sir Daran. "Maybe two or three as far as I can tell. We'll have to watch for an ambush further along. When we mount back up, we're going to start off at the same pace we've been keeping. But on my signal, ride hard until we get to the Glandey Trading Post, a few hours south of the castle. If we are indeed being followed, we may be able to outrun them and find sanctuary there.

"If an ambush is set up before that, won't it be suicide riding into it?" questioned Scurra.

"Would you rather die a warrior or a wimp?" asked Sir Daran.

"Is there another option that doesn't involve dying?" asked Scurra.

"We'll go in a few minutes but don't look harried. It may be nothing but I'm not taking any chances with the best of my freshmen," remarked Sir Daran.

"I think he just paid us a compliment!" said Bowie.

Jack shook his head. "Then we must be in grave danger."

"Saddle up," said Sir Daran.

"What if the trading post itself has been overrun?" asked Jack.

Sir Daran considered it. "Not likely. There are at least twenty soldiers on site at any given time. It would be next to impossible for a large number of Skullians to infiltrate that deeply into Andaar and overtake the trading post without arousing some sort of an alarm."

The freshmen followed orders precisely, acting casual and saddling up their horses to continue their journey. They rode the first hour at a normal pace then came around the first bend of the path. Sir Daran gave the signal and the entire group bolted as fast as their horses would take them.

*\*\**

The day after Sir Daran and the freshmen had taken off to Libertas, Dean Slade awoke early with a strange feeling churning in the pit of his stomach. Was he sensing trouble or was it indigestion from one too many nachos the night before? *Probably the later*, he thought to himself. His steward left his breakfast on the table in the sitting area outside his bed chamber. He grabbed a small piece of bread and forced himself to eat it but he wasn't really hungry.

He went down to the grounds and walked toward the main gates greeting several students along the way.

Two sophomores were sparring with wasters. He stopped their practice and addressed the two combatants. "Don't forget to maintain your posture even as you thrust so you can recover more quickly. If you land a blow but are off balance, you could leave yourself exposed." He demonstrated and they bowed in thanks. "Carry on," he said.

All three gates leading into the castle were opened and manned by student guards. Dean Slade looked out across the countryside and noticed a small speck in the distance that grew larger every second. It was a messenger bearing the sigil of King Gnarus. Dean Slade called the order to let the rider pass through without stopping.

The messenger dismounted with an acrobatic maneuver. It wasn't his first delivery. "Greetings, my lord."

Dean Slade recognized the messenger from previous correspondences. "Welcome, sir."

"I carry a message from the king." He handed it directly to Dean Slade who opened it with some urgency. As soon as he read it, he crumpled the note in a clenched fist.

"What is it, my lord?" asked the messenger.

"Were other messengers sent with the same message?" He was hopeful of a positive response but knew better.

"No, my lord. The message was not considered dire by the king."

Hawk and Deyglenn came over after witnessing the exchange. Dean Slade turned to them. "I need one infantry company and one archery company on horseback ready to go in ten minutes, leather armor and weapons. No provisions, just water."

Consider it done, my lord," said Hawk. He and Deyglenn hurried off to make the necessary preparations.

Slade's steward rushed over and stood at attention. He didn't wait for an order. "I'll ready your horse, armor and weapons." Dean Slade nodded and his steward ran off to execute the task.

The messenger looked bewildered. "Forgive me, my lord, but I don't understand? The king himself told me the message was an invitation to the castle for a celebration."

"Good sir, it is. But we received the same message two evenings back," said Slade.

"Thunder and lightning!" said the messenger. "Then they're headed into an ambush."

"And they're a day's ride ahead of us." Slade gritted his teeth.

"My lord, I know a shortcut back to Libertas through the mountains. I will alert the king and send troops from the opposite direction. I assume they're going by way of Glandey?"

Dean Slade nodded yes. He knew how dangerous it would be for one man, no matter how experienced, to ride the treacherous mountain trail at full speed but precious lives were at stake and this brave soldier was offering to take the risk.

Without another word, the messenger jumped onto his horse, swiftly pulled back on the reins and exited the castle at a full gallop.

\*\*\*

The freshman convoy rode hard, not stopping until they peaked a hill looking down on the trading post a few miles away. Something still gnawed at Sir Daran.

Jack took note of it. "Sir, you don't seem convinced we're out of danger yet."

"Aye, Jack," said Sir Daran. "Something doesn't feel right but staying out here makes us sitting ducks. Best we proceed. As soon as Sir Daran finished his sentence, two dozen riders exited the forest in pursuit—Skullians by the look of them. From the trading post, two dozen additional soldiers on horseback raced toward them. Sir Daran pulled out his telescope. They were dressed in Andaarian soldier uniforms but two particular riders caught Sir Daran's eye. "Grigori and Thorgills," he said.

The Strongthorne escort was significantly outnumbered but Sir Daran seemed non-plussed by it. "This is where we make our stand then." He dismounted his horse and called out orders. "Circle formation, shields out."

When the enemy was within a hundred feet, Kellen turned to Sir Daran. "May I suggest tortoise formation?"

"If they wanted to shoot arrows," said Sir Daran, "they could have loosed half a dozen volleys by now. They mean to take us alive!"

The Skullians surrounded them. Grigori and Thorgills dismounted with swords and shields in hand. About half a dozen archers stayed back but the remainder of the Skullians dismounted with weapons and shields at the ready.

"You overcame the trading post's guards, I take it?" commented Sir Daran.

"It took several weeks to slowly infiltrate Glandey and position ourselves," said Grigori with restrained pride.

"All this just to capture me?" goaded Sir Daran.

"I promised Thorgills he could escort you to Vile for a taste of his specialty," said Grigori.

"Hey Thorgills," said Bowie, "you've got something on your face." Thorgills immediately touched his cheek feeling around for a scrap of food but instead felt the scar Bowie had given him in the forest and realized he was being duped. He wasn't too happy about that.

"Nice," Jack said to Bowie. "Making friends as always."

"Surrender now. There's no need to spill blood," said Grigori.

"No," said Sir Daran matter-of-factly.

"No?" Grigori was amused. "Well, then ..." Grigori attacked Sir Daran which prompted Thorgills to attack Kellen. The Skullian soldiers went after the remaining Strongthorne students.

Grigori was equally matched with Sir Daran. The same went for Kellen and Thorgills. Quickly though, the mass of the enemy overpowered them. Sir Daran would have fought until his own death but the Skullians had the freshmen at sword point and if there was a chance he could negotiate for their lives, he would. "Enough!" bellowed Grigori. The fighting stopped.

Before Sir Daran could offer his peaceful surrender for the lives of his students—

"I've got an idea," Bowie said to Grigori. "Why not have just you and me settle this?"

Grigori looked surprised for a moment as did everyone else. But his surprise turned into an infectious laugh that spread to Thorgills and the other Skullians.

Bowie continued, "What's the matter, you chicken?" The Skullians stopped laughing immediately. Bowie imitated a chicken complete with chicken sounds and flapping wings. This got the Strongthorne group laughing. Thorgills hit Sir Daran in the face with his gauntleted hand. The laughter stopped.

Grigori looked upon Bowie. "That was a mistake. At first, I was just going to capture you. But now that I'm thinking about it, my sons haven't fed lately."

Through the throng of soldiers walked Grigori's cloaked and hideous sons, Darne and Ontul. Their mere presence instilled fear on both sides. They emulated the forms of goblins, their bodies mangled into foul contortions of twisted sinew, raw muscle and tortured flesh. Their teeth were like stained enamel knives and their eyes black with the unsettling glow of burning coal. No longer human, they lived as pure predators, eating the raw flesh of beast and men alike. If there was any humanity left in them, it was reserved for their father who still loved them despite their foul existence.

They looked at Bowie as a cat would look upon a wounded mouse. They licked their shriveled lips and clacked their razor teeth in anticipation of their next meal. Even Bowie was repulsed by their menacing tenor. He realized if he failed, he would be a meal for these two creatures.

Jack desperately wanted his friend to stand down. Maybe they would be ransomed. There was still a chance they could all live. What Bowie proposed was insane. Grigori was arguably the best swordsman in Atlantis. Bowie was simply no match for the brother of Master Lumens.

"Give him his sword," said Grigori to one of the four soldiers holding Bowie. The soldier complied and stuck Bowie's sword into the ground.

Bowie looked at the soldier scornfully. "I hope you didn't bend the tip," he cautioned. The guard shoved Bowie who summarily broke the grip of the other three guards and knocked him out with a right cross. The other three guards pulled their swords on Bowie. Grigori cleared his throat. The guards sheathed their swords and bowed their heads.

"Are you finished?" asked Grigori.

"Just warming up a bit," replied Bowie.

Bowie pulled his sword from the ground and wiped the dirt away on his pants. He pointed the tip at Grigori in a threatening gesture. "For Strongthorne," he declared.

There were no more words to be spoken. Grigori attacked Bowie with savage grace. Bowie deflected the first seven blows but was unable to counter and at a loss for what to do next. "You've lasted longer than I thought," mocked Grigori. For once Bowie had no reply. Jack saw fear in Bowie's eyes for the first time ever.

Grigori attacked with three more blows. Bowie used all his strength to block then feebly countered with a cross slash to Grigori's rib cage while stepping in. Grigori easily parried the blow outward and thrust his sword into Bowie's gut.

"Nooooooooo!" screamed Shaunteera. Bowie dropped his sword. The blow was painful and paralyzing but it would take time to kill Bowie, which is what Grigori had intended. It would leave plenty of time for Grigori's sons to feast on Bowie while he was still alive.

Bowie was in shock. Tears filled the eyes of his friends, all except for Jack who was numb with anger and sorrow. He couldn't believe his best friend would die today, and a horrible death at that. What pained him most was he couldn't do anything about it.

Grigori plunged deeper into Bowie's gut, almost to the hilt of his blade. Bowie held onto Grigori's sides for support. Blood filled his mouth. He looked up into Grigori's cool, ruthless eyes. "Enjoy this moment because someday, I will kill you." Bowie wiped the blood from his mouth. Grigori used his boot to push Bowie off his blade and onto the ground in a bloody heap.

Grigori turned to his sons. "He was brave though arrogant. Wait until we've made some distance before you dine." His two sons bowed in acknowledgment. "And when you're done, bring me his head. "Now, we go," said Grigori. Shaunteera cried hysterically.

The Skullians tied up their captives. As they headed out, Jack looked back at his friend lying helpless on the ground and shivered at the fate awaiting him. Bowie caught his gaze and winked. His spirit was irrepressible, even in the face of death.

When they were some distance away, they all heard the high-pitched squeals of Darne and Ontul, seemingly enjoying their meal. Jack's stomach twisted into knots and he felt nauseous.

Sir Daran looked resolute. Jack thought he must be plotting their escape but that was a romanticized version of the reality that awaited his consilium. Thorgills was no doubt savoring what he was going to do to Sir Daran once he got him back to Vile.

Grigori's ears perked up and he stopped the procession. He looked south. A large group of soldiers were riding hard in their direction. Grigori asked for his telescope and viewed the oncoming combatants. At its head was Dean Slade with two companies of Strongthorne infantrymen and archers respectively. They outnumbered his troops two to one. Before he could decide whether or not to engage them, he heard a rumble from the north. He spied two full companies of Andaarian troops also on horseback riding hard at them, led by King Gnarus himself and next to him, a soldier he did not know, the messenger who had taken the shortcut through the mountain path from the academy. The Skullians were outnumbered four to one. Fighting would be suicide.

"Circle formation!" called out Grigori. "Prisoners in the middle. Swords at their throats!" What started as a kidnapping quickly turned into a hostage situation.

Dean Slade and his troops rode up to within twenty feet of Grigori on one side. The king and his troops did the same on the other side.

"You can kill us now but we will slit their throats first," said Grigori unafraid.

"I know that," said the king. "And lucky for you these students' lives are worth far more to me than you and your soldiers. My offer is this: we will exchange all of your pathetic lives for theirs. You will leave your horses, surrender your arms and return to Skul by way of the forest. Will you abide by this pledge?"

Grigori winced at the insult and reluctantly agreed. "I will abide."

A few hundred feet away, a cloaked figure came into view carrying a sack.

Grigori smiled. "Ah, one of my sons has returned!" The pledge was made before King Gnarus or Dean Slade knew about Bowie so there was nothing they could do to avenge Bowie's demise.

The soldiers opened up as the cloaked figure walked toward Grigori. Jack looked at the creature. There was something odd about its gate.

As the figure approached, Grigori also noticed something was amiss. "My son, where is your brother?"

The figure paused and threw a bloody sack in front of Grigori. The decapitated heads of Darne and Ontul rolled out, giving him a start and making his horse rear back. Grigori looked at the figure as he pulled back the hood of his cloak. It was Bowie, alive and well.

He looked at Bowie with hate and bewilderment. "But how?"

Bowie smiled. "Missing something?"

Instinctively, Grigori reached for the pouch on his belt, the one that *had* contained the amanata crystal given to him by his wife which could heal a mortal wound. Bowie allowed Grigori to stab him in the gut so he could get close enough to pick-pocket the crystal. It hurt like hell to have a sword run through his body, but Bowie figured if he could endure that, he could execute his plan. When he wiped the blood from his mouth, he also ingested the crystal.

Bowie's wounds healed quickly and he stealthily retrieved the dagger concealed in his boot. When Grigori's sons descended on him to feast, he slashed the throat of Darne, rolled over to his sword and was able to hold it straight up and brace it against the ground as Ontul jumped on him thus impaling himself.

Knowing that Grigori would wait for his sons to catch up, he thought he could pose as one of them and get close enough to Grigori to kill him. He never thought he'd have a chance to save himself, but maybe his sacrifice in taking out the leader of Skul would help sway the war in favor of the good guys. But when he saw Dean Slade with Strongthorne soldiers and another group which he assumed to be the king's army, he thought he'd go for a dramatic entrance instead and cheese off Grigori in the process.

Grigori was plenty cheesed. He wanted to attack Bowie outright even if it meant his own death. Not only had Bowie killed his two sons, he had also taken the one remaining symbol of love and sacrifice his wife had given him.

But revenge was a much sweeter proposition and he committed himself to exact it on Bowie, Strongthorne, Andaar, his brother, Fronisi—anyone or anything that stood in the way of his plan.

King Gnarus looked at the heads of Grigori's sons. "Collect their bodies and go," he directed at Grigori. "I will leave you with one of your horses to carry their remains."

Grigori knew he had been beaten for the time being. He motioned his soldiers to cut the students loose who all ran to hug Bowie. The Skullians dismounted and laid down their weapons. One soldier put the heads back into the sack and tied it to the one horse they were allowed. Grigori, Thorgills and the Skullian soldiers headed toward the forest. Grigori paused for a moment. "This is not the last of it!" he announced.

Thorgills starred at Bowie with buggy eyes and a psychotic grin on his face. He would get even with Bowie when the time was right.

Bowie locked eyes with Thorgills then wiped his cheek with his finger indicating Thorgills had something on his face. Thorgills went to wipe whatever it was off then felt the scar Bowie had given him. He got duped again.

Grigori turned to Thorgills shaking his head. "You really have to stop falling for that."

# Graduation

The senior class spent several days preparing for graduation culminating in a ceremony in which they officially became knights. It was rumored the graduation ritual involved cleansing of the body, mind and soul, quiet contemplation and meditation but the specific details of the rite of passage were kept private from the other students and public at large.

Of the one-hundred boys who started at Strongthorne Academy four years earlier, fifty-four men remained, forged into some of the finest warriors in Atlantis. After graduation, most would be assigned to various positions throughout the continent, some as diplomats representing Andaar in other regions. Others would go straight into frontline military service and on rare occasion, a select student was assigned to the Andaarian king's personal guard, which was far more than a glorified security detail. The King's Guard was comprised of the best of the best. They were recognized as the bravest and most skilled soldiers in Andaar. In addition to performing special assignments that put their lives in constant peril, when the king himself entered into battle, it was up to members of the King's Guard to protect him.

Comprised of two hundred elite soldiers, there were usually three or four open spots per year due to attrition. Soldiers in the regular army who had proven themselves worthy were the first to fill those positions. A Strongthorne student hadn't been directly assigned to the King's Guard in over five years. The last one, Glave Cornes, was an exceptional fighter and diplomat, besides playing a mean shawm.

While the seniors readied themselves for graduation, the other cadets were assigned to grounds preparation. Parents, dignitaries and invited guests of the graduating seniors would be in attendance, including King Gnarus. To remind them of their plebe status, the freshmen were assigned the most disgusting and despicable tasks such as cleaning the latrines, stables and guano throughout the castle. In all fairness, it would be their last time engaged in such chores. They had survived their first year at Strongthorne and would become sophomores, replaced by one-hundred new "dung huggers."

The morning of graduation, Jack and Bowie headed down to the kitchen to help Beurk prepare vast amounts of nachos for the arriving guests. Beurk had made a special spicy chider cheese for the occasion.

The graduation took place in the stadium which was decorated with garlands and banners. Embroidered seat pads were placed at each spot to provide some layer of comfort on the hard, stony seats. It was a formal occasion and the students were dressed in their best (or at the very least their cleanest) attire. A stage was constructed up front. There sat the dean with the class consilia and next to them King Gnarus in a modest throne. Behind them sat the other faculty and staff.

The guests included King Gi'tal and his brother Arma along with a small group of other Kentauros dignitaries as well as attendees from Astoria Academy which included Lady Hesper, Lady Kiran, Lexi and Kate. King Broc of Laidir was invited but politely refused due to an ensuing battle with Skullian forces at the Wedge River. However, he sent his son Prince Davie in his stead which was a gesture of good faith between Laidir and Andaar. Also, rumor had spread that one of Strongthorne's top new students spoke with a Laidirian accent and King Broc was a bit curious about whether or not one of their own was represented at the academy.

King Cloyce of Fens refused his invitation by courier and sent no dignitary or other representative in his place. Of course, no one from Skul was invited though it was assumed a spy or two would be in the audience.

Musicians played a triumphant piece to indicate the beginning of the ceremony. Everyone took their seats and Dean Slade approached the podium in formal armor and cloak. He spoke into a small fixed megaphone that amplified his voice.

"I am Lord Galdus Slade, dean of Strongthorne Academy. The men who stand before you today have proven themselves worthy of knighthood. They have trained hard, acquired wisdom and skill, and will in a moment pledge their loyalty to Andaar. I and my staff have guided their education, trained them in all facets of knighthood and have led them into battle on more than one occasion. Of the one-hundred students who began four years ago, fifty-four remain. Those that perished are heroes. They sacrificed their lives in the pursuit of a greater good, a higher ideal. They will always be remembered as our brothers in arms and with that we pay them tribute."

Dean Slade pulled out a scroll and one by one, read off the names of those who had died, starting with the most recent and going back to their freshman year. He gave pause between each name, lest each individual's sacrifice be trivialized.

Following the memorial, each consilium in turn gave a small speech about the seniors' progression from freshman year to graduation. After the last speech, Dean Slade resumed his place at the podium. "With great pleasure, I present the graduating class." The audience applauded as the seniors entered the stadium, each wearing a white vesture, red robe, black hose and shoes. The white symbolized purity and the red, nobility. Black symbolized death.

Each senior was flanked by two classmen of their choosing to aid in the ceremony. Kellen had asked Bowie and Jack to be his wingmen as it were. As the procession of graduating seniors walked onto the stage, the applause and cheers amplified. On the stage rested fifty-four newly forged swords and shields bearing the Andaarian coat-of-arms, a blue and white gyronny background with a radiant golden sun in the center, each set custom-made for the senior student receiving it.

Once everyone settled down, Dean Slade took his position in front of the consilia and to the right of the king.

Sir Glavin took center stage and read from a scroll. "On this day, we recognize the skill and honor of these men. In service of Andaar and of Atlantis, embodying both martial mastery and the code of chivalry, and cultivating that within which distinguishes right from wrong, do these men achieve their new rank." Sir Glavin sat down.

Dean Slade resumed his position at the podium and addressed the seniors. "Do you accept the accolade of knighthood offered to you on this day?"

The seniors responded in unison, "We do, my lord."

Dean Slade took a moment before responding. "This pleases us."

Sir Glavin approached Dean Slade and handed him a scroll listing the graduating seniors, from which the dean read. "We call upon Lavin Anzo to come forth, bearing witness to this court and company." The senior student approached Dean Slade and went down on one knee. The escorts on either side bowed.

Dean Slade pulled out his sword and touched Lavin on each shoulder with the flat part of the blade as he spoke these words, "For honor, for courage, for clarity of mind and purity of heart, I dub thee *Sir* Lavin Anzo. Arise and be counted among the Alumni of Strongthorne Academy and Brotherhood of Andaarian Knights."

The newly christened knight stood, bowed to Dean Slade and then to the king. Sir Glavin handed Sir Anzo's attendants a sword and shield respectively, who in turn handed them to Sir Lavin. He raised his sword to the audience and proclaimed, "For Andaar!" then placed it over his heart to finish the salute. He took his place stage left to await the other graduates. His attendants retreated to their position behind the faculty and stood at attention.

Each senior student in turn was called out and knighted in the same way.

Toward the end, one remaining senior stood. Dean Slade sat down and the king stood up. All students, faculty and attendees stood up and bowed. King Gnarus took his place at the podium and motioned everyone to resume their seats.

"It is my great honor to attend today's graduation and bear witness to these extraordinary men accepting the accolade of knighthood. No doubt they will serve Andaar with the honor, respect and bravery they have brought forth as students of Strongthorne Academy. Any one of them would make a fine addition to the King's Guard. However, there is but one vacancy I need fill at this time. And so it is that I ask Kellen Aquilam to become a knight and join the King's Guard."

Flanked by Bowie and Jack, Kellen came forth and kneeled in front of the king. "Kellen, do you pledge your life to the knighthood of Andaar, and as a member of the King's Guard protect your king to the best of your ability in both battle and diplomacy, and take on any assignment of which your king deems worthy of your attention until that service is no longer required or until your last breath?"

"This I swear with all my heart!" responded Kellen.

"Good answer," jested the king. Then he pulled out his sword and dubbed Kellen as he recited, "For honor, for courage, for clarity of mind and purity of heart, I dub thee Sir Kellen Aquilam. Arise and be counted among the Alumni of Strongthorne Academy, Brotherhood of Andaarian Knights and member of the King's Guard."

Kellen stood. In turn, Bowie and Jack handed him the special sword and shield given to members of the King's Guard. Kellen raised his sword to the audience and proclaimed, "For Andaar and for the king!" then placed it over his heart and finished the salute before joining his classmates.

The king sat down again as Dean Slade came forth. "Ladies and gentlemen, I present you with Strongthorne's graduating class of 207!" The audience rose to their feet in thunderous applause.

Dean Slade cued the musicians to resume playing. Graduation was over and Andaar had its new knights.

# Summer School

Jack and Bowie were summoned to the dean's chambers after the ceremony. Terrim and Scalt stood guard at the entrance.

"Hey, I remember you guys. You were going to kill us!" asserted Bowie.

Terrim didn't miss a beat. "We weren't going to kill you. We were taking you to be killed."

"Tortured first, of course," added Scalt.

"My bad," said Bowie apologetically. The four of them exchanged warm greetings.

"From what we've heard, it's been quite a year for you two!" said Terrim.

Jack sensed something—it should have been regular Strongthorne students or perhaps members of the King's Guard standing watch, not Fronisian soldiers. "When did Master Lumens arrive?" asked Jack. Terrim and Scalt smiled at each other.

"You are quite astute, Jack," replied Terrim. "He is expecting you. Both of you." He and Scalt each took a handle of the double door to let them in.

Upon entering, they observed Master Lumens conferring with King Gnarus and Dean Slade. Several other dignitaries were also in the room as well as servers weaving in and out of the guests. The three men turned toward the two boys. Jack and Bowie bowed. Master Lumens spoke first. "It is good to see you both again. We were just discussing your plans for the summer."

Jack and Bowie looked at each other. So much had transpired recently, they hadn't even considered what they would do over the summer. Most of the students went home for the break. Not exactly an option for Jack and Bowie.

"We would like you to attend summer school," said Master Lumens.

Both boys frowned a bit. From where Jack and Bowie were from, summer school was usually reserved for those kids who needed to compensate for screwing up during the regular school year. "Begging your pardon, Master Lumens, but did we do something wrong?"

"Not in the least!" said Master Lumens. "In fact, you both have exemplified extraordinary valor and skills we wish to cultivate."

Dean Slade spoke directly to Bowie. "Summer school for you will be an internship with the King's Guard." Bowie's eyes lit up.

"Kellen suggested it," said the king.

"He's not a bad sort after all, is he?" said Bowie.

Dean Slade cleared his throat. Bowie corrected himself, "I mean he's not a bad sort after all, is he, *your majesty*?"

The King swallowed a smile. "No, Bowie, not a bad sort at all."

"It's quite an honor, normally reserved for a select few between their junior and senior years," said Dean Slade. "You will be the youngest student to have such an honor bestowed upon him. Don't make us regret it!"

"I won't, my lord!" said Bowie.

"Congratulations, Bowie!" said Jack. "Well deserved!"

"Your majesty, what about Jack? He's more clever and very skilled—"

Master Lumens cut him off. "It is not for you to question his majesty." But before Bowie could protest further, "I requested that Jack join me in Fronisi for the summer and the king has graciously allowed it. Rest assured your friend will not miss out on combat training, but he will also be instructed in meditation and other such practices."

"He's better suited to that sort of thing than I am," confessed Bowie.

"Indeed," said Master Lumens.

"Pack right away and be discreet," spoke the dean.

Jack looked concerned. "May I ask why the secrecy?"

Master Lumens's expression turned grave. "The goblin attack in broad daylight and your two separate run-ins with Grigori suggests to me he's got his eye on you two. I believe he's had one of his prophetic dreams and that you're part of it."

Dean Slade added, "I have faced Grigori on numerous occasions in battle and never once have I seen fear in his eyes—until that day in the forest."

"We think capturing Sir Daran after the war games was a cover for his intention to kidnap you two specifically," added the king.

"Why not just kill us when he had the chance?" asked Bowie.

Jack remembered what Master Lumens had told them about Grigori's dreams. "Because he may not have known what his dream meant. We could have become martyrs had he killed us which could have led to his demise."

"My suspicion as well, Jack," said Master Lumens. "But when Bowie challenged him to single combat, I believe it altered the perception of his dream and he thought Bowie's death would put an end to the threat."

"Nice work," Jack said to Bowie sarcastically.

"It's a gift," retorted Bowie.

Lumens continued, "However, once he realized Bowie survived the ordeal, he may have reconsidered the martyr scenario."

"Becoming a martyr isn't exactly on my bucket list," said Bowie.

"Not on my bucket list either!" confirmed Jack.

"What is a 'bucket list?'" asked the king.

Master Lumens whispered to the boys, "What did I say to you both about introducing things from your world into this one?"

"Care for some nachos, sire?" came the untimely question from a server holding a platter piled high with them.

"So these are the famous nachos I've heard so much about!" said the king.

"Nachos?" questioned Master Lumens as he shot a menacing glance at Jack and Bowie.

The king pulled back the sleeve of his royal robe as he took a chip piled high with cheese and peppers. *Crunch!*

"Very good!" said the king. "And they've got a kick to them! Who came up with such a thing?"

Fortunately for Jack and Bowie, Dean Slade interjected, "If Grigori used capturing Sir Daran as a cover story, that means he didn't tell Thorgills about his dream either."

"Most likely he did not," said Lumens. "He would not want to appear vulnerable or weakened in any way, even to Thorgills, one of his most trusted advisors."

"And there's another reason why we think Thorgills is not privy to Grigori's dream," said the king. "Rumor has it he has a bounty on your head," he directed at Bowie. "He wants you dead or alive, but is paying better if you're alive. No doubt he'd prefer to take you to Vile and execute you in public."

"What's my head worth these days, your majesty?" asked Bowie.

"A thousand ghip alive and five hundred dead," said the king.

"No too shabby. I'd turn myself in for that kind of money!" said Bowie.

Master Lumens spoke, "There are still many unanswered questions. Knowing my brother as I do and in light of what happened this year, I believe he is plotting something epic and has been for quite some time. I suspect he is using his dark powers on the goblins and forming some sort of alliance, if that's even possible. To what extent, I cannot say nor what he plans to do with them. He has also made several long journeys by sea as well and we've not been able to discover where he's traveled to or why."

"Boys, why don't you go prepare yourselves for your respective journeys ahead," said the dean.

Jack and Bowie excused themselves. Outside in the courtyard, their friends were gathered around. Shaunteera was packing up her horse. Her father and uncle talked quietly with her brother. Their escort back to Kentauros was comprised of twenty Centaur soldiers.

"You weren't going to leave without saying good-bye, were you?" Bowie asked Shaunteera.

"Of course not!" she said annoyed. "I heard you were both in the dean's chambers. I was going to wait."

"I wasn't," Jemm said from his mounted position.

Shaunteera tightened up one last strap. "I guess that's it!" She first went over to Scurra and gave him a hug, then to Gaul. She approached the twins who took on mock battle stances. She struck her own pose—they growled at each other, laughed and hugged good-bye. She then went over to Jack. "We've been through much. You are a good friend, Jack. I will miss you this summer." She gave Jack a warm hug.

"You didn't say you'd miss me this summer," said Scurra.

"I know," said Shaunteera, which drew laughter all around.

Scurra grabbed his neck as if he had been choked. "Tough crowd."

She turned to Bowie and suddenly felt like several dozen eyes were watching her, which they were.

There was a long moment of awkward silence. If she didn't hug him, it would be obvious she was hiding her true feelings for him. If she hugged him, it would confirm her true feelings for him.

Bowie may have been proud but he was also chivalrous and didn't want Shaunteera to feel embarrassed. "May I have permission to hug one of the best, and certainly most attractive, warriors at Strongthorne?" he asked her.

Shaunteera was taken back. She had no choice but to say, "You may."

Bowie turned to Scurra and hugged him instead. While everyone laughed, even Jemm, he let go of Scurra and hugged Shaunteera. "I might even miss you a little bit this summer."

"A little bit, huh?" she smiled.

"A little bit," he confirmed.

"Thank you for saving my life more than once this year," she said sincerely.

For a moment, he lost himself in the truth of his feelings for her. "There will never be anyone else," he said barely above a whisper.

"What?" but when she looked into his eyes, she knew exactly what he said and what he meant by it.

He helped her mount up. The Centaur escort proceeded to leave with waves and good-byes going back and forth. Shaunteera looked back at Bowie and smiled. "There will never be anyone else," she said softly.

"What was that?" her father asked.

"Nothing," she said and trotted ahead.

# EPILOGUE

In addition to Master Lumens and Jack, the Fronisi escort was comprised of thirty armored Centaur horsemen led by Terrim. The escort to Libertas was larger with forty of the King's Guard plus the king, Kellen and Bowie.

Jack and Bowie said their good-byes to the remaining freshmen and then approached each other.

"I couldn't have done any of this without you," said Jack.

"I know," teased Bowie.

"I think you're going to have an awesome summer training with the King's Guard," offered Jack.

"Likewise with Master Lumens," said Bowie. "I'll bet he's got some real fancy stuff planned for you! When we get back for the start of the school year, we'll exchange notes."

"Totally," said Jack.

So much had transpired between them but words fell short of communicating the bond of their friendship and the gratitude they had for one another. Jack's eye filled with tears. "Bowie, I just want to say—"

Bowie cut his friend off, "All right then, let's not drag this out all day." He looked a little misty-eyed himself. "Give us a hug!" Bowie said and opened his arms. Jack complied.

"That's one of the things I like about you," commented Jack.

"What's that?" asked Bowie.

"You always know how to take an uncomfortable situation—and make it even worse!" joked Jack.

They parted ways for the summer and headed off to more adventures.

# NOTE FROM THE AUTHOR

Word-of-mouth is crucial for any author to succeed. If you enjoyed the book, please leave a review online—anywhere you are able. Even if it's just a sentence or two. It would make all the difference and would be very much appreciated.

Thanks!
Richard

# About the Author

At the age of nine, the eponymous *Richard Lohrey's Fabulous Stories* became his first published work, albeit distributed exclusively to family members. In addition to a comedy romance novel and several screenplays, Lohrey spent over two decades writing professionally in advertising and social media. When he's not writing, he's either scuba diving, cooking, studying martial arts or convincing his wife to see movies she would normally avoid at all costs.

Thank you so much for reading one of our **Fantasy** novels.

If you enjoyed our book, please check out our recommended title for your next great read!

*War of the Staffs* by Steve Stephenson & Kathryn M. Tedrick

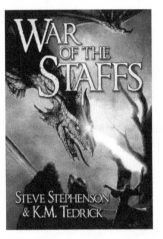

"Offers an enjoyable romp for high fantasy fans." *-KIRKUS REVIEWS*

CPSIA information can be obtained
at www.ICGtesting.com
Printed in the USA
FSHW021635151019
63021FS